# THE PRINCESS GAME

# THE PRINCESS GAME

## A REIMAGINING OF SLEEPING BEAUTY

MELANIE CELLIER

Luminant Publications
PO Box 203
Glen Osmond, South Australia 5064

melaniecellier@internode.on.net
http://www.melaniecellier.com

Cover Design by Karri Klawiter

*For my readers*
*you encourage and inspire me*

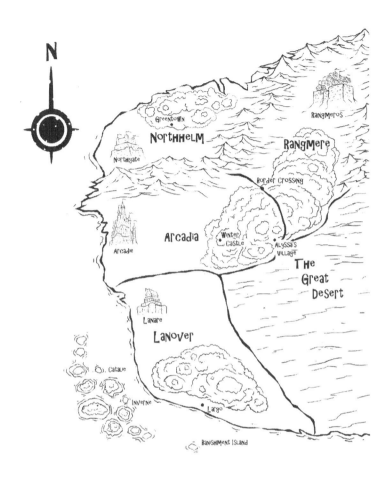

N

Greentown

Northhelm

RangMeros

RangMere

Northgate

Border Crossing

Arcadia

Winter
Castle

Alyssa's
Village

The
Great
Desert

Arcadie

Lanare

Lanover

Catalie

Inverne

Largo

Banishment Island

# Royal Family of Lanover

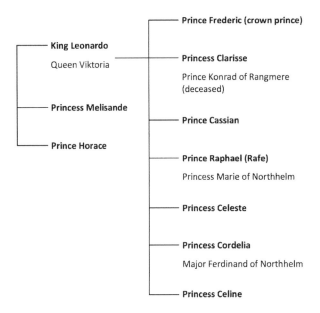

King Leonardo
Queen Viktoria

Princess Melisande

Prince Horace

Prince Frederic (crown prince)

Princess Clarisse
Prince Konrad of Rangmere (deceased)

Prince Cassian

Prince Raphael (Rafe)
Princess Marie of Northhelm

Princess Celeste

Princess Cordelia
Major Ferdinand of Northhelm

Princess Celine

# PROLOGUE

*P*rince Frederic frowned down at the report the steward had just handed him. He would need to take the news to his father as soon as possible.

"There you are, Frederic!"

He looked up and forced a smile for his younger sister. There was no point worrying Celeste about it, she wouldn't understand anyway. "Have you been looking for me?"

She nodded happily. "All over."

He watched her expectantly, but she just smiled at him. "Did you want something?" He kept his voice gentle. He didn't want to upset her, but the bad news he'd just received made it hard to concentrate.

Her face crinkled in confusion. "I suppose I must have…"

After a moment's awkward silence, which she didn't seem to find awkward at all, she pointed at the report in his hands. "What's that? Something lovely, I hope."

He bit his lip and glanced back down at the report. Once he would have happily gone to his young sister for advice, but that time had long since passed. Now he just wanted to shield her from unnecessary worry.

"Oh!" She clapped her hands, not seeming to notice his hesitation. "Is it another wedding?"

He stared at her. "Wedding?"

"Don't you remember? The last letter for Mother was about Cordelia's engagement. Silly!" She giggled.

He wanted to roll his eyes at the idea of Celeste calling *him* silly, but he stopped himself. It wasn't her fault she'd been cursed, after all. He considered trying to explain to her that the letter about their sister's engagement hadn't been the last letter their mother had received, just the last one she had shown Celeste. Or that he held a report, not a letter. But he decided the effort would strain them both far too much.

He couldn't resist a small joke, however. "Who would be getting married? Cassian, perhaps?" He suppressed a chuckle at the idea of his reserved younger brother in love.

"Cassian? Getting married? Is he really?" Celeste looked excited at the idea, and he groaned.

"No. I spoke in jest. Who would he be marrying?"

"I don't know." She frowned before brightening. "But I didn't know who Cordelia was marrying before her letter, either."

Frederic resisted the urge to massage his aching head. "Yes, but Cordelia has been in Northhelm the entire winter. Cassian lives here, with us."

With each passing year, it became harder to remember that Celeste had once been the brightest of them all. The memory of what had been stolen from her, from their whole family, brought an unusual moment of rage. Once she had challenged him, now she just exasperated him. And he worried that one day he would forget and lose all patience with her.

"It's Cassian's birthday today," said Celeste, apparently ignoring what was too complicated for her to understand.

Frederic stiffened. Cassian's birthday celebration. He'd almost forgotten. A good thing Celeste had come to find him, whatever her original reason had been. He could talk to his father about the report while they ate.

"You're right," he said, taking Celeste's elbow and steering her in the right direction. "And we're going to be late for his birthday meal."

# PART I
# CELESTE AND AURORA

"*T*he latest shipment of medical supplies for the palace doctors never arrived." My brother directed the comment at our father.

I carefully kept my eyes on my plate. So, that had been the news in the report. The one he wouldn't talk to me about. At least I'd managed to get him to Cassian's meal on time.

*But another missing delivery? That was...what? The third this month?*

King Leonardo frowned at his eldest son and heir. "That's unusual. Does the fault lie on our end or with the merchants?"

I glanced at them both out of the corner of my eye. It wasn't the first shipment to go missing, but apparently it was the first that the steward had reported to my family.

Even I had attributed the first one to natural causes. But the first one had been two months ago, and I had been concerned for some time now. It seemed the steward had a less suspicious nature.

I looked over at Cassian, my second oldest brother. He seemed unperturbed at having his birthday meal disturbed by such a conversation. He hadn't wanted anything extravagant for the day; he never did. Perhaps it still felt strange to him to cele-brate without his twin, Clarisse, who had long since married and was living in Rangmere.

"Did the merchants have an excuse?" he asked. "They're usually reliable."

*They claim to have delivered the supplies to the palace gate,* I thought.

"Apparently, they're claiming they made the delivery," said Frederic. "And they want payment."

I hadn't received a report on this particular incident yet, but I didn't need to. I'd read about four previous ones.

My father sighed. "Lanover may be the wealthiest of the king-doms, but that doesn't mean we will let ourselves be cheated."

I stiffened. Something strange was definitely going on, but I hadn't been able to trace it to its source yet, and trouble with the merchants was the last thing we needed right now. If my father refused to pay, every traveling merchant caravan in the kingdom might decide to head for the borders as fast as they could go.

I opened my mouth, and then shoved a spoonful of cake in before anyone noticed. I knew better than to try to contribute to the conversation. The curse would never allow it. A splitting headache wouldn't help anything, and I needed to hear my father's decision.

"Blatant disrespect!" barked my uncle. Uncle Horace disap-proved of irregularity. "Don't pay them a single coin."

I forgot myself for a moment and snorted, but the sound twisted in my throat and emerged as a giggle. My uncle glared at me.

I rushed to cover up my lapse. "I don't think one coin would be enough." I giggled again, this time intentionally. "The merchants always charge so much for the beautiful material they bring for my dresses."

Everyone stared at me.

"They might get angry if you only paid them one coin." I

smiled around at them all with an innocent expression, hoping they would understand my hint.

A momentary pause ensued, as everyone tried to think of a response. My youngest sister, Celine, rolled her eyes, and returned her attention to her slice of cake. Frederic shook his head slightly and Cassian looked at me pityingly.

After an extended silence, my brothers turned back to my father. I maintained my artless smile, although my teeth clenched behind it. I had clearly been dismissed, the foolish child interrupting the conversation of the adults. The three of them were about to let Uncle Horace's pride precipitate them into a kingdom-wide crisis and, thanks to my curse, I was powerless to stop it.

I knew more about what was going on than any of them, and yet they had all looked embarrassed for me. The poor Sleeping Princess. Foolish Celeste, thinking she could contribute something to the conversation.

I knew it wasn't their fault. I knew it was only because of the curse but, for a moment, anger and frustration overwhelmed my good sense. I opened my mouth to speak and was instantly seized by a coughing fit.

Once again, I had the attention of everyone at the table, with the exception of Celine who seemed far too focused on her plate. I suspected she was plotting something, but I struggled to bring my thoughts into line while the coughs still wracked my body.

I held up my fork, and the curse loosened its grip, allowing me enough air to speak. "A crumb." I smiled weakly, my eyes still watering from the attack.

My father sighed and recommended I have some water. I meekly obeyed, my eye catching on one of the footmen, who had come to clear away the empty dishes. I recognized him immediately. He didn't usually wait on our family meals, but then we didn't usually eat the midday meal together at all. Extra servants had been brought in for the special birthday occasion.

He was one of my agents and a good one, too. If I hadn't known to watch him closely, even I wouldn't have noticed him slip the note into the loose crack of the sideboard, the hiding place where we regularly exchanged messages. My fingers itched to retrieve it, but the curse kept me in my chair. I had already forgotten myself once tonight, and I didn't look forward to the consequences if I slipped up again.

Surely the note held information about the latest missing shipment. Perhaps it even included some new clue. It might contain some piece of evidence that would convince my father not to make a rash move. But it remained hidden away, impossibly out of reach.

Of course, my agent had no idea his spymaster sat so close to him. He believed, like my own family, that I was nothing more than the Sleeping Princess. All thanks to my aunt.

A wave of icy cold crept down from my scalp, although my face remained calm. I had long ago subjugated my external reactions. Stillness and a smile were always the safest postures when a wrong look or word could produce a coughing fit or crippling pain. I assumed the pose instinctively now whenever my mind or emotions threatened to break free of the lie I was forced to live.

And nothing threatened my calm façade like the thought of my absent aunt. Which is why I generally tried to avoid thinking of her. I needed a clear head, not one clouded by hatred.

Unfortunately, it's hard not to hate someone who tried to serve you a death sentence when you were only a few days old.

I took a deep breath. I usually kept my emotions under better control. I had to since I was only truly safe from the curse when I was alone. In public, the more I played along, the more license the curse seemed to give me. These days, I usually uttered foolish statements and gave empty smiles without even thinking about it.

"I suppose we'll have to pay first while we investigate what happened to the supplies," said my father, pulling my attention back to the table. "It's best not to upset the merchants over something that may turn out to be a misunderstanding."

I let out a silent breath of relief as everyone began to get up from the table. Perhaps I didn't give my father enough credit.

Celine rushed over and grabbed my arm. "Come on. I want to show you something."

I let her pull me awkwardly toward the door, giving me the opportunity to bump against the sideboard. With a quick, subtle movement, I retrieved the hidden note and tucked it into my dress. I wanted to slip away alone, so I could read it, but Celine had a firm grip on my arm and whispered that it was about a dress. So I could hardly refuse—everyone knew Princess Celeste loved nothing so much as gowns and fashion.

When we reached her room, Celine gestured for me to sit on the bed and then threw me a book.

I fumbled the catch on purpose before looking down at it in confusion. "This isn't a dress."

Celine slumped down beside me. "Thanks for that observation, Celeste, I never would have realized."

I suppressed a sigh. "I'm sure you said something about a dress..."

"What's the hurry? It's not as if we have anything else to do." She glanced sadly at the rain falling against her window. "I found this book in the library and wanted to show you a hilarious bit. Have you read it? Back before, I mean."

I examined the title. A history of my family. I had read it, of course. I had spent a lot of time in the library before I turned sixteen. Now, I could only study in private—the curse deemed studying an unsuitable occupation.

I frowned down at it in concentration, and Celine shook her head. "Never mind. I'm sure you wouldn't remember, anyway. It's about our family. Read it, and I'll tell you when you get to the right bit."

I began to read, Celine peering at the page over my shoulder.

*Once upon a time, in the southernmost kingdom of Lanover, a handsome king married a beautiful queen.*

The first line jolted my memory. This was the history book that read more like a fairy tale. What about it had caught Celine's interest?

*Everyone said that their children would be the most beautiful princes and princesses that the kingdom had ever seen. And, in due time, the king and queen had a handsome little boy. The young prince was soon followed by twins—another handsome boy and a beautiful princess. The whole kingdom exclaimed at her beauty.*

I forced my breathing to remain even. Celine had grown up with this story and was obviously so familiar with it that it had lost its significance for her. It didn't even seem to occur to her that it might be a painful topic for me.

A sudden urge to throw the book away gripped me but, if I did, I would suffer the consequences. The curse wanted me to play along, to act as oblivious as Celine clearly believed me to be. And a small part of me wanted to reread the disaster that had been my birth. I could sense the imminent tragedy hovering over the story as he described my older siblings' arrivals.

*The people soon celebrated the arrival of a third prince, and when the queen fell pregnant again, they began to call the royal family blessed. Their fifth child was another girl, and the court exclaimed that she was as beautiful as her sister had been.*

I paused for a moment, closing my eyes. If only my story had ended there. Another equally beautiful princess, and they all lived happily ever after.

*The king and queen planned a lavish Christening for their new daughter, who was to be named Celeste, and invited all the nobles in the land.*

I shook my head. If only that had been true, if only they hadn't made one, very notable, exception. I wished, as I had a thousand times, that I understood why they had failed to invite my aunt. My parents had always refused to talk about her at all.

But perhaps they had already guessed the craziness that obviously lurked within. Perhaps they had simply picked the wrong way to try to protect me.

I turned back to the page, expecting to read about what had happened next, but instead found several paragraphs describing the decorations of the great hall, the clothing of the guests and my infant beauty. I witnessed my own stunning beauty every day in the mirror, yet even I didn't quite believe the extravagance of his descriptions. And I somehow doubted that my Christening had been more lavish than every other event my parents had hosted in the nineteen years since.

Celine, still reading over my shoulder, snorted. "You really haven't had a single ugly day in your life, have you, Lettie?"

I smiled at her use of my nickname, but otherwise ignored the comment. Celine had only been a child when my curse had taken effect. She knew the cost of my beauty and had never envied it.

I watched her while she returned to reading. She had no need to be envious. At fourteen she was already as beautiful as our other sisters, Clarisse and Cordelia. I pushed aside the wish that I could have had an ordinary beauty like theirs. The thought was so well-worn it was starting to lose its effect on me.

Celine let out a hearty laugh, and then pointed at a spot on the next page in response to my enquiring look.

*The court hummed when the two godmothers present both stepped forward to gift the young princess. Such an extravagance, when her older siblings had each received only a single gift at their Christenings. The first gifted her with great beauty and the second with great intelligence. Had a child ever been more blessed? She would outshine even her siblings.*

"For the record, Lettie, I don't feel outshone—whatever that even means."

"Of course not! You're very beautiful as well, Celine. And you didn't need a godmother to gift it to you, either."

Celine snorted. "I notice that you say nothing about intelligence. But it gets better." She pointed back at the page.

*But even as the court exclaimed their delight, a strange hush fell over the proceedings. The huge doors of the great hall had been forced open, and a single figure stood in the doorway. Princess Melisande. A gasp rippled through the crowd.*

*The princess strode straight to the baby in her cradle and gazed down upon her. Then her voice rang through the room as she uttered a curse on the child. Clutched in her hand was an object of power, and she used it to pronounce death over the baby. On her sixteenth birthday, she would die. The whole room stood frozen, too shocked to prevent the king's sister from leaving the room. She was neither seen nor heard of again.*

Celine paused, a thoughtful look on her face. "What do you think happened to Aunt Melisande? I've always wondered. I mean, she can't actually have disappeared."

I smiled at Celine blankly while inside I fought a resurgence of my earlier turbulent emotions. It didn't normally hit me like this, twice in one day. My aunt was rarely mentioned at court, and even more rarely in front of me.

I forced myself to respond. "I'm sure I don't have the slightest idea. It's a very tricky puzzle."

Celine sighed. "Of course you don't. But never mind that, listen to this next bit." She pulled the book out of my hands. *"The queen immediately became hysterical."*

Celine chuckled with delight. "Mother, hysterical! Can you imagine?"

I shook my head, my own chuckle only slightly forced. That had to be a fabrication. Or at least a large exaggeration. Our mother never did anything as fatiguing as hysterics.

She threw the book aside, not bothering to watch where it landed. "Whoever wrote it must have been an idiot."

"Does being overly dramatic make you an idiot?" I asked the question in a tone of exaggerated innocence, watching for her reaction. She rolled her eyes and didn't answer, standing and stretching instead. She was either entirely unbothered by my wry question, or she didn't grasp that I was poking fun at her. Knowing Celine, it could easily be either one. She wasn't in the least sensitive and was more likely to laugh than feel hurt when our older siblings criticized her.

But on the other hand, since my sixteenth birthday, when the curse had taken effect, no one ever attributed a hidden meaning to my words. It was the only way I managed to get through some of the more boring royal functions. I enjoyed seeing how far I could push both the curse and the credulity of the courtiers. My sly humor amused me if no one else.

Celine disappeared into her wardrobe and my eyes found the discarded book on the floor. I didn't need to read on to know the rest of the story. I had made my parents tell it to me often enough that I could easily picture the scene.

After my aunt had pronounced death over me, the court had been thrown into chaos. Until another unexpected figure had emerged. It turns out three godmothers, not two, had attended my Christening. And the third had yet to give her gift.

After some thought, she had offered my parents a modification of the curse. "Death is powerful," she had reportedly said. "And only the High King himself can entirely defeat it. But as his servants, we have been given the power to fight against it where we can. If you desire, I can give the gift of sleep. Instead of death, she will sleep, and a kiss of true love shall awaken her."

"How long will she sleep for?" my father had asked.

The godmother had looked a little uncomfortable. "That's hard to say, Your Majesties. It could be many years."

"Many years! Is she to awake to find her family old and gray—she robbed of us, and us robbed of her?" For all her placid disposition, my mother's love for her children is warm and genuine.

The godmother had asked, somewhat scathingly, I imagined,

if the queen would prefer that the whole court slept along with the princess. No one had even bothered to reply to that sally.

It had been the Duchess of Sessily, newly arrived at her title, who had suggested an alternate solution. "If you are able to offer sleep instead of death, could it be just her mind that sleeps? She has been gifted with great intelligence. To rob her of that, after only sixteen years, would be a fate like enough to death, would it not?"

My parents hadn't been enthusiastic about that suggestion, either, but no one had managed to come up with a better one. So the final *gift* had been given, and my fate had been sealed. Or so everyone in Lanover thought. I alone knew there was more to the story. And trapped inside my own mind, there was no one I could tell. It had been a lonely three and a half years.

# CHAPTER 2

*I* fell back to lie on the coverlet and gaze at the ceiling. The story had another chapter, one that I would never find written in any book.

Before the curse had taken effect, I spent my spare time training or studying. I trained because I was determined to master a skill that hadn't been magically gifted to me. And since Rafe spent all his time training, it had been easy to convince him to teach me whenever our tutors weren't paying attention.

I studied because I was determined to find a way around my curse. I couldn't bear the idea of the coming transformation. What would it be like to lose the best part of my mind? Would I even still be me? I had been the smartest and the best for as long as I could remember. I couldn't bear to lose it all.

I didn't tell anyone, even Rafe, about my secret determination. I pored over books in the library until late at night and pestered our tutors with questions.

Two nights before my sixteenth birthday, I had summoned my godmother in despair. She had been older than I was expecting, the gray in her hair matching the gray of her wings, and with a clear no-nonsense air. I guess when you had seven princes and princesses to deal with, a bit of no-nonsense was required.

"I wondered how long it would be before I heard from you." She looked me up and down.

I hadn't been able to escape the sense that she didn't quite approve of what she saw. It had been a novel sensation. Already, at age fifteen, I was used to a very different reaction.

"I need your help. Is there no way I can free myself from this curse?"

"You're leaving it a bit late to ask, aren't you?"

I bit my lip, unwilling to admit that I had wanted to find the solution for myself. I had been sure I would find one.

She nodded knowingly. "A proud young thing, aren't you?" She sighed. "I suppose it was inevitable given your Christening gifts."

"Surely you can do something!" With my birthday only days away, I was desperate enough to beg, if that was what she required.

She regarded me silently for a moment. "The High King has seen your searching." A knot that had been tightening in my chest for the last several weeks loosened. "But actions have consequences. And your curse is the consequence of a great many actions." The knot tightened again.

"Not *my* actions! I was only a baby."

She sighed. "Unfortunately, consequences don't always fall on those who most deserve them. The innocent suffer along with the guilty." She shot me a stern look. "Although how many are truly innocent? You have lessons of your own to learn. And much good can still come to your kingdom from this curse."

"But what about me?" I knew I should be brave, and willing to sacrifice anything for the kingdom, but I had been too scared. Perhaps courage was the lesson I had needed to learn.

"Yes, well, that is why I am here. Your searching is to have some reward."

I held my breath, my eyes fixed on her face.

"The kingdoms will believe that your mind sleeps. But inside," she reached out a finger to touch my forehead, "you will remain yourself. Would you accept such a thing?"

My desperation pushed me to nod agreement.

"Very well, then. It is done." She smiled at me a little wryly. "Somehow, I imagine that when next we meet, you will be a little more humble, my dear."

I had been too relieved to consider her words at the time, but their meaning had become clear once my birthday passed. And I had begun to suspect it was in the area of humility, not courage, that my godmother had found me wanting.

It took me nearly a year to learn the full limitations of the curse, and to learn to follow its guidelines instinctively. A painful year of coughing fits and cramps and sudden splitting headaches.

But all of that had seemed nothing compared to the far more painful blows to my pride. Once I had been universally admired —the most beautiful and intelligent of all my peers. Standing far above even my own siblings, who had been born with every advantage gifted to royalty.

Once I turned sixteen, everything changed. The eyes turned on me were still full of admiration for my beauty, but the other emotions they now held were pity, scorn or, worst of all, dismissal. The sting of it took a long time to fade. Sometimes I felt it still.

But interestingly, I found a few advantages to the change. No one watched their words around me. Those at the palace who had grown accustomed to my breathtaking beauty often stopped noticing me at all. My education in human nature grew by leaps and bounds until it rivaled the book learning I already possessed.

When the rumors of Rangmeran aggression became too loud to be ignored, I recruited my first agent and the spymaster, Aurora, was born. I discovered that as long as my face was covered, my identity obscured, the curse would let me act to protect my kingdom. I could speak freely then, too, as long as I didn't give myself away.

I had thought long and hard about how Lanover could protect itself from the war hungry kingdom of Rangmere. We were rich, but our army was small, and we were ill-prepared for any assault. My father hoped the marriage alliance between Clarisse and the heir to the Rangmeran throne would be enough, but the rumors suggested otherwise.

Northhelm had a strong military but lacked our wealth. A trade treaty with them, negotiated on terms favorable to them rather than us, would ensure their economic dependence on Lanover. If Rangmere ever moved against us, Northhelm would stand as our allies.

The woman I had recruited was a minor aide to the Duchess of Sessily, and she made my suggestion to the duchess. In an amazingly short period of time, the treaty was signed. I obviously hadn't been the only one concerned about Rangmere.

The positive reception of the idea ensured the loyalty of my new agent, and I began to build a network, spreading my eyes and ears further abroad. Eventually the duchess grew tired of the charade and demanded to know the source of her aide's ideas. The woman had admitted that she served Aurora, and the duchess had demanded a meeting.

I had met her at night in the garden, hanging back, to ensure she didn't recognize me and had no chance to snatch off my scarf. It took some work, but I managed to convince her that my loyalty to the crown was absolute, and my anonymity maintained for personal reasons. Reluctantly she agreed to work with me, feeding my information to the king and queen for the good of the kingdom.

In the two years since then we had even grown close, in a strange sort of way. Bound together by our secret service to the crown.

Our kingdom had grown lax in the many years of peace. It shouldn't have taken a curse for us to develop a spy network. The foiled threat from Rangmere had proved we needed to anticipate the dangers that might seek to destroy our people.

My mind turned to the missing supplies and the note still tucked in my dress. I glanced toward the wardrobe, wondering how much longer before Celine returned.

"I have no idea what is going on right now, Celine," I called out.

She popped her head out, smiling cheekily. "Do you ever?" I didn't respond. "I'm trying out a new dress because there is absolutely nothing else to do."

That elicited a sympathetic smile. It had been raining for three days straight, and I knew that Celine was missing Cordelia, our middle sister. As the youngest Lanoverian royals, it would usually have been the three of us in here. And, since the curse, Cordelia was a lot more fun than I was.

But Cordelia had traveled to the kingdom of Northhelm for our brother Rafe's wedding and had fallen in love with a Northhelmian noble. Celine had been wild with jealousy at being left behind, and now Cordelia wasn't coming back.

I, on the other hand, had been glad not to go. I was needed here. And I'd had my own royal visit two years ago to the kingdom of Arcadia. I had only begun to build my network of agents then, so my absence had been less critical. It hadn't been a particularly enjoyable trip, though. How could it be? Lanover had kept my curse quiet, so the Arcadians had thought me nothing but an empty-headed fool.

Of course, that was exactly what the Lanoverians thought of me, too, but at least they knew why.

Celine disappeared back into her wardrobe, so I rolled onto my stomach and pulled out the note, shielding it from view with my body.

For a moment, I let myself fall into my other persona. My bright, empty smile dropped away, and I could easily picture the expression that took its place. Confident, commanding, determined.

The message was short and to the point.

> The night sentry roster has been switched for the small western gate. The new sentry has received several reprimands in the past for drinking and sleeping while on watch.

I frowned down at it. Most people didn't realize how much servants saw. How many little details they knew about the lives of everyone who lived in the palace. It was something I used to my advantage. My agents knew to keep me informed of anything unusual. Any changes to routine, however minor. And this one certainly seemed suspicious. It wasn't what I'd been expecting, though.

I tucked the note away and rolled over, smoothing my thoughts from my face as my sister emerged.

"Celine!" I gasped, the contents of the message momentarily driven from my mind.

My sister gave a satisfied smirk and spun in place. She wore a magnificent deep blue dress, with a plunging back and bare shoulders. She looked exquisite. But our mother would never let her wear it.

"Where did it come from?" I knelt down in front of her to examine the material of the skirt. All of the palace seamstresses knew to take their instructions from the queen when designing the gowns of the youngest princess.

"There's a new seamstress in the city. She was delighted to receive a commission for a royal gown."

"Oh, Celine." The poor woman would be so disappointed when the dress was never worn.

"Don't give me that look, Lettie. I need you to help me convince Mother. Everyone in the family trusts your judgment on clothes." She lowered her voice before muttering, "Even if they don't on anything else."

I laughed and shook my head. Celine didn't have a hope. The dress was clearly designed for an older woman, not a young teen. Our oldest, married sister Clarisse would look magnificent in it. But Celine wouldn't even reach the beginning of adulthood for two more years. Our mother would never let her wear it in public.

"The material is beautiful." I ran my fingers over the soft silk again, sidestepping her request for help. I didn't feel like an argument. The curse made them difficult, and my mind kept returning to my now-hidden note.

"The whole dress is beautiful. It's a triumph." Celine grinned into the mirror in satisfaction.

I shook my head, unable to repress a smile of my own. Dinner would be interesting. Watching Celine clash with our mother was like watching a raging sea beating against a solid rock. Our mother would remain calm and placid and entirely unmoving. She wouldn't argue or rage—she was far too laid-back for that. She would simply let Celine storm on, unheeded. If called upon, she would calmly state her position, and at the end of the whole process she would remind Celine that the servants had been instructed to ensure the queen's wishes were carried out.

Celine knew from experience that the servants had been given permission to carry her back to her room and lock her inside if she tried to do something the queen had forbidden. I just hoped Celine didn't spend too long sulking this time. I missed Cordelia, too, and didn't look forward to being stuck inside the palace with no one but a moping Celine for company.

A guilty thought snuck through my mind. I was five years

older than Celine. Perhaps Mother would let me wear the dress. It was a little daring, yes, but I wasn't fourteen. After a moment's consideration, I shook my head regretfully. Celine would be so angry with me that it wouldn't be worth it.

It was a pity for the dress to go to waste, though. The deep blue reminded me of the dress I had worn for my introduction to the Arcadian court nearly two years ago. The color was a perfect complement to my golden skin and dark chestnut hair. Of course, that was why Celine had chosen it since she shared the same coloring. Most of us in the south did. The few northerners in our court stood out, looking pale and faded next to our darker tones.

Celine drifted over to where I sat and plopped down beside me. Her glee fell away as her gaze once again locked on the window. "I thought it was supposed to be spring." She sighed loudly.

"It is spring, silly." I laughed.

Despite how many times I was forced to misuse it, I still secretly liked my laugh. The musical sound always managed to convey a sense of joy, regardless of how I actually felt. And other people found it irresistible, responding with a smile or laugh of their own.

Celine rolled her eyes.

All except for my family, of course, who spent so much time with me. Celine rarely tried to restrain her impatience, but the rest of them had mostly learned to ignore my strange ways. As the baby of the family, Celine didn't believe in hiding her feelings.

She claimed she was being true to herself. Frederic, my oldest brother, said she was looking for attention. I could easily imagine his serious, disapproving face as he said it, too. Frederic didn't approve of dramatics.

Secretly I agreed with him a little. Only I didn't blame her for wanting to stand out. It couldn't be easy being the youngest of seven. Of course, I couldn't exactly relate to her situation, either. I would give almost anything not to stand out—to just be one of the many Lanoverian princesses.

But whenever I began to feel overwhelmed, I reminded myself that it could be worse. I could be dead.

# CHAPTER 3

*S*everal hours later, as I reluctantly trailed my extravagantly-dressed sister down to our family's private dining room, I reminded myself again that I couldn't steal the dress. I would have to be satisfied with giving the new seamstress a commission of my own.

My mind turned back to the message from my agent. Too many unusual things had been happening around the Lanoverian palace of late. And too many unsettling rumors. Unfortunately, I had yet to find anything sufficiently concrete to bring to my parents' attention.

And it didn't help that their primary advisor, the Duchess of Sessily, was in Northhelm discussing the treaties surrounding Rafe's marriage to Marie, the Northhelmian princess. Which meant I was without my usual conduit for information from my secret spy network to my parents.

I frowned. Perhaps I could gain some more concrete information tonight.

It didn't take me more than a second to decide that I would investigate the situation myself rather than assigning one of my agents. I was aching for some action after days of inactivity, and this seemed like a perfect opportunity. Why put a negligent sentry on a lone guard shift unless you were planning for him to fail?

I pushed the food around on my plate, still contemplating this question as our meal dragged on. Our mother's reaction to Celine's garb had been predictable, but I'd been surprised at Celine's mild response. She had hardly complained at all when she had been forbidden to wear the gown again.

Her restraint had made for an unexpectedly quiet meal. Maybe everyone had exhausted their conversation at our earlier meal. My father sat at the head of the table and my mother at the foot, in their usual places. To my father's right sat Frederic, my oldest brother, and Cassian the next oldest. They both dedicated themselves to the task of eating, too serious, or in the case of Cassian, too reserved, to offer much light conversation.

An empty chair sat next to Cassian, belonging to his twin, Clarisse. Clarisse had been living in Rangmere for years, yet still her chair sat there, empty. As if my parents couldn't quite let go of any of their children.

Across from my brothers sat Celine and me. The empty seat between us belonged to Cordelia, and the one between me and my father to Rafe. My brother had gone adventuring before he met Princess Marie of Northhelm, so his place had also been empty for some time. I missed him most of all. Rafe was only two years older than me, and he and I had been best friends before the curse had taken effect.

Of all my family, he had been least able to accept the consequences of the curse, and he had confided in me that his adventuring had a purpose—to find a way to break my curse. He hadn't expected the sentiment to mean much to me—my cursed persona never expressed any dissatisfaction with my empty-headed state —but secretly I had been deeply touched. Every now and then we received a letter with a suggested cure. Nothing had worked so

27

far, and I didn't expect it to. I knew the only way to break the curse, even if Rafe did not.

And I supposed now that he was married the letters would stop. At least he was bringing his new wife on a tour of Lanover before they settled down, so I would get to see him soon.

Just as this thought crossed my mind, the door of our dining room swung open. My heart skipped a beat in surprise. Standing there in the empty doorway stood the object of my thoughts.

"Rafe!" I jumped to my feet, for once able to show my true feelings of delight. I raced around the table and almost fell into his arms.

He swept me into a giant hug and then set me back down. "Goodness, where is your decorum, sister dear?" His eyes laughed at me. "Who raised such a ruffian?"

He turned to our parents with a cheeky twinkle. "Mother, Father." He gave them both a half bow.

"Raphael. It is a pleasure to see you again, son." King Leonardo provided the model for Cassian's reserve.

"Yes, indeed, Rafe. But we weren't expecting you until tomorrow." Our mother's mild complaint only made Rafe grin and go to give her a hug. He clearly knew better than to expect her to get up and come to him.

"We made excellent time and decided to push on rather than spending another night on the road. I told the rest of our party to head straight for their various accommodations, but I couldn't resist coming to greet you all. And to introduce you to my wife."

Pride sounded in his voice as he pulled a tall young woman forward through the door. I examined her curiously. She looked nothing like I had expected. Tall and pale, even for a northerner, she was pretty rather than beautiful. But I could tell that Rafe would disagree with that assessment from the way his eyes shone when they rested on her. I determined immediately to love her for his sake.

Celine rushed forward to receive her own greeting. Rafe had

always been her favorite brother, too. As she moved, her new dress swished, and her face glowed with triumph. So, it hadn't been boredom that had inspired Celine to change into such an outrageous dress on this particular evening. Her earlier acquiescence now made sense. The girl was sneakier than I gave her credit for. Perhaps I should consider recruiting her. It would do her good to have a productive direction to channel all that energy toward.

An unfamiliar young man followed Marie through the door. Tall and broad-shouldered, he carried himself with confidence and command. He had a handsome face, in the golden-haired, blue-eyed fashion of the north, and I could only assume he was Marie's brother, Prince William. I hadn't realized he would be accompanying them to Lanover.

Rafe confirmed my suspicions by announcing William's name, but he was too busy introducing Marie to Celine and our parents to bother naming the rest of us. I was still standing next to the door, so Prince William turned to me first.

He took my hand. "I hardly think I need an introduction. One glance at your face tells me that you must be the infamous Sleeping Princess. Allow me to tell you that you're even more beautiful than the stories say." His eyes glowed, and I couldn't tell whether it was with humor or admiration. Or perhaps some mix of both.

Was he mocking me? Assuming I was too empty-headed to be offended by his greeting me with a reference to my curse? It took all of my control to keep the outrage off my face.

I curtsied, my smile friendly and oblivious.

"A pleasure to meet you, Prince." I looked up at him through my lashes. "I'm afraid I haven't heard anything at all about you."

His brows rose at the simple, artless words. But clearly he knew of my curse. He could no more take offense than I could. I let my smile grow, keeping my expression innocent.

He regarded me hesitantly for a moment and then grinned,

spreading his hands wide. "What can I say, Your Highness? I am undone by your beauty."

He kissed my hand and then continued on to greet the rest of my family. I pretended to be absorbed in Princess Marie's conversation with my mother, but I didn't miss the way his eyes kept returning to me. Sometimes bemused, sometimes suspicious, but always admiring. I couldn't keep a slow smile from creeping over my face. I would have to be careful with this handsome newcomer. He wasn't as used to my curse as the Lanoverians. A challenge, then.

~

After everyone else had retired to bed, I slipped out of my rooms and into the darkened corridor. I was dressed in the comfortable, loose outfit of a guard, dyed black to blend into the shadows. A long black scarf wrapped around my head, covering my hair and shielding everything but my eyes.

The lingering humidity in the air made the material uncomfortable against my face, but I didn't even consider removing it. Once, at the beginning, I had decided to reveal my true identity to one of my agents. As soon as my hand moved toward the scarf, I had been hit by crippling stomach cramps. I had been incapacitated in bed for three days, terrified the whole time that I would never recover. The warning had been clear.

Fear of permanent disablement and pain was a convincing motivation to ensure no-one ever discovered the true name of the mysterious spymaster, code named Aurora.

Slipping from shadow to shadow, I visited each of my message caches. Hidden in plain sight, like the sideboard in the dining room, my agents used these nooks to pass information on to me. Tonight they were all empty, which left me free to follow up on the change in guard shift.

I rolled my shoulders and moved toward the western gate. An

unexpected glow appeared around a corner, followed by the sound of feet and the low murmur of voices. Moving silently, I eased open one of the doors lining the corridor and slipped into a storage cupboard. I knew where every door in the sprawling palace led and could find my way around every corridor blind.

I left the door open a crack so I could see who else was roaming the palace at such a late hour. I instantly recognized the three figures. I had been wrong—not all of my family were already in bed. My two oldest brothers, Frederic and Cassian, strode along, deep in conversation with my father's brother. Uncle Horace always kept late hours, and, from their dress, it looked like he had been refereeing for a sparring match between my brothers.

Frederic and Cassian both took their responsibilities to our kingdom seriously and were wont to engage in physical training late at night if other duties had kept them occupied during the day. I had often dreamed of competing against my brothers, wildly curious to know if I could hold my own against them. But Cassian was four years older than me and Frederic six. Before the curse they had deemed me too much a child to duel with them, and afterward I couldn't afford to let anyone know I had continued and expanded my training.

I waited until they had disappeared from sight and then continued on my way. I soon arrived at the western gate.

Everyone in the palace called it a gate, but it was really only a door. The other kingdoms all had high walls surrounding their many-storied palaces. But in Lanover, our royal residence was single-story, a huge sprawling building built of the same reddish sandstone as the rest of our city. The only things that distinguished it were its size and its location. Built on top of a large hill, and surrounded by extensive gardens, the palace looked out over the entire city.

Apparently, my ancestors had felt that the hill provided enough protection and had never enclosed the building and gardens with a wall. Personally, I suspected they had liked the view. It helped that Lanover had a much more relaxed culture than our northern neighbors, and our capital had never come under attack.

But on occasions like this, I felt the danger of having nothing but a single guard and a small wooden door between the palace's inhabitants and the outside world. Of course, that was why Aurora existed—to keep the royal family and the kingdom safe.

The guard was stationed outside the door, but I decided to wait inside, hiding myself behind a large potted plant a small way down the corridor. I settled down to await events.

The first two hours passed peacefully, my greatest challenge being to stay awake. I practiced hand strengthening exercises, and when my muscles tired, I played mind games designed to sharpen my senses. By the third hour, I was thinking longingly of my comfortable bed and grumbling silently to myself.

Why had I chosen to spend my night sitting in an uncomfortable corridor, again?

A sudden noise jerked me out of my head. The door was slowly opening from the outside. Something that most definitely was not supposed to be happening in the middle of the night.

I eased onto the balls of my feet and waited there, crouching in place. A man, also dressed in black, came through the doorway. He carefully shut the heavy door behind him and surveyed his surroundings. After only a moment of hesitation, he took off down the corridor.

I waited for several breaths and then followed behind him. As I padded along the stone floor, I admitted to a moment of relief. Part of me had wondered if I was making a mistake by watching the door alone. I had been honing my skills for years now, but I was still only one person. If an actual assault had come through the door, I couldn't have stopped it.

But I had put my trust in my intelligence network, and it had not let me down. I was sure I would get more warning of anything as serious as an attack on the palace. Whatever was being planned, it was still in its early stages.

For over an hour, I followed the man silently around the palace. I became increasingly tense as the minutes passed. What was his purpose? He had opened many doors but hadn't entered any of the rooms. We had nearly circled back around to the western gate when a brown furry figure slunk around the corner.

The cat ignored the stranger but headed straight in my direction. I froze. I recognized her immediately—she had been raised in the palace since kittenhood and was an excellent mouser. Unfortunately, I was one of her favorite people.

She marched straight up to where I hid in the shadows and rubbed against my leg, purring. I stifled a curse.

"Mrrow," she said, pressing in closer. She was hoping for a treat.

My eyes flew to the shrouded figure ahead of me.

He hadn't appeared to notice the cat at first, but at the sound, he turned and strained to see in the darkness. His body stiffened when he spotted me.

He took off, sprinting in the direction of the gate. I growled and started after him, pushing my legs as fast as they could go. He had nearly reached the exit when I leaped forward and tackled him to the ground.

I quickly rolled out of reach. The man was taller and heavier, and I couldn't afford to get pinned down. I jumped up and then lunged forward, kicking out before he had a chance to regain his balance.

He staggered backward before grunting and charging toward me. I stepped aside at the last moment and used his momentum to swing him over my hip and back down onto the floor. I skirted around him, positioning myself between him and the door.

He was warier the second time, striking out with his fists and feet, but not committing his whole body to the attacks. I blocked him, slowly falling backward. I needed to finish the bout. I didn't want to let him escape when I still had no idea what he wanted in the palace, but I also had no idea what to do with him once I'd managed to overpower him. I could hardly turn him over to the guard myself.

He must have seen my mental hesitation reflected in my stance, because he made a second, desperate charge. I blocked him, using a well-timed kick. But this time, as he fell, he grasped at my face, his fingers tangling in my scarf.

I snatched at the material, whirling around to put my back to him while I replaced it. I didn't think he had seen my face.

A shoulder in the middle of my back sent me sprawling. I flipped over in time to see him disappearing through the external door. By the time I had regained my breath enough to follow, he was long gone.

I ground my teeth as I looked out over the shadowy gardens. He had only escaped because of the stupid curse. And if he ever came back, he would know my weak spot now. I glanced down at the guard. The man slumped in a sitting position, his back to the wall.

I nearly turned away in disgust, but something made me pause. I crouched down and examined him. To my surprise, the smell of alcohol was missing. I lightly shook his shoulders, but his head simply lolled further to one side. Wrinkling my nose in distaste, I leaned in close and sniffed his breath.

Well. I rocked back on my heels. I recognized the scent. A sleeping potion. So whoever had arranged the change in the sentry roster had left nothing to chance. It was a clever plan. Given his history, the man would be too scared to report any lapse of consciousness. And if anyone discovered him, they would assume he had overindulged and fallen asleep.

I considered calling for a fresh guard but decided it was unnecessary. Dawn would arrive soon and with it a change of guard. I was confident the stranger I had fought wouldn't return to the palace via this means.

I hurried back to my room, my mind whirling. Why go to all that trouble just to wander around the palace? Had the man found what he was looking for, or had I disturbed him before he had the chance?

I changed into my nightgown and hid my Aurora outfit in its usual hiding place in a box under my bed. Slipping between the sheets, I admitted to myself that I had no idea what had just happened. I didn't like the feeling.

From my earliest memory, I had been smarter and more aware than other children my age. I had asked my parents in confusion why the others were so slow, and that was the first time I had heard about my Christening gifts. They didn't tell me about the curse until later.

By thirteen, I could out-think most of the adults that I knew. Confusion was, therefore, an unfamiliar and unwelcome sensation.

I tossed in the bed, knowing that I needed to be sleeping, but unable to stop thinking about the strange events of the night.

Something was happening in Lanover, something bad. The signs were subtle but, in my role as Aurora, I was perfectly placed to see them. Somehow I knew that the missing supplies and the strange intruder were at the heart of the danger, but I couldn't yet see anything clearly. How did they connect to each other?

At times like this, I recognized the value of Aurora. I could even see the value to the kingdom that had come from my curse. But, personally, it continued to bring me nothing but despair.

Before the curse had taken effect, I had been beloved of the whole court. I had entertained no doubt that by the time I turned eighteen, a kiss of true love would free me. But, as time passed, I realized the flaw in my plans. I had become two people. Aurora who lived in the shadows, a fighter and strategist, coldly confident and authoritative. And Celeste who lived in the open, who loved dresses and dancing, and who laughed as easily as she breathed.

Since I was both of those people, no one truly knew me. The whole me. So how could anyone truly love me? I would be trapped forever between Celeste and Aurora.

I don't know when my thoughts had turned from the danger threatening my kingdom to true love. I only knew that when I fell asleep, my dreams reflected the warm glow of blue eyes rather than the shadows that usually inhabited my sleep.

# CHAPTER 4

*T*he next day my parents held a proper court reception for their new daughter-in-law. Celine and I had cornered Rafe first thing in the morning and made him and Marie tell us the whole story of their doings in Northhelm. He had written to us previously with a short version, since he had hoped the means they had used to defeat the powerful bargain-maker plaguing Northhelm might have freed me also. But, of course, in my case, the effort had met with failure.

The full story had taken a long time and my admiration for Marie had grown significantly by the end of it. Outside forces had shaped and changed her life before she had even been born. But despite them all, she showed determination to take her position as princess seriously, to bring value to her kingdom. I felt a strong sense of kinship.

Celine threw a cushion off the small sofa she had been lounging on. "So much excitement! Everyone else gets to have all the fun." She moaned. "When will it be my turn to get out of this boring kingdom?"

I looked at her significantly and then tilted my head toward

Marie. Didn't she care about making a good impression with our new sister-in-law? Celine ignored me.

Thankfully Marie laughed. "I was feeling bored and wishing for some excitement before I met Rafe, too. But the sad truth is that the excitement isn't much fun when it's actually happening. I know I certainly regretted my wish soon enough."

Celine sighed, and I could see in her eyes that she wasn't convinced.

"So it's true that Dellie isn't coming back?" I asked Rafe.

He nodded. "I'm awfully sorry to steal her away to Northhelm with me. I know you girls will miss her. Her fiancé is a great sort, though. You'll like him."

"Cordelia insisted their wedding be here, in Lanover." Marie seemed to be trying to appease Celine. "She's visiting Ferdy's estates and family at the moment, but they'll join us here before we return to Northhelm next winter."

"I suppose that's something," admitted Celine. "I'd like to be a bride's attendant again." She had a faraway look, as if imagining her dress.

Marie caught my eye, and I could see that she was trying to stifle a laugh. Unfortunately, my own giggles were always close to the surface in my Celeste persona, and I couldn't keep one from bursting out.

Once I'd started, Rafe and Marie couldn't hold themselves back, either. Marie had yet to be exposed to the contagious music of my laughter, and she was soon gasping for breath. Celine regarded us all with narrowed eyes and then, when we didn't stop, she flounced out of the room muttering under her breath about insufferable older siblings.

"Oh, dear." I mopped my eyes. "Poor Celine. I shouldn't have laughed at her."

Rafe shrugged it off. "She'll recover and be causing mischief soon enough."

Later, though, as I prepared for the official reception, my mind returned to Celine. It couldn't be easy growing up as the baby at court. And somehow, she had known Rafe was going to arrive the night before, when even I hadn't heard about it. Maybe it really was time to introduce Celine to Aurora.

I hesitated for two reasons. Her safety and mine. Information gathering was not without risks, and Celine was still young. I would feel terrible if any harm befell her. And, as my sister, she knew me better than almost anyone. Would she see through my disguise? Would some small mannerism or quirk give me away?

I was still pondering the question when the herald announced my arrival to the court.

Several of the young men rushed to surround me, as they always did. But, after my dream the night before, I couldn't help searching out William with my eyes. I told myself it was only because he represented a new challenge at an otherwise boring event.

If I had hoped he would approach me quickly, I was soon disappointed. He certainly had no need to seek me out. A gaggle of court girls surrounded him all evening. I could hardly blame them. He was novel and handsome and would one day be a king.

I ignored the group around him and smiled at my own companions. I laughed often and wondered in my head how my inane conversation didn't drive everyone away. It had become a little tiresome to be so valued for nothing but my beauty.

The whole time, out of the corner of my eye, I watched the Northhelmian prince. He made no obvious move to acknowledge my presence. But his eyes betrayed him. They followed me wherever I went, his expression too difficult to read at this distance. A couple of times my cheeks grew warm, and I chided myself for my foolishness.

Celine, dressed much more somberly than the night before, convinced my parents to allow some dancing. As she took the instructions to the musicians, William's eyes met mine across the room. This time neither of us looked away, and a charming grin spread across his face. Without a word he abandoned the group at his side and strode across the floor to me. Somehow he found his way through the crowd surrounding me, and when the first strains of the music began, it was his hand that reached for mine.

I looked up at him mischievously and let him lead me away from my protesting admirers.

"That was smoothly done, Your Highness," I murmured.

He laughed down at me, holding me close for the dance. "I've been waiting for my chance all evening."

"Have you indeed? Despite your admiring flock?"

"Ah, but none of them compare to you."

"Careful, Prince, you'll make me blush." I looked up at him. "And then all of my admirers will wonder what you've said to me. They might challenge you to a duel."

"I would welcome a good match." He spun me around. "I've spent too long on horseback or stuffed into a carriage lately."

I couldn't help admiring his confidence. For an insane moment, I opened my mouth to tell him I would be happy to have a practice match with him. As long as I got to choose the weapon. But the barest tickle in the back of my throat stopped the words before they began. What was it about this man that made me forget the part I had to play?

The memory of our meeting the night before surged, and my resentment flared. The prince was overconfident if he thought he could win me over by admiring my beauty while he mocked my limitations.

"You complimented me last night, too, Your Highness. I think you might be a flatterer. I should probably ignore everything you say."

"Then I will simply have to keep saying it until you believe me."

He didn't seem in the least dismayed by my ingenuous rejection, and I wanted to grind my teeth together in frustration. If I hadn't been hedged in by the curse, I could have quickly put him in his place.

Then I reminded myself that the curse just made it more of a challenge. The prince would be here for months, so I could take all the time I needed.

I smiled up at him. "You're far too kind, Prince. I shall look forward to seeing you fight for my favor."

He looked a little startled, and I congratulated myself on catching him off guard. He looked down at me with the barest hint of suspicion, so I increased the innocence in my expression and batted my eyelashes at him.

"If that is your desire, Princess, it will be my honor to fight. And, please, call me William."

I regarded him for a moment. "Well, your sister is married to my brother, which makes us family of a sort, so I suppose that would be perfectly appropriate, William."

"Family!" He actually faltered for a moment in the dance, and I congratulated myself on a small victory. I would enjoy catching out this confident prince.

But he recovered in seconds and smiled down at me. "My name sounds charmingly on your tongue, Princess."

The music finished, and I swept into a deep curtsey. "Thank you for the dance, William."

"The pleasure, I can assure you, is all mine."

A member of court came forward to claim my hand for the next dance, but I continued to watch William from the corner of my eye. His gaze remained fixed on my retreating form until the next dance drove him from the floor. I smiled to myself and my dance partner sighed with pleasure. I barely refrained from rolling my eyes.

~

The next day a maid was finishing putting up my hair when Celine came crashing into my chamber. "Quick! Celeste, hurry!"

When I didn't move, she ran forward and tried to pull me out of the chair.

"Celine," I said reprovingly. "Rosie is still finishing my hair."

"Never mind that!" My sister waved the maid away. "You have to come right now."

Sighing, I let her drag me out into the corridor. "What in the kingdoms is going on, Celine?"

"It's Prince William." She smiled dreamily. "Cordelia wrote me that he was handsome, but I didn't expect him to be quite so…"

I snorted and let the curse do the work of transforming it into a giggle. "I didn't see that letter. When did it arrive?"

"Only a few hours before they did. She sent it via royal messenger with the rest of the official missives, but it must have gotten held up somewhere."

"Oh! So you already knew they were coming!" I said, as if the thought hadn't occurred to me before.

She nodded, still pulling me along. "I saw the messenger arriving in the rain and pumped him for information. He'd passed them on the road earlier that day."

"I'm still not entirely clear why the prince's dreaminess requires me to be pulled out of my room with my hair half done."

Celine snorted. "It looks done to me. You look gorgeous—as you always do."

I ignored her since she still hadn't answered my question and dug in my heels, pulling her to a stop. "What is going on, Celine?" And then I quickly added to satisfy the curse, "A princess should never run, it's inelegant. She might arrive at her destination red and breathless."

Celine rolled her eyes but began walking at a more reasonable pace. When it came to beauty, my sisters considered me a reliable source.

I fell into step beside her but poked her side, reminding her I still didn't know where we were going.

"William put out a general challenge to the young men of the court. He said he was doing it under royal orders or some such thing." She eyed me sideways as we walked. "Something about winning a certain princess' favor."

I stared at her. "Now? This morning?"

"Apparently he's a man of action."

"Celine…" I wasn't quite sure how to phrase my point without offending her. "You remember that you're only fourteen, right?"

Celine grimaced. "Seriously, Lettie? Even for you that's bad. *Of course* I remember my own age." She glared down at the stone passing beneath our feet. "And even if I didn't, I get reminded of it often enough."

"I…I'm sorry." I gripped her arm, regarding her with concern.

She shook me off and looked up with a determinedly enthusiastic expression. "Oh, never mind. I know that the prince wouldn't seriously look at me. But Lettie," she dropped her voice to a whisper, "they're fighting shirtless!"

My laugh rang through the corridor, and I slid my arm through hers. "Well, we'd better hurry then, we wouldn't want to miss that." I winked at her, and she giggled and picked up the pace.

The practice hall buzzed with sound as we stepped through the doors. A large group of young men stood around the edges, talking loudly and boastfully of their different areas of expertise. Most of them were watching a bout going on in the middle of the room.

I briefly noted Frederic, Cassian, and Rafe grouped together to one side, all of their eyes trained on the match, and then my own eyes caught on the fighters. William was matched against a young Lanoverian noble, and Celine had been right. His chest was bare.

A part of my mind noticed his excellent form and the clean lines of his blade as it swept through the air. The rest of my focus was absorbed by the muscles in his back and shoulders and the smooth look of his pale skin.

"Careful, Lettie," said Celine in my ear. "Don't start drooling."

I stiffened and tore my eyes away. "I don't know what you mean." It was a weak defense, but my mind seemed to have lost its usual sharp edge.

Celine dragged me around to the far side of the room, and I noticed that she carefully placed the largest group of nobles between us and our brothers. She was clearly afraid that they might kick us out of the hall if they noticed us.

"Are we sneaking in?" I asked in a whisper.

"Of course not. He's fighting for you, isn't he? Who has a better right to watch?" But I noticed she spoke quietly and cast an uneasy glance at our brothers as she said it.

I pulled her down onto a simple wooden bench against the wall and returned my attention to the match. Now that the first shock had passed, I focused on the competition itself. William fought well. His opponent outweighed him slightly, but the prince seemed to have the edge in skill. After another couple of minutes, he brought the match to an end, lightly resting the tip of his blade against the other man's neck.

The Lanoverian lowered his weapon, and I could read his lips as he congratulated William on his victory. Several of the other nobles clamored to fight him next, but Rafe stepped forward, and they all ceded to him.

"You said any weapon, did you not, my friend?" Rafe's eyes were dancing, and I knew exactly what he was going to choose.

"Ah!" Apparently William did, too. "So you're finally willing to fight me and prove your supposed mastery, are you?"

"I was waiting to ensure you'd made a full recovery from your adventures in Northhelm," said Rafe. "I don't want you to have any excuses when you lose."

William grinned. "We'll see about that."

Both men went over to a large weapons rack on the wall and chose a pair of knives. I sat up straighter. I had never seen William fight with knives, of course, but I didn't doubt the outcome for even a moment. As a child, Rafe had bemoaned receiving the useless Christening gift of grace. And then he had started weapons training. I never heard him complain about it again after that.

And while Rafe had mastered the sword and the bow, his real expertise lay with knives. The captain of our guard said he had never seen someone fight like Rafe. Given my brother had been my teacher, it was no surprise I favored knives myself. Well, that and I didn't have the strength and reach to be an effective sword fighter against men.

I shivered in anticipation. It had been far too long since I'd seen Rafe engage in a practice bout against anyone who could hold their own. I only hoped William could achieve a decent match.

They faced off from each other, and Frederic called a start to the bout. William darted forward, sounding Rafe out, and within moments they were exchanging slashes and blocks at deadly speed. I held my breath, enjoying the thrust and retreat of the lethal dance. William was even better than I had hoped, although I knew Rafe was holding back. The two began to call out friendly insults to each other as they fought, and I couldn't resist an amused smile.

Entering into the humorous spirit, Rafe threw one of his knives, slicing a gash in the fabric covering William's left leg. He used his remaining blade to maneuver William around in a wide circle and then called a challenge for William to emulate his feat.

"You can go for my arm if you like. It's my least favorite shirt, I assure you." His back was to me now, but I could easily imagine his laughing expression egging William on.

My smile grew wider.

And so, when William glanced up, his arm pulled back in the middle of his throw, he saw me leaning forward on my seat in breathless interest, a genuine smile lighting up my face. A jolting shock passed over his face, and I knew instantly that something was off with his throw.

# CHAPTER 5

*I* leaped to my feet as his hand released the knife, and it began to spin through the air. It missed Rafe completely and came straight toward Celine and me sitting directly behind Rafe. My mind shut down and my instincts took over. Jumping forward in front of my sister, I grabbed the knife from the air, halting its dangerous flight.

For the briefest second, I looked down at the blade in my hand, and then up into William's eyes. Something passed between us, but before I could decide what it was, the first wave of pain hit my stomach.

The shocked silence in the hall gave way to a sudden uproar as most of the men present rushed over to ensure we were unharmed. My mind raced, struggling to think past the crippling pain.

I dropped back onto the seat and let the knife fall to the ground. In the circumstances, the tears came easily. Far more easily, in fact, than sitting upright and ignoring the pain in my middle.

"Oh! What happened?" I cried, eyes shut. "Did it cut me? Is there blood? I can't look. Am I going to die?" I gave a little, endearing sob and cracked my eyes open just enough to see Rafe in front of me. I stood up and tipped myself into his arms, crying against his chest.

He patted me on the back and tried to shush me. "That was amazing, Lettie." I could feel his head move to glance around at the crowd. "She and I used to practice together before the curse. Her muscles must have remembered what her mind didn't."

A quiet murmur passed through the group, and I slumped against Rafe in relief as the cramps subsided. I'd managed to convince them; the curse was satisfied. I berated myself silently. I had grown too comfortable with my familiar routine, and now the arrival of the Northhelmians had thrown me off. I needed to be more vigilant. No more drooling over bare chests or expert knife moves. Something was going on in Lanover, and I couldn't risk being out of action for days, or worse. I needed to keep a tighter rein on myself.

I wiped away my tears and beamed at the small crowd. "How amazing! Maybe I can beat you all now."

They laughed obediently, and I turned to my sister, my tone full of excitement and amazement. "Did you see, Celine?"

Celine stared at me with round eyes. "I seriously thought I was going to die. You saved me Celeste!"

I gave her a hug. "It was terrifying, wasn't it? I have no idea what came over me."

"You're lucky that Rafe taught you how to handle knives. No one ever taught me how to fight." She clenched her jaw before adding, "Always the unwanted baby."

"Yes, I am lucky, aren't I?" I poured all the innocence I could muster into my expression and then held her gaze.

She was the first one to look away, muttering something inaudible.

I turned toward the others, satisfied. My sympathy for her situation as the youngest had its limits.

I nearly collided with William, who was standing much closer than I had realized. He still hadn't put his shirt on, so I took a hurried step backward.

"I'm so sorry, Princess." His voice was low and earnest, all trace of his usual humor absent. "I don't know what happened, but it was entirely unacceptable. I would never want to put you or your sister in danger." He shook his head. "You on the other hand were incredible. I don't know how you did that."

The sincerity in his eyes proved even more disconcerting than his usual charm. I swallowed and tried to compose myself.

"I don't know, either. But if it hadn't happened, I might not have had the chance to play the hero. It was quite thrilling, to tell you the truth." I smiled as disarmingly as possible. "Now Celine will have to be grateful to me and do whatever I say."

His eyes stared down into mine, his body still. After a long moment, that may have been only a second, he took a shuddering breath. His quiet whisper was for my ears alone. "What? Doesn't everyone already do whatever you ask? I thought you had us all under your spell."

My heart beat unaccountably fast, and I tried to tell myself it was nothing but the usual flirting I had long since grown accustomed to. "I don't know," I whispered back, "do I?"

He opened his mouth to reply, but Rafe clapped him on the shoulder, breaking us both out of the moment.

"An unfortunate accident, but all's well that ends well, hey? I told you our Celeste was a remarkable girl." He smiled at me proudly, and I realized how much I had missed his approval.

Frederic came up behind him, frowning. "I don't know what you girls are doing in here, but it isn't safe. I think that much has been proven. I don't want to see you in here again."

Celine jumped to her feet. "You aren't our father, Frederic. And you aren't king yet. Leave us alone!"

Her glare suggested she was ready for a fight, so I took her arm and began to lead her from the room. She followed me, merely turning her head to continue glaring at our brother.

"Honestly! Who does he think he is?" She fumed all the way down the corridor, muttering to herself about her excess of parents.

"At least we got to have a bit of excitement," I offered, trying to calm her down. "Didn't you say you wanted excitement and danger?"

She glanced over at me, and for a moment a vulnerable young girl looked out through her eyes.

"I really thought for a second there..." She shook herself. "Perfectly thrilling—wasn't that what you said? Maybe I won't have to leave Lanover to find some adventure, after all. Maybe the adventure has come to us."

The next two weeks seemed positively boring after the unexpected excitement. Our mother asked Celine to help her plan an extravagant masquerade ball in honor of the newlyweds, so even my youngest sister was quietly occupied.

William continued to give me extravagant compliments, and since our interaction in the practice hall, he watched me even more from afar, speculation mixed in with his blatant admiration. Something about his gaze sparked an answering challenge in me, and I couldn't seem to stop myself from dangerously skirting the edges of the curse's limits.

Every double meaning and barbed exclamation only deepened the gleam in his eyes, and I told myself to stop before he began to question me in earnest. But despite my fears of the curse, I continued in our weaponless duel.

But William only received half my attention. Every night, I dressed in black and slipped from my room to roam the corridors of the palace. Now, not a single night went by when I didn't find messages from my agents. The kitchen staff reported food stores mysteriously vanishing, and my recruits from the ranks of the guard noted more shifts changed at late notice. I had charged two of my agents with finding out who was making these changes, but they had yet to determine the source. The two palace quartermasters each thought the other responsible and saw no reason to question the situation.

Since I had yet to identify the purpose of the changes, I kept my agents from bringing it to anyone else's attention. I kept hoping the mastermind would make a wrong step and reveal themselves. Every night I pored over the reports, looking for some kind of pattern, anything that would shed light on the mysterious activity. I found nothing.

If the duchess had been in Lanover, I would have turned to her in my desperation. But she had stayed behind in Northhelm to finalize some negotiations.

Two nights before the ball, I once again pushed the food around on my plate, too frustrated to eat. Our normal family dinners had been expanded due to our visitors, so the conversation flowed easily around me. I listened with only half an ear.

"Is it necessary to make the day of the ball a holiday for the entire kingdom, Leonardo?" My Uncle Horace sounded like a curmudgeonly old man, rather than the relatively young one he actually was.

"Really, Horace! The people deserve a holiday as well as the nobility." My mother was a perfect counterpoint to my uncle's tough views. "They will work all the harder for it on the other days, you'll see."

Horace shook his head. "You're too soft-hearted the both of you. The people of Lanover should have more respect for the crown and for good hard work."

"I, for one, enjoy the more relaxed attitude here in Lanover." William paused as he brought his fork to his mouth. "And your kingdom doesn't seem to suffer for it. From what I can see, your wealth must fall from the trees. I only wish we were so fortunate in Northhelm." He smiled to remove any scent of resentment from his words. I suspected he was trying to turn the conversation to lighter topics.

Frederic quickly backed him, launching into a conversation on Lanover's chief resources and exports. He liked our uncle and hated it when he clashed with our parents.

Horace glanced from one to the other and then picked his fork back up. But he muttered quietly to himself about young people and their irresponsible ways while his eyes lingered on Celine.

I swallowed a mouthful of food. Our poor uncle would never be convinced of the responsibility and serious work ethic of my generation if he looked to Celine as an example.

My father's younger brother had toured the other kingdoms in his youth and been greatly impressed by their formal, hardworking ways and the respect they showed to authority. He had returned to Lanover full of new ideas to increase our productivity and, despite the years that had passed, he still sought to convince my father to implement some of them. Apparently my uncle would never grasp what seemed to come so instinctively to my parents—an understanding of our people and culture. We saw no reason to work harder when no one among us suffered serious want.

Of course, some of his suggestions had been good ones, and I had even seen a few of them implemented under Aurora's careful influence. If I had not been hampered by the curse, I would have sought my uncle directly so that we could work together. As it was, he continued to complain over every new holiday or welfare measure, and I could do nothing to influence him.

Growing up, I had assumed that the other kingdoms must be full of people like my uncle. But my time in Arcadia, and now the visit from the Northhelmians, had taught me that this was not the case. Not everyone from the north was serious and dour and devoted to hard work.

The thought made my eyes lift involuntarily to William, and I found he was watching me play with my food. His eyes lit up when they met mine, and he gave me a special smile that seemed just for me.

I compelled myself to smile in return before looking back down at my food. I had no time for our games while I tried to crack Aurora's problems. Still, I couldn't resist peeking back up at him. Concern shadowed his face as he continued to look my way. He could tell something was wrong.

I took a deep breath. I needed to try harder.

"Tomorrow should be a beautiful day." I cut across all the different conversations at the table, forcing myself to look oblivious to the confused and resigned expressions turned my way. "Marie and William must be sick of the palace and gardens by now. We should show them the rest of the city."

⁓

The next morning, our horses made their way down the steep, well-worn path that led from the palace to the capital.

"No grooms or guards?" asked Marie.

"We don't bother with such things here." Celine almost bounced in her saddle, full of pleasure at escaping the palace. "There are enough of us to look after ourselves."

The northern princess digested this sentiment and then sat up straighter. "Yes, indeed."

We called friendly greetings to the various people making their way up toward the palace, and William drew his mount close to mine. "Lanover is certainly unlike the other kingdoms. What did you think of Arcadia when you were there?"

"It was delightful, of course. How could it not be? They threw me a great many balls and parties." The curse turned my tone of sarcasm into sweet earnestness. I winced inside, wishing the curse would let me mirror the internal frustration on my face. He must think me a complete fool.

I paused. Of course he thought me a complete fool. Everyone did. And I'd long ago become accustomed to the idea. So why did it hurt so much to know that William saw me that way?

Despite my continued internal warnings, I was letting myself be swept away by our game, and I wasn't going to like the consequences if I let myself go too far.

I pulled my horse a little away from William's, and he let me go, although I could feel his eyes burning into my back.

I tried to view my city through the eyes of a stranger. I suspected it was drier than they had been expecting. The capital was located in the north of Lanover and was by far the driest city in the kingdom. An effect only enhanced by the prevalence of sandstone. Still, it was nothing compared to the vast sandy desert that bordered Lanover to the east. I had traveled there once as a child, and the stinging heat had convinced me never to return.

To the south, however, our kingdom only grew more beautiful. The further you traveled, the more green surrounded you, until you reached true jungle in the farthest reaches. Even this far north, bright flowers lit up our homes and markets, and a hint of water always lingered in the air.

We weaved through the streets, pointing out buildings of interest and calling greetings to the inhabitants of the city. No one paid us much mind; they were used to seeing us roaming around.

"If you want true beauty," said Rafe to his wife, "I'll take you out to see some of the islands. My parents said I might plan our wedding tour myself, so I'll ask them if they have a boat and crew available."

I sighed silently. I could hardly leave the palace at such a crucial time, but it had been far too long since I'd visited any of the many islands strung along the Lanoverian coast. Their brilliant turquoise waters and white sandy beaches provided the perfect location for a relaxing escape. I tipped my head back to take in the blue of the sky above us and imagined the beautiful scene.

"Perhaps we might join them, Princess," said William, who had drifted toward me again.

Could he read my thoughts? I tried to think of a way to put him off. "Sadly, that won't be possible. I get sea sick."

"Sea sick?" Celine stared at me. I hadn't seen how close her horse had wandered. "No you don't!"

I clenched my teeth together and suppressed my glare. Why did she have to stick her nose in?

"Don't I?" I looked at her with mild confusion. "I must have been thinking of something else, then."

William glanced between us curiously, and Celine rolled her eyes at him. "Ignore this one. She can't help herself."

Humiliation washed over me, as intensely as it had done during the first year of my curse. My own sister—dramatic, childish Celine—had no problem dismissing me, and in front of an outsider, too. Her condescension hurt more than Frederic or Cassian's would have. Even a fourteen-year-old deemed me too foolish to warrant the slightest consideration.

And there wasn't a single thing I could do about it. My continued survival depended on everyone coming to exactly that conclusion. I glanced sideways at William. Did he agree with Celine?

I shook myself and took a deep breath, digging my hands into my horse's mane and grounding myself in the steadiness of the animal. Celine didn't know how her words hurt me. And it didn't matter what other people thought of me. I knew my own value, and that was enough. It was just strangely hard to remember it with those blue eyes trained on me.

"Perhaps we will go to the islands after all, then," William said, before letting the matter drop.

# CHAPTER 6

*T*hat afternoon I wandered the corridors of the palace aimlessly, glad for once that my curse enabled idleness. I hoped that something would come to me as I walked, some spark of comprehension that I kept missing in the darkness of night.

Nothing came.

Eventually my feet led me to the practice hall. The clash of blades made me peek inside. Rafe and William fought alone, dueling with swords this time. I watched them unseen, wishing I could burn my frustrations off in a similar fight.

The sweat dripped down their faces, and they seemed evenly matched. Until eventually William gave a strong lunge, ducking in beneath Rafe's guard. Both men dropped their blades, panting for breath.

"Well, well, well. There's always a first time, I suppose." Rafe wiped his arm across his face, his light-hearted tone showing he didn't resent the loss. "Your fight seemed full of *passion* today."

William growled something I couldn't hear.

"I wish you could have met her before the curse." Rafe strolled over toward the weapons rack. "She was incredible."

*I'm still here inside.* I wanted to scream it out and let the sound echo off the distant walls.

William shook his head. "Maybe it's better that I didn't. She already manages to haunt my every thought as it is."

Warmth crept up my neck and face.

He growled again and thrust his sword onto the rack with more force than was necessary. "No, I don't mean that." He looked sideways at Rafe. "I've decided I'm going to stay." He tried to sound casual but failed.

"Stay? In Lanover?" Rafe frowned at him. "What will your parents say?"

"I don't care. I can't go back and leave her like this. It's wrong. There has to be a way to break the curse. I'm determined to find it."

Rafe smiled, but the expression looked grim. "I've been looking for a way to break it for more than three years. That's why I went to Northhelm in the first place, remember?"

I wished my parents would tell Rafe the truth. But the curse wouldn't let me request it of them, any more than it would let me tell him myself. Rafe, along with the rest of Lanover, believed that the curse was permanent. They thought that the provision of a true love's kiss had gone when my parents talked my godmother out of putting me into a true sleep.

Mother and Father had left it that way on purpose. They were afraid I would be besieged by young men attempting to kiss me. All in the name of breaking the curse, of course, but in truth, they would be seeking the ultimate prize—marriage to a beautiful princess, and the princedom that accompanied it. I appreciated my parents' protection, but surely they could safely trust my siblings not to spread the story?

Rafe clapped William on the back and tried for a lighter smile. "Don't tell me that the great crown prince of Northhelm has fallen in love with a beautiful face."

William shifted uncomfortably. "I don't know about love..."

He walked over to one of the side benches and picked up a towel. "She's the most exquisite thing I've ever seen, of course—and Northhelm has its fair share of beauty, in both people and nature. But it's not just that. She makes me laugh. And there's something else about her." He wiped his face with the towel. "It's like there's something lurking, just below the surface. Except I can't quite seem to put my finger on it." He threw the towel back down. "I feel like we're old friends and, in just a moment, I'll remember who she is. Only the moment never comes."

I drew back quickly, my heart beating fast. I took two steps away from the door and then took off running. He was even closer to seeing through me than I had thought. And it terrified me that the discovery produced more elation than fear.

Their conversation echoed through my mind, and I tried to remind myself that eventually the novelty of my beauty would fade, and William would flee my empty conversation. But when I slipped into bed that evening, a single frangipani rested on my pillow.

I stared at it. I had told William that morning that the frangipani was my favorite flower.

"Rosie," I said to the maid banking the fire. "Where did this flower come from?"

She looked up with a twinkle in her eye. "A certain young prince may have tasked me with placing it there, Your Highness. How could I say no to such a handsome face?"

"How indeed?" I sank back against the pillows. Rafe had spoken to William of love. Was it possible? Could William grow to love me truly? But he only saw a beautiful face. True love would value me regardless of my appearance. And how could anyone truly see me apart from my striking looks? Especially when the curse ensured nothing else was visible.

I shook myself. A flower changed nothing. It merely served as a warning that William was more observant that most.

~

It took more effort than usual to slip into Aurora that night.

Then I found two reports from my agents. One reported that the latest shipment of weapons for the castle armory had never arrived. The royal weapons maker in the capital swore that he had sent them, but both quartermasters denied receiving them.

That got my attention. Missing food supplies and medicines were one thing. But missing weapons? I still hoped I was dealing with a thief within the palace hierarchy—someone who was selling the items for their own profit. Unfortunately, I feared that was wishful thinking.

I had never worked out what the late-night visitor to the palace had been after, and I felt sure a missing puzzle piece eluded my grasp. I slipped a reassuring hand down to feel the hilt of the dagger I had taken to wearing in my boot. I didn't want to be caught at a disadvantage again.

The second note detailed yet another change in the guard roster. I decided the time had come to investigate the two quartermasters. Both men had held their positions for most of my life and neither had ever shown the slightest disloyalty to the royal family. But with missing supplies and odd changes to the guard, I couldn't keep ignoring them. Especially since neither man had brought the missing items to my parents' attention.

Those guards who lived in the palace inhabited the furthest wing, separated from the main part of the building by several unused corridors and an internal, open courtyard. I didn't often visit their wing since the night watch ensured there were always guards awake. I would need all of my concentration to enter and leave undetected.

I decided to approach from the outside since the garden provided far more hiding places than the corridors. Working my way around the massive building, I drank in the beautiful scent that permeated the air. Marie had told me that in the north, most of the plants were dormant for half the year. The thought made me sad.

Flowers and dresses were the only two of my real interests I had been able to keep after the curse. I couldn't imagine life without either one of them.

When I reached the distant wing, I counted the windows and then took a final moment to tuck my scarf more firmly around my face. Waiting for a cloud to pass in front of the moon, I moved out of hiding. Running swiftly but silently, I approached the fourth window from the end.

Counting my breaths helped to calm me as I pulled out my set of lock picks and used them to prize open the window shutters. It was a handy concentration trick I had learned years ago. As soon as the shutters were open, I swung myself over the sill and into the room, pulling them quietly closed behind me. I stood there, still counting, until I heard the sentry walk past on his rounds.

Once his footsteps had faded, I looked around the room. While I had been focusing on my ears, my eyes had adjusted to the lower light, and I could clearly see the space that served as both a sitting room and an office for our longest standing quartermaster, Ercole.

Everything looked exactly as it should, and snores emanated from the adjoining bedchamber. A second inspection locked the position of everything in my mind. I would ensure that before I left, the scene looked exactly as it did now.

I stepped away from the window and paused. Turning back to examine the windowsill and shutters, my eyes caught on a long, white hair illuminated by an errant ray of moonlight. I leaned down and picked it up from the floor, rolling it between my fingers. Ercole's gleaming bald head appeared in my mind.

I ran through the rest of the guards stationed at the palace and could think of none that had gone white. I carefully placed the hair back on the sill and then strode over to the other window. I found a second hair, this one resting across the clasp of the shutters. A quick glance at the door revealed a third hair. My gut sank.

I could think of no good reason for Ercole to set up an intruder alert system in his office. *Unless he also suspects something is wrong and is being cautious.* I still wanted to believe the best. I didn't quite convince myself, however.

My heartbeat picked up as I crossed over to his desk. A quick examination of the papers on top revealed nothing of interest. I carefully replaced them and bent to search the drawers. The bottom one was locked.

My lock picks re-emerged from where I kept them hidden in my hair, and I soon had the drawer open. A small leather book rested inside. I picked it up and examined the spine. *A Quartermaster's Guide to Supplies and Inventory.* Nothing suspicious there.

So why did he keep it in a locked drawer?

I flipped through the pages and a thin piece of parchment drifted out of the book and toward the floor. I caught it before it landed. Crossing over to one of the windows, I read it in a shaft of light that had managed to squeeze through a gap in the shutters.

A letter. My eyes skimmed the words and found a description of the most recent harvest and the health of several family members. The paper itself was dirty and worn, folded in multiple places.

It looked completely innocuous except for several small notations made in odd places. Several individual letters had also been circled.

I had spent the entire second year of my curse teaching myself how to make and decipher codes. I easily recognized the markings. They were the same sorts I had made myself in my early days of coding. Ercole had clearly needed some visual aids when he had deciphered this message.

A loud snore from the next room made me hesitate. Should I

leave the note or take it with me? I needed to decipher it, but I wasn't ready for Ercole to discover someone had raided his rooms.

One of the drawers had held a stack of blank parchment. I would simply have to hope he didn't know exactly how many were in the pile. Whipping one out, I found a pen and began to carefully copy the letter. Every mark on the page was repeated on my copy, and I then carefully folded my own sheet to match the folds on the original.

I looked at it and sighed. It wasn't as good as taking the letter itself, but it was a necessary compromise. Tucking the copy into my shirt, I returned the original and relocked the drawer.

A quick search of the rest of the room revealed nothing else of interest. I had intended to depart through the internal door, since Antonio, the other quartermaster, resided directly across the hall. But the hair balanced on the door handle made that impossible.

I examined the way he had laid the hair across the untouched shutter handle. I couldn't emulate the exact positioning on my window, but I picked up the hair I had dislodged anyway and wrapped it around one side of the internal clasp. Hopefully once I was through the window and the shutter was closed, the hair would look close enough to undisturbed.

I hadn't been meant to notice the hairs at all, so its presence on the shutter should be enough to allay suspicion. If Ercole was expecting anyone, he was clearly hoping for an amateur. Not surprising since he had been around long enough, and was senior enough, to know Lanover was sorely lacking in the spy arena. Clearly he hadn't heard of Aurora's arrival.

And, thankfully, I hadn't even considered sending one of my agents to do the job. They hadn't been trained for this sort of thing since I only used such methods as a last resort. The situation had never called for it before, with the one exception of my own agents. Anyone who volunteered to join my network had their room searched by me. I couldn't risk having my agents infiltrated by anyone disloyal to Lanover. I walked a particularly fine line since my spy network lacked official sanction.

I waited by the window until the sentry had made a pass and then slipped out into the night. A long walk through the garden to the far side of the wing gave me plenty of time to wonder what I would find when I decoded the message. It was still possible Ercole was only a thief and not a traitor. I feared I was clutching at straws, though.

I had to admit to a small thrill as I swung myself into Antonio's office. Another smooth entry. It had been too long since I had practiced these skills, and I'd forgotten the rush that came with them. The hours I spent doing strength and knife exercises in my bedchamber kept me in physical condition, but they did nothing to alleviate my boredom. In the early days, before I had expanded my network of agents, I had done more of the work myself. I hadn't realized how much I missed it.

It didn't take long to see the obvious differences in Antonio's room. No hairs or sand marked the entrances, and none of his drawers were locked.

The relief must have made me careless because I forgot to wait for the sentry to pass before I let myself back out the window. I had secured the shutter and taken only two steps away when he rounded the corner.

# CHAPTER 7

or a frozen moment we stared at each other. Then he gave a loud shout, and I took off into the gardens, as fast as I could run. My pulse hammered, and my breath thundered through my throat as I weaved through the plants. How long did I have before more guards heard his shout and joined him?

I screamed at myself silently for getting lax and overconfident.

I knew the gardens as well as I knew the palace, and I managed to put a little distance between us. My mind raced as I tried to think how I could use that to my advantage.

I rounded a tree, my attention focused on my pursuit, and failed to notice a shadowy figure in front of me. I collided with the man just as the moon sailed out from behind a cloud and illuminated the scene.

I staggered back in shock, recognizing the arms that reached out to steady me. William.

He looked me over quizzically before focusing on my eyes. I tried to wrench myself free to keep running, but his fingers tightened on my arms. Another shout from the pursuing guard brought his head up. He looked down at me once more and then thrust me behind him, keeping one hand firmly wrapped around my wrist.

I considered breaking his hold, but he didn't seem to be restraining me for the guard. I made the risky split-second decision to trust him. He had slowed me down enough that I had lost my lead, anyway. My options had narrowed considerably.

The guard, who had been joined by a comrade, barreled around the tree and jerked to a halt. The moonlight still shone strongly enough to light William's face. The second guard glanced at the first uneasily.

"Y...Your Highness," he stammered. I could easily read his thoughts as he glared at his companion. *Have you been chasing the prince this whole time? Didn't you recognize him?*

The original guard had noticed me sheltering behind William, however.

"Excuse me, Your Highness," he said, more confidently. "We have a few questions for your...companion."

William raised both eyebrows. "Come, come gentlemen. You've already frightened the poor thing half out of her wits. I really can't allow you to intimidate her any further."

"Her?" The guard clearly hadn't recognized I was a girl. The news seemed to throw him off stride. "We wouldn't wish to inconvenience Your Highness in any way, but we have our duty."

William treated them to his easy smile. "And a credit you are to Lanover, I'm sure." He leaned forward and lowered his voice. "But this particular young flower is nervous for a reason. A strict father, you understand. One who would take exception to even a simple stroll through the moonlight." He winked. "I can assure you, however, she's no risk to Lanover." He chuckled as if even the thought amused him.

"I...I see." The guard leaned around William to look at me. "Is that right, miss?" He moved his weight uncomfortably from foot to foot. He now seemed torn as to whether he was supposed to be protecting William from me, or me from William. The whole situation was so ridiculous, I nearly laughed.

I raised the pitch of my voice as high as I could and added a nervous wobble when I assured him that all was well with me and I truly, *truly* hadn't meant any harm. He'd just given me such a fright.

The second guard gave a small start when he got a good look at me, and as the moonlight fell on his face, I easily recognized why. I glared at him, trying to send a message with my eyes.

He tugged at the other guard's arm. "Come on. We're clearly not wanted here." He gave William a knowing look and a wink of his own. I reminded myself to commend him on his acting skills later. As one of my newer agents, I hadn't had the chance to see him in action before.

Reluctantly the first guard allowed himself to be dragged away. I waited until the sound of their retreat had fully faded before I let out a deep breath. I looked up into William's twinkling eyes.

"As a prince, rescuing fair maidens in distress is quite my usual occupation. I can't say I've ever rescued one dressed like you before, though."

I lowered the tone of my voice, as instinctive a part of my Aurora persona as giggling had become to my princess one. "Thank you."

"I generally like to know the names of the women I rescue."

"Aurora," I said without thinking.

"Ah." He regarded me with a smile. "And are you as lovely as the dawn underneath that scarf, Aurora?"

I quickly stepped backward. "I'm afraid that will have to remain up to your imagination."

He examined me from top to toe, taking in my dyed outfit.

Thank goodness the scarf hid the warmth flooding my cheeks. Aurora didn't blush.

"I sincerely trust you haven't made a liar out of me, Aurora, when I told those guards you meant no harm to Lanover. You have to admit your appearance looks a little...shifty."

I hovered on the balls of my feet, ready to run if I needed to, but curiosity kept me in place. "I can assure you I have only the good of the kingdom at heart. But tell me, why did you help me?"

His brow scrunched in thought. "That is an excellent question. I can't say exactly. It was the decision of a moment." His gaze focused on my face. "I suppose it was your eyes. They were so obviously pleading for help, I couldn't abandon you."

"A chivalrous princeling, then."

He didn't seem to take offense at my condescending comment. "You grow more interesting by the minute, Aurora. You see me simply burning with curiosity. What sends a young woman, dressed in black from head to toe, fleeing from the palace guards in the middle of the night?"

I shifted my weight, preparing to leave, but he caught the movement.

His hand shot out to grip my wrist again. "Oh no you don't. I've sullied my honor for you. Who knows what terrible rumors are circulating among the guards even as we speak?"

His eyes didn't lose their twinkle, so I decided not to waste any pity on him.

"I'm afraid the cost of my assistance is an answer of some sort." He looked at me meekly. "It need only be a small one. I assure you I'm not in the least greedy."

A reluctant laugh escaped me. "Will you accept the promise of a large answer tomorrow night, Princeling?"

"You tempt me, Oh Mysterious One, but how do I know you'll reappear?"

I stiffened. "I'm offering you my word."

He let go of my arm and held up both hands in surrender. "No need to glare fire at me." He regarded me silently for a moment. "Curiouser and curiouser. Very well, Aurora, I accept. Tell me where to find you tomorrow night, and your humble servant will await you there."

I thought for a moment. "Meet me in the gazebo on the other side of the garden. The spot will be more believable for a lovers' meet up if anyone happens upon us. Come at three bells past midnight."

He made no protest at the late hour, so I turned to leave. I took several steps before turning back around. He was watching my retreating back.

I knew I should stay silent and escape while I had the chance, but I couldn't resist. "You're very trusting, Princeling."

He spread his arms out wide, the moonlight glinting in his golden hair. "What can I say, Aurora? You inspire trust." He gave a deep chuckle. "Or is this my warning that I should be more suspicious? I can call the guard back if you would prefer."

"I'll be there tomorrow night. Don't keep me waiting." I slipped away, exercising all of my self-control not to look back over my shoulder.

～

I didn't see how sleep would be possible after the events of the night, but I knew I had to try. Tomorrow would be a long day, and the night even longer.

Even so, I had several stops before I could return to my chambers. My discoveries in Ercole's office would require the resources of my entire network, and some at least of them would need to receive their instructions in person. Coded notes were left in all of my hidden message caches, my last stop being the library. I scanned the shelves, fighting against my drooping eyelids. The earlier rush had faded, leaving me unusually exhausted.

I finally located a copy of *A Quartermaster's Guide to Supplies and Inventory* and made my way toward my bed. The book and the copied letter I tucked safely under my pillow. Part of me wanted to stay up and begin deciphering the message, but the saner part of me knew it was far too late. I would make quicker work of it in the morning.

Rosie woke me when she came in to draw back the curtains and stoke the fire. I moaned and covered my eyes with my arm.

"A big day today, Your Highness." She crossed the room with a bounce in her step.

I lowered my arm and stared at her in confusion, one hand stealing beneath the pillow to check for the book and parchment.

She shook her head at my blank expression. "The ball, I mean, Your Highness."

Oh. The ball. I put my arm back over my face. Yet another thing to fit into the night. At least I would have an excuse for looking tired the next day. A slight twinge in my stomach reminded me that everyone knew Princess Celeste loved balls.

I pushed myself into a sitting position. "Has my new dress arrived, Rosie?"

"Just this morning, Your Highness." She pointed to a carefully wrapped bundle draped across a wing chair. "I hope Your Highness doesn't mind, but I took a peek as I brought it up. I think you're going to be right pleased."

Returning Rosie's good-natured smile was an easy chore. The maid took almost as much interest in my clothes as I did and never betrayed the least bit of jealousy that they belonged to me instead of her.

"What will you be doing tonight, Rosie?" I dragged myself out of bed and tottered over to the small table where she had laid my breakfast tray. I sank into a chair.

I had long ago decreed that I would take my morning meal in my room. Officially, I needed the extra time to prepare for the day. Unofficially, I had spent more mornings in the same sleep deprived haze than I cared to remember.

"Their Majesties have declared a holiday for the whole kingdom. There are to be all sorts of celebrations in the capital, and even a dance in the servants' hall."

"Will you be going into the city?" I asked, aware that she was being courted by a young shopkeeper. I tried to send her on as many errands to the city as I could justify.

She looked at me sideways. "Well, if Your Highness didn't mind…"

"No, no, of course not." I grasped eagerly at the opportunity. "You should go and have fun. I can undress myself."

"If you're sure…" I nodded, and she beamed at me. "I'll leave a basin of water for you to wash and make sure the fire is banked up before I leave."

She floated out of the room, obviously picturing the delightful night to come. I took a long sip of tea. My evening would be a little easier without Rosie around. I wouldn't need to pretend to go to bed before emerging as Aurora.

I took another sip of tea and noticed a bright spot on my breakfast tray. Another frangipani. I picked it up.

Twirling it, I admired its colors and clean lines. A smile played around my mouth. Despite the danger, speaking my mind to William had been almost as much of a rush as breaking into the quartermasters' rooms. Already I looked forward to seeing him again as Aurora.

He must have been nearly as late to bed as I had been. When had he given the flower to my maid? My hand stilled as a more important question surfaced. What had he been doing in the garden in the middle of the night?

I shook my head. William wouldn't be the only one with questions when we met at the gazebo.

I hurried through my breakfast, my eyes continually returning to the flower. As soon as I had taken the last bite, I wedged my makeshift doorstop under the door. All of the servants for this wing of the palace knew about my old door, and the way it periodically got stuck.

Once my privacy was ensured, I withdrew the book—surely the key to the letter's code—and settled in to start deciphering.

# CHAPTER 8

$\mathcal{T}$he code was more sophisticated than I had expected and took a long time to crack. Thankfully the ball provided an excuse for staying holed up in my room. No activities had been planned for the day since everyone was busy preparing for the various evening festivities.

When I finished, I sat back and read the whole message through. My eyes widened. I had been hoping that the situation would prove less drastic than I feared. Instead, it was worse. Several things now came into focus in my head.

Ercole was using his position as quartermaster to increase the number of guards. At the same time, he was intercepting shipments of supplies, selling them off quietly, and using the proceeds to fund a mercenary army. The mercenaries were hidden in plain sight among the rank of the guards, to all outside appearance merely loyal guards fulfilling their duties. But in reality, he paid them a second salary in exchange for giving their true loyalty to the rebellion.

I paced up and down my chamber, my churning mind demanding physical movement. I thought of all the times I had seen Ercole fulfilling his duties during my childhood. He had always professed full loyalty to our family. What had turned him against us?

My decision to leave the original letter behind in his desk had been a good one. Now, when my father sent guards to arrest him, they would find the proof of his treason.

I stilled. No. I couldn't let my outrage override my strategic sense. If we moved against Ercole now, we might prevent the spate of thieving. We might even severely limit the growth of his mercenary army.

But we wouldn't have the head of the rebellion. Ercole clearly took his orders from someone else. But the letter gave no indication of who that might be. If I had him arrested, we would have to rely on gaining a confession. And while we tried to secure one, the true villain would have time to flee or obscure his plans in some way.

For now, finally, I had the advantage. With my network behind me, I could use this new information to uncover the rest of the plot. I frowned. With the duchess absent, I would also have to devise a way to convey the details of the plot to my parents.

My eyes fell on an ugly ornament sitting on a side table. I picked it up and hurled it, as hard as I could, into the fireplace. It smashed with a satisfying crash. If only I wasn't limited by the curse.

I closed my eyes and tried to retrieve a sense of calm. I was starting to act like Celine. I shook myself. I had no time for dramatics—there was far too much to be done.

I had to stop planning when Rosie arrived to help me into my gown for the ball. Reluctantly I turned my attention to dressing. It would be harder than ever to play the foolish princess this evening.

But my Celeste persona came so easily these days, that within minutes I found myself distracted by my new gown. The seamstress from the city had outdone herself, and it was even more striking than the one she had made for Celine. Her fabric had an unusual sheen, and I reminded myself to ask her about the source of her material. Of course, that would have to wait until I had dealt with the mercenary militia gathering at our door.

I swept into the ballroom, my anger over the rebellion heightening my color and lending an extra edge to my movements. Everyone who saw me stopped in their tracks, and I couldn't help a savage satisfaction. Despite everything the curse had stolen from me, I retained a certain power. Willing or not, everyone responded to my beauty, unable to look away.

Ercole and his mysterious leader had underestimated me, just as the whole court did. And I would use every tool at my disposal to bring them down.

Men clamored to dance with me, and for the first few dances I lost myself in the physical exertion, ignoring their attempts at conversation or answering at random. Thankfully the curse let me get away with such inconsiderate behavior.

By the third dance I noticed a glaring absence from the crowd surrounding me. My eyes found William dancing on the other side of the ballroom. Why hadn't he approached me yet?

"Careful, Lettie." Celine gave me a knowing smile. "Someone might think that was jealousy in your eyes."

I sucked in a breath, opened my mouth to respond and then closed it again. None of the responses that came to mind sounded enough like my cursed self.

"I'm sure he'll be over here soon enough. He's only glanced this way about fifty times already."

I suppressed a smile.

"And he spent the whole day prowling the palace like a caged animal. Something to do with your absence, perhaps?"

I wasn't entirely sure if Celine was jealous herself or trying to be encouraging. I watched William and, sure enough, he did glance my way twice during the dance. Still, despite Celine's words, I couldn't help feeling he was a little less attentive than usual.

A sudden thought stilled my restless hands. Last night, William had met Aurora for the first time. And in only a few hours, he would meet her again. Could that have anything to do with the subtle change in his demeanor toward me?

I bit my lip, wishing the thought had less power over me.

Minutes later, the prince was bowing over my hand. The fiery admiration in his eyes made me doubt my earlier conclusion.

"You outshine the entire room," he murmured. He shook his head. "No, you outshine the sun and the moon. I have never seen you look so beautiful."

After so many years of compliments, I usually received them with equanimity. But I couldn't ignore the light in his eyes and the throb in his voice. My cheeks burned.

"Ah," he said, softer still. "Not made of stone after all." His grin seemed to devour my face, and I blushed darker still.

A pale young man who had been watching us from afar stepped forward and bowed in my direction. "I regret that business has kept me in the city these last few weeks, Your Highness. I have missed the sight of you, like a man misses food and wine. The sight of your beauty is like a refreshing drink in a parched desert. My soul is lifted up and enriched merely by gazing upon you."

Rafe strolled up to us, thankfully cutting off whatever response Celine had been about to make.

"Ah, Rivers! It's been too long."

They exchanged greetings, and I took the opportunity to step on Celine's foot. She glared at me and crossed her arms, but at least she looked like she wasn't going to say anything. She knew that Celeste hated conflict.

The Arcadian noble was even more elaborately dressed than most of the women, and he was certainly more than a little ridiculous. But I didn't like her mocking him. He had been a devoted admirer for years without ever making the least demand on me. He merely wished to be allowed to gaze upon my beauty.

Celine thought he was a bigger fool than I was. But I'd seen his shrewd gaze and heard him in conversation with some of the merchants of the court. He and I were alike in many ways. An intelligent interior hidden behind a flippant façade. I didn't understand the motivation behind his mannerisms, but I felt the kinship all the same. Perhaps his love of beauty was simply a part of him, the same way my love of dresses and flowers was a true part of me.

"I'm glad you're enjoying Celeste's appearance, Rivers," said Celine. "It took her most of the day to accomplish." She turned to me, all innocence. "I don't know how you can bear to spend so much time making yourself beautiful. *I* would be bored to tears."

Normally my family tried to shield me from the foolishness of my cursed personality, not draw attention to it. Apparently, she hadn't taken my reprimand well. Still, I preferred she took it out on me than on Rivers.

"Beauty is its own reward." I beamed around at the group.

Rivers nodded in complete agreement, but Rafe looked like he wanted to vomit. Truthfully, I agreed. But I needed some reason to account for the hours a day I spent hidden from court life. This excuse was simple and, most importantly, believable. Thank goodness that in reality my appearance needed little upkeep.

William looked surprised, but he quickly recovered himself. "Beauty such as yours is worth every minute."

Rivers eyed him with dislike. I giggled and, for once, the sound was real. Rivers probably resented William for stealing his line.

The Arcadian gave a stiff bow, and moved to the other side of the ballroom, throwing the occasional dark look over his shoulder.

"Who was that?" William looked equal parts fascinated and revolted.

"Oh, that's just Rivers. I'm surprised you haven't met him yet. He's Arcadian. He followed me back to Lanover after my state visit two years ago and has been here ever since."

William gave a low whistle. "Two years! He must be very much in love with you." He cast me a sideways glance, clearly assessing what I thought of the Arcadian.

I gave a snort, which the curse turned into a giggle. "It's beauty that he worships." I gave a second giggle, voluntary this time, in the hopes the curse would let me get the next line out. "His own mostly."

William quickly turned a bark of laughter into a cough. "Well, he is very beautiful," he said gravely once he got his breath back.

Rafe choked on his drink and shook his head at William with a significant look. I wished my brother had simply been amused, as William had been, but I understood his expression easily. I spun away before I could be tempted to respond. Even my brother, who loved me, wanted to remind William how foolish I was. How impossible that I could purposefully make a witty comment. Just a beautiful face, not worthy of William's regard.

The first notes of a new song drifted across the crowd, and I watched William out of the corner of my eye. Would he ask me to dance? Or had Rafe put him off? He seemed to be looking my way; surely he had come over with that intention in the first place.

Celine stood in my direct line of sight, and I watched the direction of her gaze. The row of full-length windows had been thrown open for the evening, giving the dancers direct access to the gardens. Small decorative lanterns nestled among the plants for a short distance, but after that, the moon provided the only light. Several couples already strolled the gently-lit walkways.

"Don't even think about it," said Rafe to Celine. He had obviously noticed the same thing I had. "You know Mother would forbid it."

Celine rolled her eyes.

"A princess is never indiscreet." I said, then lowered my voice. "And just because you're only fourteen, doesn't mean that some awful person won't try to use you to get closer to the crown."

Celine spun around to face me. "Honestly, Celeste! You might be the most beautiful girl in the palace, but that doesn't mean every single man here is in love with you. It is possible that the rest of us might honestly attract someone's interest, too."

"That's not what I meant…" I didn't finish since she had already stormed away.

My conscience twisted as I watched her go. I hoped my words wouldn't goad her into doing something outrageous. I had spoken thoughtlessly, my mind too full to properly handle my tempestuous sister. And I had let some of the frustration at my own situation leak out onto her.

Rafe stepped forward and patted me on the arm. "Don't worry, Lettie. We'll all keep an eye on her. And I'm fairly certain Mother has told the guards not to let her out into the gardens."

I still felt bad, but his reassurance provided some relief. I eyed the ceremonial guards lining the walls and decided that he was almost certainly right. My mother wouldn't leave Celine unsupervised at such an event.

"Ah," said William, "the gardens. A dangerous place indeed for any young woman…or young man for that matter." He smiled, as if joking, but I noticed that his eyes lingered on the windows, and he joined Rafe at the refreshment table instead of asking me to dance.

For the first time in weeks, my eyes followed him around the room instead of the other way around. I wished I could see into his mind. The memory of my earlier humiliation burned. Had he been put off by the lie I was forced to live? By the disdain of my own siblings? Or was it his upcoming meeting with Aurora that gave him pause? What, or rather who, consumed his thoughts as he gazed at the couples outside?

~

I had set up a series of meetings with my agents that would take me half the night to accomplish. And since the ball would almost certainly continue on until the late hours, I made the unprecedented move of excusing myself early with a headache. Nothing delighted Celeste more than dresses and dancing and balls, but I couldn't afford the time.

My mother patted me on the hand and told me to tuck myself into bed. She promised to visit me in the morning before sailing off toward a group of nobles. I only hoped the rest of the court joined her in her unconcern.

At least between the ball and the dance in the servants' hall, the corridors were mostly empty. Still, I paid extra attention as I made my way to my first rendezvous point.

Some of my agents towered above me, but none of them would ever consider disrespecting or challenging me. After three years, they believed me infallible, and followed me with almost slavish devotion. Despite the advantages my Christening gift had given me, some nights I could hardly sleep from the pressure. I couldn't afford even the smallest mistake. And now the stakes were higher than ever.

Every single one of my agents in the palace soon had a new assignment.

The guards had been given instructions to tail Ercole. "I don't care what lengths you have to go to," I told them. "Between you all, you need to keep him under watch, at all times. I want to know every single person he speaks to and everywhere he goes."

I could see the burning curiosity in their eyes, but I ignored it, and no one voiced their questions.

The maids and grooms and footmen and under-cooks were

tasked with ensuring no more deliveries or supplies went astray. Now that I knew the stolen items were supplying a rebel army, I couldn't allow the bleeding to continue.

"I want one of you manning every delivery and watching every storeroom. Manipulate your shifts any way you have to. I don't care if you change the rosters while everyone else sleeps. Make it happen!"

None of them asked how to accomplish such a feat. They knew I valued them for their initiative, and I had trained them for such a crisis. Their eyes shone with their desire to prove themselves.

"Lanover needs you," I said quietly. "Don't let your kingdom down."

By the time my last rendezvous had finished, I had to jog to the gazebo. The third bell sounded moments before I arrived, so I slowed, keeping my eye out for any stragglers from the ball or servants' dance. I could still see the glow of the ballroom windows in the distance, so at least some revelers remained.

I barely had time to wonder if William would keep me waiting before he stepped out of the shadows.

# CHAPTER 9

"*S*he appears." His voice held the barest hint of relief.

"Tell me, Princeling." I let the smile sound in my voice. "Have you been fretting all day over whether you made the wrong decision?"

"I will admit the smallest doubt crossed my mind. But I see now that I wronged you. How foolish of me to suppose that you might dance the night away and forget all about me. I had forgotten that you're not the type for gowns and dances."

I snorted, and satisfaction washed over me at the indelicate sound. With my face hidden behind a scarf I felt free and light. My true feelings tasted sweet on my lips.

That honesty compelled me to admit that service to my kingdom had been a secondary motive in the creation of Aurora. All day I craved the freedom that night brought.

"You're a presumptive princeling, aren't you? How do you know I don't dance as well as I sneak? A girl can wield a blade and a dress at the same time, you know."

The moonlight reflected off the gleam in his eyes. "I would love to see you in a gown, Aurora."

For a wild moment, I wanted to rip off my scarf, but it didn't need the warning burst of pain in my head to dissuade me. Lanover and my family were in imminent danger, and it didn't matter how dashing this foreign prince looked in the moonlight, or how sick I was of living a lie. Aurora didn't lose her focus because of a pair of blue eyes, and Aurora was as much a part of me as Celeste.

I had spent most of the day considering what to tell William and, in the end, had decided that the situation was dire enough to warrant the truth.

"Tell me, Princeling, did you put your daylight hours to good account? Did you ask around about a mysterious girl called Aurora?" It's what I would have done in his position.

"I'll admit that I did." He followed me into the gazebo where we were less likely to be seen by any particularly adventurous couple. "And I got some interesting reactions. It seems that the servants didn't appreciate a foreigner asking questions about their precious spymaster."

He said the word lightly, but I felt the weight of it and smiled. My tale would be much simpler if he accepted my identity.

Choosing my words carefully, I outlined the situation and my recent discoveries. "Lanover needs your help, if you're willing to give it." I stepped closer and lowered my voice, gazing up into his face with brimming eyes. "*I* need your help."

His breath hitched. For a moment, I thought I had him, but he stepped back and shook his head slightly.

I couldn't help feeling pleased. It might have been more convenient for him to follow me blindly, but I respected him more for not doing so.

"A rebellion is a serious thing. And I could hardly refuse Lanover my aid. Not when one of your princes recently helped Northhelm defeat our own rebel. But I'll admit to a little curiosity as to why you're trusting me so freely." The challenge in his eye was tinged with humor. "For all you know, I might be involved. Are you sure you don't want to search my room, too?"

I said nothing, regarding him steadily.

Slowly his eyebrows rose. "I'm not sure whether to feel violated or impressed."

"If you're asking for my opinion, I would recommend going with impressed. All new recruits get vetted. I wouldn't be standing here now if I had found anything suspicious." Taking the time to check his rooms before meeting with the first of my agents had been the right decision. My reputation had been earned through moves like that.

"I'll admit that your youth made me doubt you." William ran his hand along his jaw. "But clearly your king knew what he was doing when he assigned you the role. It will be a pleasure to me to repay something of my debt to your kingdom."

I decided he didn't need to know that I had assigned myself the role. I wasn't even sure if my father knew of Aurora's existence. If he did, he seemed content to let the matter stand.

"You can start by answering a question for me. What exactly were you doing in the gardens in the middle of the night last night?"

William ran his hand along his jaw, his eyes drifting in the direction of the ballroom. "I couldn't sleep and decided to go for a walk to clear my mind."

I raised one eyebrow, and he grimaced before chuckling. "That doesn't exactly sound convincing, does it? It wasn't rebellion or intrigue keeping me awake. It was entirely romantic in nature."

I froze. I wasn't entirely sure I was ready to talk to William about Celeste as Aurora. My deception had never been so complicated.

He sighed. "I'm busy fighting an attraction that doesn't feel entirely natural, but I promise I won't let it interfere in this."

"Not natural?"

"I can't seem to shake it, no matter how hard I try, or how many times I tell myself she's not right for me." He looked at me and one side of his mouth crept up. "I sound like a crazy person, don't I? Not exactly the impression I was going for."

A flash of movement behind William caught my attention before I could reply. I held up a hand to silence him, and he stilled instantly.

Someone wound through the garden. His clothing proclaimed him a reveler, but he walked alone, and his movements seemed too careful and calculating. And, more than that, something about his gait seemed familiar. It didn't take me long to place him. I had followed him through the palace for an hour, after all.

My interest pricked. I had made no headway whatsoever in trying to fit the actions of the mysterious intruder with the rebellion. But I felt sure they were somehow connected.

I watched him head toward the palace and gestured for William to follow me, never taking my eyes off the trespasser. The prince fell in behind me, and I felt a moment of gratitude that he knew how to move silently. He had told me he served in the royal guard back home. Obviously the position was more than ceremonial.

We followed the man halfway around the palace until we approached one of the entrances near the servants' hall. The intruder's bearing changed, and he began to sway slightly as if he had drunk too much. He waved at the guard and called out a greeting, his words almost too slurred to be comprehensible. The guard shook his head but made no move to bar the man's entry.

So he hadn't achieved his purpose last visit. And now he was trying a different approach.

I hung back, wishing I could rip off my scarf and follow the man through the door. But, dressed as I was, I couldn't make such a straight-forward entrance. Trusting that William would follow, I made a sharp right and hurried around a corner. Out of sight of the guard, or any other doors, I removed my lock picks and opened the closest shutters. I glanced at William as I tucked them back into place. His face conveyed nothing but appreciation.

I hoisted myself onto the windowsill and jumped down into the corridor. I could hear the faint scrape of William's boots as he followed me, and the slight click as he relatched the shutters. I ignored him, trying to get my bearings.

Given the door he had entered through, the intruder could have taken two directions. But only a small section of the palace had been left unsearched on his previous visit, so I took a gamble and headed in that direction.

My instincts proved correct. We found him only a single corridor further on from where the cat had given me away on the last occasion. He obviously felt secure enough in his disguise since he carried a candle.

The light made him easy to spot as he once again tried every door he encountered. Except this time, after only three doors, he paused.

He had reached his destination, and my instincts told me his next move. I had made a mistake. When he checked up and down the corridor, we would be fully exposed. We had nowhere to hide.

But apparently William thought even faster than I did. Slipping his arms around my waist, he pressed me to his chest and pinned me against the wall. Angling us so that his back faced the intruder, he lowered his head until his face hung the barest breath above mine.

A soft snicker sounded from the intruder, followed by the sound of a closing door. William didn't let me go.

My heart pounded furiously, and I told myself it was only because of our narrow escape. It had nothing whatsoever to do with being held so tightly in William's arms.

"Quick thinking." I wished I didn't sound breathless.

His chuckle made no sound, but I could feel the vibration in his chest. "If it wasn't for that blasted scarf of yours, I could have given a better performance."

His words made my eyes drop to his lips, and I swallowed.

They looked soft and inviting. I tore my mind away from the suddenly burning question of what it would feel like to have them pressed against mine.

Placing my hands on his chest, I firmly pushed him away. He yielded easily, stepping back and giving me space. I stepped into the center of the corridor, carefully ignoring him.

The faintest tinge of light leaked out from under one of the doors. This part of the palace held various offices, and it took me only a moment to remember what lived on the other side of this particular door.

I rocked back on my heels. Interesting.

I slipped inside the room on the other side of the corridor. William followed me. Pulling the door most of the way closed, I settled in to wait.

"Now what?" asked William, in the faintest whisper.

"Now we see what he does next."

We didn't have to wait long. Within minutes, the door reopened, and the man stepped back out into the corridor. He strode quickly toward the nearest exit, his goal obviously completed.

I let him get a decent head start and then trailed behind, wanting to make sure he left without further activity. I itched to be back at the room he had just vacated, but I couldn't afford to get sloppy now.

He left the palace without incident, and I rushed back the way we had come. I began to emulate the intruder, opening each door we passed and sticking my head inside. It took five doors before my search was rewarded.

"Ah huh." I strode into the room and took the glass of water off the desk. It was half-empty with finger marks on the sides, but it would serve my purpose. I grabbed a lantern off a second desk and paused to light it. From the looks of things, the officials who worked in this office kept long hours.

"Feeling thirsty?"

I ignored William—he would understand soon enough.

Reaching the room in question, I removed a handkerchief and carefully opened the door without touching the handle.

The door swung wide to reveal a small room, not much bigger than a storage cupboard. Every wall was lined with shelves and most of them were filled with heavy leather tomes. An empty desk stood in the middle of the floor.

William peered in over my shoulder. "A records room?"

I nodded. "For the palace magistrate. The trial outcomes and the details of the sentencing of every major criminal in the history of Lanover is recorded here." I stepped inside and placed the lantern on the table.

William surveyed the number of books with a frown. "Are the records sealed?"

I shook my head. "Any citizen of Lanover may request access from the magistrate."

"In that case, why would anyone break into the palace for these? Unless they wanted to change one, perhaps?"

"It's for historical purposes only." I set the glass down beside the lantern. "Changing the record would change nothing. As to why someone would break in…the answer seems obvious to me."

"Then please, enlighten me."

"Whatever information he was after, he didn't want anyone knowing he wanted it."

William looked sheepish. "Now that you say it, that does seem rather obvious."

I grinned at him. "That's why I'm the spymaster, and you're the prince. Some things should be left to the experts."

"I was wondering why I liked you so much—now I remember. It's because of your charm." I refused to be baited, so he continued. "I suppose now you're going to tell me how we work out which record he wanted to access."

"Of course." I dipped my fingers into the glass and began flicking water onto the spines. After my fourth flick, I paused.

William stepped closer. "Did that book just turn orange?"

He exaggerated, but several spots of bright orange had appeared on the spine. I removed the book and carefully cleaned them off with my handkerchief. I placed it on the table, but William dropped his hand down onto the cover, holding it closed.

"As your humble assistant, I'm completely lost. What just happened?"

"The door handle is coated with a special powder. Made from a jungle flower from southern Lanover. It's so fine that it becomes invisible unless wet. Then it forms a bright orange paste. When our intruder opened the door, his fingers picked some of it up and transferred it onto this book. All I had to do was add water."

"And it just happens that this particular door was coated with this powder?"

"Of course not." I tried not to let my impatience show. "All the doors of all the record rooms in the palace are coated with it. For such an occurrence as this, I might add."

"Why isn't every book in the room coated with the stuff? You must have very lax record keepers."

I sighed. I wanted to know what was inside the book. "First of all, this is a *historical* record room, remember. The current volume is kept in the magistrate's office. And, secondly, his junior aide is one of my agents. He removes the powder and reapplies it as needed."

I shifted uncomfortably under the awe in William's face. "Is there anything you haven't thought of?"

I shrugged. "I wouldn't know, would I? Since I haven't thought of it. Now, can I open this book and find out what that man wanted?"

"Please do." He removed his hand.

The second page had a list of the names of every criminal

recorded in the volume. I scanned it, hoping something would jump out at me.

The names looked strangely familiar. I had the vague feeling I'd read this book before. But only one entry in this room had ever interested me...

# CHAPTER 10

Bile rose in my throat as I found her name on the list. Princess Melisande. My father's sister. The woman who had sentenced me to death out of resentment. Who thought wishing destruction on a baby was an appropriate response to being excluded from a Christening.

I didn't need to flip to her entry, but I did it anyway. I already knew her fate. Like Celine, I had been entirely dissatisfied with the story of her disappearance. And like the intruder, I had chosen to visit this room at night, without going through the magistrate to get my answers.

My aunt had been banished to one of Lanover's most remote islands. At first, she had received regular shipments of supplies. But after a year, the boat captain had reported a strange phenomenon. A tall hedge had grown out of nowhere to surround the entire island. It started at the place where the sand of the beaches stopped, and the thorns were as long as a grown man's forearm.

The first time, he had left the supplies on the deepest beach, out of reach of the tide. When he returned, months later, the supplies were still there. Picked over by birds and half rotten. He didn't bother leaving the next shipment. Once a year, he sailed past the island to check if the hedge remained. It had only grown taller and thicker.

No one knew what was hiding behind the hedge, or what fate had befallen my aunt. Personally, I hoped she had died slowly and alone, short on food and medicine.

William read over my shoulder, letting out a low whistle when he reached the end of the record. "Is that…?"

"Yes." I didn't want to discuss it. Instead my attention focused on several lines that had been recently added to the entry.

For the last three years, the captain had been instructed to try various methods of removing the hedge. It had so far proved resistant to flame, sword and ax.

I snapped the book shut and shoved it back on the shelf, too distracted to move quietly. After all this time, someone was trying to break through the hedge and contact my aunt. Someone official. And, apparently, someone unofficial was very interested in the methods being employed. Someone who didn't want anyone to know about their interest.

I slapped a hand to my mouth, my eyes going wide. Several things began to make sense. Ercole's father had been quarter-master before him. Ercole had grown up around court, almost the same age as my father. And everyone said that Melisande had been as beautiful as any of my sisters. The princesses of Lanover always were.

Perhaps he hadn't lost his loyalty to our family, perhaps his loyalty had always been to a different member of the family. My aunt had used one magical object to curse me. Perhaps she had access to more. Perhaps she had built the hedge herself, only now she had lost control of it and needed to be rescued. Perhaps the two of them had been laying plans this whole time, biding their time, preparing against the day when Melisande could have her final revenge on my family. If only Ercole could find a way to free her…

The woman must be unhinged, of course. But I knew better than anyone the power of a beautiful face. And how much people were willing to overlook when faced with great beauty. I had wondered who led the rebellion but had somehow overlooked the most obvious answer. Only one person had ever attempted to bring death to my family before.

But that still left the question of who had made the official order. Were my parents trying to contact my aunt after all this time? Why would they attempt such a thing?

I ushered William out of the room. I knew he must be curious, and I appreciated his restraint.

"It would appear that our intruder has an interest in Princess Melisande, her whereabouts, and the means being used to reestablish contact with her." I didn't mention that I had no idea who had given the original order to test the hedge. Or how far my suspicions extended.

"We need more information. If you're still willing to help, start nosing around. You can get away with asking questions no local could ask. Use that. Find out if any of the nobles are harboring dissatisfaction with their monarchs. But, most of all, get me any information you can find on the princess."

My anger and hatred toward my aunt, which I normally tried to keep buried deep, now roiled so close to the surface that I lived in daily fear of it bursting through my Celeste persona. I walked through the palace under a dark cloud and pushed myself harder than ever each night. The frangipanis that continued to appear on my pillow and beside my plate no longer brought a smile to my face. They merely served to remind me of the life I should have had. The life Aunt Melisande had taken from me.

In the past, Rafe would have noticed my abstraction. But his life had changed, and now his new wife absorbed the majority of his focus. And understandably so, when they had been married so recently.

Celine should have seen a difference as well, but she barely spoke to me anymore. My fears for her had proven far from true. Instead of reacting outrageously, ever since the ball Celine had become quiet and withdrawn.

If I hadn't been so consumed by the rebellion my aunt had somehow managed to conjure up from the other side of the kingdom, I would have been extremely concerned. And even with my distraction, every now and then a twinge of guilt hit me as I looked at my sister across the dining table. But I always brushed it aside. I was only one person, and I could not be responsible for everything. Parenting Celine was my mother and father's responsibility, not mine.

I didn't have time to teach William code, so we met in person every second night. Each time he tried to engage me in conversation, but I wasn't in the mood for pleasantries. I received his report and then slipped away, off to do my own investigations.

Unfortunately, he hadn't been able to discover anything particularly useful.

"There's something more to the story. I'm sure of it," he said, at one point, frustrated by his own failure. "But I think the king and queen might be the only ones with answers. And I can't ask them directly." He looked at me apologetically. "I hope you understand. There's just no way to subtly ask a person about that time years ago when their sister tried to murder their baby."

I wanted to rail at him, but I restrained myself. Especially since he was right. And I couldn't ask them, either—Celeste didn't feel curious about such things. There had to be a way though, if only I could think of it...

The idea came to me while we all strolled through the garden one afternoon. I was telling Marie about all the flowers that were new to her, and William was attempting to decide which bloom I should wear in my hair. Marie and I pointedly ignored him, but he continued his one-sided conversation, plucking and then discarding every variety we examined in favor of the next one.

He declared himself determined to find the one that best brought out my eyes. I would have lost all patience with him if I hadn't known of his secret service to Aurora. I, better than anyone, knew that those of us who lived half our lives in the shadows put on acts all the time. I would make myself a hypocrite if I faulted him for it now.

Celine trailed behind us, running her hand along the bushes, but offering no comment unless directly called upon. The sight of her boredom reminded me of the now distant day in her chambers when she had read to me from the history book. What was it she had said?

*"What do you think happened to Aunt Melisande? I've always wondered. I mean, she can't actually have disappeared."*

Despite her current state of unusual withdrawal, Celine was the one member of the family who could be counted on to ask an awkward question. I just needed to stir her curiosity.

I led the group toward a far corner of the garden, a section I hadn't visited for more than four years. Steeling myself, I pointed to a bush covered in fragrant blossoms. "And that is the Melisande flower. Apparently, it was first grown the year that my aunt was born, so the gardeners named it in honor of her."

William, who had been reaching out to pluck one of the flowers, let his hand drop back to his side.

"Really?" Celine pushed forward to examine it more closely. "I never knew that. In fact, I don't recognize the flower at all."

I scrunched up my face as if thinking hard. "Don't you? Perhaps Mother and Father requested the gardeners not to include it in their arrangements." I smiled around at everyone as if proud of myself for thinking of this possibility.

"That would make sense, given..." Marie met Rafe's eyes and trailed off. I pretended not to notice her words or the unhappy look they shared.

I turned to Celine. "Did you ever find out what happened?"

Her fingers had been stroking the petals of one of the flowers, but she jerked her hand away at my words. "What happened to what?"

"Not *what*, silly." I giggled. "*Who*. To Aunt Melisande, of course. You asked me what had happened to her, only I didn't know the answer." I sighed. "I generally don't."

"Cheer up, Princess," said William, stepping closer to me with a comforting smile. "No one expects you to have all the answers."

"No one expects you to have any answers," Celine muttered under her breath.

Rafe glared at her and put a protective arm around my shoulders. "I think we should keep moving. There's no reason to be upsetting Lettie."

"Oh, I'm not upset." I smiled around at them brightly. I had seen William's spark of interest when I had initiated the topic, and I knew I was treading dangerously.

"Of course she's not." Celine led the way, stomping down the path ahead of us. I followed close enough behind to hear her quiet words. "But we should all be worried about upsetting her, anyway. Not about me, though. No one should worry about upsetting me. I'm of no account whatsoever."

I knew I should feel bad, but I felt elated instead. A riled and careless Celine was exactly what I needed.

My careful maneuvering paid off that night at the evening meal. When the servants had finished serving the sweets, Celine turned to face our father, casting a defiant look at Rafe as she did so.

"Father, what happened to Aunt Melisande? She can't really have disappeared, can she?"

Instant silence fell. Except for the clatter of Uncle Horace's fork hitting his plate. He glared at Celine. The few times I had ever heard the topic of his older sister mentioned in his presence, he had responded with a similar look.

Celine glared straight back at him. She had never had much patience for what she deemed his 'fusty old ways'.

Melisande must have been the Celine in their family. My aunt certainly couldn't be accused of lacking in dramatics, a quality Uncle Horace seemed to hate. A sign of an undisciplined mind. It didn't help that his sister had betrayed her family in the worst possible way, either.

My parents responded more calmly, but then they always did. My mother's placidity and my father's reserve protected them from such emotional outbursts. I had always wondered what they truly felt in their hearts toward my aunt. She had tried to kill their daughter. Surely they hated her as I did.

Frederic frowned at Celine and then glanced uneasily toward me. I had orchestrated the conversation, but I still had to put all my efforts into maintaining my unconcerned expression. My emotions churned, fighting to break free.

Cassian didn't look at either of us but trained his attention on our father. I got the sense he wanted to know the answer himself.

My father cleared his throat and shared a look with my mother. I forced myself to breathe normally. What secrets did they share about my aunt?

"My sister did not disappear, no." My father's voice was heavy. "She attempted to kill a member of the royal family; we could not let her walk away."

Frederic nodded once. "The penalty for such an attempt is death. We have not needed to inflict such a punishment for over a hundred years, but that does not change the law."

My father cleared his throat and looked at my mother again.

"It was a complex situation." Our mother looked around at us all. Was the sadness in her eyes for me?

"What do you mean, complex?" Frederic's faint tinge of outrage satisfied me. He believed strongly in the rule of law and sometimes seemed oblivious to shades of gray. But in this case, I agreed with him whole-heartedly—I couldn't see anything complex about it.

Cassian narrowed his eyes, looking between Frederic and our mother. His mind was more devious than Frederic's, even though he generally kept it to himself. The two of them balanced each other well, and I had no doubt that Cassian would one day be Frederic's Chief Advisor. I had never been close to either of them, but I expected Frederic's future rule would be a successful one. After all, respect for the law was an excellent quality in the heir.

Mother sighed. "Your aunt is a member of the royal family herself, remember."

"Is? I take it she wasn't executed, then?" asked Cassian.

"No, she wasn't. Against my recommendations at the time, mind you." Apparently, Uncle Horace was as unforgiving toward her as I was. That made one of the family at least.

"Come, Horace. She's our sister." Father frowned at his younger brother. "And you know the circumstances."

Uncle Horace looked like he was about to protest, but after a moment he thought better of it and returned to his food. His dark expression remained, however.

I hoped my eyes didn't betray the same gleam I could see in William's. What circumstances? I had never been able to find out why my father had failed to invite his own sister to my Christening. Had she already begun to show signs of losing her mind? Was that why he had wanted to keep her away?

Was madness what mitigated her attack on me? Certainly not even the most doting brother could consider her reaction anything but crazed.

I willed Celine or one of my brothers to ask for an explanation of his comment. But my mother spoke before anyone had the chance. "Your aunt was banished to a remote island. As far as anyone knows, she is living there still."

"As far as anyone knows? Doesn't anyone ever check on her?" Frederic sounded incredulous.

"The island is protected by a magical barrier." Father worded it as if the hedge was part of the prison rather than a mysterious later addition. Was he the one who had ordered it to be breached? If so, why now after so many years? Or had the orders come from a rebel hiding within the palace hierarchy?

"So that's how you stop her from escaping the island?" Celine seemed far too fascinated by the whole thing.

"The island itself does that." Uncle Horace still looked displeased with the conversation. "The whole thing is surrounded by dangerous reefs and submerged rocks. There is only one safe harbor and only three local captains know how to navigate the passage to it. Their loyalty is absolute. The knowledge has been passed down for generations since the island has always been used for political banishment."

"Are there other prisoners there now?" asked Celine with wide eyes. "Do they have to battle each other?"

"Battle each other?" My mother's graceful eyebrows rose. "Really, Celine, of course they do not. The island has never accommodated more than one prisoner at a time. It stood empty for many years before..." Her eyes flicked to me.

"Oh." Celine looked disappointed. "Will you ever bring her back? Will she be pardoned?"

I froze as I battled to keep my emotions hidden. Bring her back? The thought had literally never occurred to me. Surely Father would not consider such a thing.

He looked almost as taken aback as I felt. "I do not know. Perhaps...perhaps if..." His eyes wandered to me, still and silent in my chair. He shook his head. "No, I do not think she will ever return."

I could barely breathe. It was easy enough to read the missing parts of his sentences. Perhaps if my curse were ever broken, he would think of pardoning his sister. But he had no hope of such an event occurring.

I wasn't sure which thought enraged me more. That my own father thought I was trapped forever, or that he would even consider pardoning the monster who trapped me in the first place.

I noticed William's eyes on my face and forced myself to breathe. It would be interesting to hear how he reported this conversation to Aurora. I would have to ensure I seemed sufficiently interested when he did so, too.

"I think that is quite enough of this conversation," said my mother. "Let us turn our minds to a more cheerful topic. Rafe, I understand you are wanting to take dear Marie and William on a tour of the islands?"

I let the sound of her words fade away as I attempted to regain my calm. I *would* break this curse. And after I did, I would devote my not inconsiderable abilities to ensuring my aunt never received a pardon for her crimes.

# PART II
# WIND AND WAVES

# CHAPTER 11

"This is new. Should I be worried?" William strolled over to join me at the weapons rack. His quiet words seemed to reverberate through the dark practice hall. I glanced over and saw with relief that he had closed the door behind him.

I went back to strapping the knife to my arm.

"Are you sure you don't want to go for something bigger?"

I was almost certain he was joking. "This one is just fine." I kept my head down, focused on my task. "Along with the two in my boots and the two at my back."

William shook his head. "Did I ever mention that I like a well-armed girl?"

I finally looked up to meet his eyes. "No, I don't believe you did."

"My favorite kind, I assure you."

I pointed to the weapons rack. "Arm up."

He straightened. "The plot thickens."

I rolled my eyes. "Tonight is different. I'd rather not do it on my own, but I will if I have to."

"Absolutely not. Whatever it is, I'm in." He chose a sword and sheath and began to buckle them around his waist. "Why me, though? Is this a recognition of my superior fighting skills?"

"You can do something for me that none of my other agents can—provide legitimacy."

"So I'm officially one of your agents now? Do I get special privileges? What about a secret handshake at least?"

I ignored him. "You've already done it once, the night we met. If anyone discovers us, you need to invoke your royal authority and remind them that you're not to be questioned."

He raised one eyebrow. "I'm not to be questioned? I think I missed that memo. I think *you* missed that memo."

I bit my tongue to hold back a giggle. Aurora didn't giggle, that was Celeste. What if William recognized the sound? "Not to be arrested on the spot, at least."

"That I can probably manage. I'm glad you're seeing my true depth and worth at last."

I turned back to the task at hand. He seemed determined not to take the situation seriously, and I had no idea what had evoked such a playful mood in him. But it was clearly dangerous, as evidenced by my near giggle. A sound I shouldn't have been at all tempted to make given the seriousness of our mission and the lurking tension that fueled it.

When I looked back up, he was watching me. And the laugh had dropped out of his eyes.

"Thank you for trusting me, Aurora. I was starting to feel pretty useless. And I don't want you to see me as useless."

His eyes locked onto mine, and I put a self-conscious hand up to my scarf. I kept thinking he was going to recognize me when he looked at me like that. As if I had all of his attention. As if I were the most captivating thing he'd ever seen.

Then I remembered that he looked at me like that during the day, too. I scowled. He had no business giving Aurora that look when he was busy pursuing a beautiful princess. It was most likely just another tool in his princely arsenal. It probably meant nothing.

Of course, the princess he pursued was me. But he didn't know that. I squeezed my eyes shut and took a deep breath. I needed to refocus. A man's life might depend on it. And not any man—one of my own.

I watched as William tucked a small throwing dagger into each boot and then gestured for him to follow me. I spoke quietly as we walked.

"Two of my agents among the guard have been recruited into the mercenary shadow army. The rebels have been hiding in plain sight among our own guard, ready to move on command. Apparently no one has noticed how much the royal guard has grown in size over the last year." I shook my head before continuing.

"Their recruitment was a major breakthrough. I finally have a good idea of the size of the army and how they're being supplied, recruited and paid. But last night one of them failed to report in. I can't ask the other one what happened because they don't know about each other. It's safer that way for both of them."

"So you think he might have been discovered?" William's grim tone suggested he knew exactly how bad that would be.

"It's possible. For now, all I know is that he hasn't reported in for two nights now."

"Could he have betrayed you?"

I shook my head. "He's one of my oldest and most loyal agents. He would never betray me." My voice gave the slightest wobble. "And that loyalty goes both ways. If he's in trouble, I need to get him out. He trusts me, and I won't let him down."

William reached over to squeeze my hand, quickly letting go again afterward. "We'll find him, Aurora. And, if we have to, we'll fight our way out."

I nodded once. "That's why we're armed. I'm hoping you can talk us out of any trouble we get into. But if not…"

I was still uneasy about my decision to involve the prince. The whole situation had the potential to become extremely messy. But concern for my agent had overridden my concerns. If they had discovered his double dealing, then he needed my help now. And I needed back up.

The rebellion wouldn't want the enmity of the other kingdoms. They had enough to deal with here in Lanover. I trusted that they wouldn't risk hurting the Northhelmian heir.

I signaled for silence as we left the palace and made our way through the gardens. I had arranged a meeting with the second guard who had infiltrated the mercenaries, and I didn't want to alert any passing sentries to our presence.

We arrived to find the guard already awaiting us. He saluted me and eyed William warily but offered no comment. I didn't waste time introducing them.

"I've lost contact with one of my agents. I need to locate him as a matter of urgency." I paused, regretting the need to inform him of his compatriot's existence. "He had also been recruited. Have you heard anything? Any rumors at all about a mole?"

He gave no visible reaction to the news that I had another agent among the rebels. But I would have expected no less from one of my people.

"Nothing, I'm afraid. But then, I haven't been on shift with any of my best sources for the last few days. Certainly there's been nothing widespread." He paused and frowned. "But I've heard stories about things in the past. A few rebels who take it on themselves to vet others. They're troublemakers—both as guards and as mercs. They've received plenty of reprimands, but nothing serious enough for any of the guard sergeants to actually dismiss them. They know how to tread the line and keep their worst doings out of sight."

I shifted my weight from foot to foot, eager for action. "If they did grab my agent, where would he be?"

He shook his head. "I couldn't say for sure."

"Make a guess."

"I've occasionally seen some of them coming and going from the gardens. But they don't look like the flower-loving types to me."

"Which direction?"

"The back northwestern corner."

The city spread out below the palace on the southern side of the hill. The northern side faced nothing but further hills. The gardens encircled the entire building, but the largest and most frequented parts sat between the southern facing palace and the city.

I pictured the gardens in my mind. I had walked them an untold number of times as the flower-loving Celeste. "There's a small gardeners' building, little more than a storage hut, in that section. Perhaps they use it as some sort of base."

"It will be easy enough for us to find out." The guard turned toward the northeast, ready to investigate.

"No."

He turned back toward me.

"If something has happened to him, your role is more important than ever. I can't risk having your position in the guard, or among the mercenaries, compromised in any way. You need to return to your barracks. We have come prepared to deal with whatever situation we find." I could only keep my words strong and hope I wasn't being overconfident.

William said nothing, but his silent presence at my back boosted my assurance.

I could see the guard wanted to argue, but I knew his good sense would prevail. It did. IIe saluted me without another word and took off at a jog back toward the main building. I had seen the strange juxtaposition before. My agents felt protective toward me but, at the same time, they had a firm belief in my limitless capability.

I turned to William. "We have a lead and that's better than

nothing. And the situation could be worse. Our job will be much easier if we only have to deal with some troublemakers and not the main facilitators of the rebellion."

I started toward the hut. William took a moment to follow and had to jog to catch up. "Shouldn't we get that guard of yours to check if these troublemakers are safe in the barracks before we proceed? It is the middle of the night, prime time for criminals to be out and about their business. Your man did say that what they're doing is unsanctioned by either their guard command or their rebel leaders..."

I shrugged. "It doesn't matter. We have to move ahead even if the men are there. I can't leave my agent with them any longer than absolutely necessary. And anyway, Princeling, that's why I brought you."

"Your confidence in my abilities is flattering." His wry tone was unmistakable, but I didn't hesitate.

As we approached the hut, all of my senses tingled and strained. The small building had been constructed of solid stone, and we had to approach quite close before we heard the sound of voices inside.

I leaned against the latched wooden door, pressing my ear to the slats.

"I don't know what you're talking about. I keep telling you, I'm just like you." My eyes flew to William's. I recognized my man's voice easily. He was here. And he sounded under stress.

"Aye, but are you really?"

Someone else said something I couldn't hear, and a loud round of laughter broke out. A sound like a foot hitting wood was followed by a loud clatter and the thud of something heavy hitting the ground. I drew back.

"He's in there."

"Are you sure?"

I didn't bother to answer, my mind taken up with a new concern. "We're dealing with offshoot troublemakers here, not the rebel leaders. I can't guarantee they'll even recognize you, let alone hold back. I can't ensure your safety in there."

I ground my teeth. Everything in me wanted to kick the door down immediately and retrieve my man. But I had a responsibility to my kingdom and to Northhelm. Who knew what the outcome would be if the crown prince was killed while visiting Lanover?

A tiny voice in the back of my head asked if that was really the only reason I was so worried about William. I squashed it ruthlessly.

William shrugged, entirely undaunted. I could even have sworn that his eyes gleamed in the small amount of moonlight. "That's why we came armed, isn't it?"

I couldn't resist returning his smile, even if he couldn't see it underneath my scarf. My scarf. "If your identity is no use to us, we're better off if they don't recognize you. Do you have something to cover your face? If we can get in and out of there quickly, and with our identities intact, they won't be able to do a thing. They can hardly report the attack to their superiors if they're doing something illicit."

William produced a handkerchief large enough to cover his face. I grinned. He looked like a bandit.

He drew his sword, and I drew the knife from my arm and one from my boot. I looked across at him, and he nodded once. Ready to go. I strode forward and kicked open the door.

# CHAPTER 12

*J*had a second's advantage as five pairs of startled eyes flew to the doorway. Two men dressed as off-duty guards lounged on wooden chairs drawn up to a simple table. The other two stood over a fifth man, my agent. He lay on the floor beside a chair that had clearly been kicked out from under him. His bound hands twisted up behind him, and he sported a magnificent black eye.

He alone seemed unsurprised to see me. In fact, he was the first to move, pushing himself into a sitting position and scooting away from the men. As soon as he had begun to distance himself, I seized my momentary advantage and launched into action.

Running forward, I kicked one of the men in the chest. Too slow to bring up his defenses, he staggered backward. His foot caught the fallen chair, and he joined it on the floor. But the seconds it had taken me to fell him had given the second man time to draw a weapon.

In the close confines of the hut, he chose to mirror me, drawing a long dagger from a sheath at his belt. I smiled in anticipation and a little relief. I didn't like the idea of using my daggers against a sword, not while I had three of his comrades at my back.

He slashed toward me, clearly trying to use his height and longer reach to end the encounter quickly. I danced away from him, careful to avoid the chair and the winded guard. I caught a flurry of activity out of the corner of my eye. William had rushed the seated men.

My blades flashed as I fended off the attacks of my assailant. I wouldn't be foolish enough to let him draw me out unless I had the right opening. Instead, I carefully maneuvered him around to clear the path between my agent and the door.

My man had managed to get to his feet, which thankfully weren't bound, and he made a run for the opening. The winded guard had also scrambled back up. He cursed and set off in pursuit.

I threw myself into a forward lunge, catching the other knife man off guard. He fell back before my blades, and I pulled back at the same moment, putting distance between us. Turning, I threw the knife in my right hand. It landed in the shoulder of the pursuing guard, who had made it two steps out the door.

He roared in pain and dropped to his knees. I whirled toward William. He had disarmed one of his opponents, and the man slumped against the wall, nursing a long gash in his right arm.

But the other man had managed to corner the prince, limiting his ability to effectively use his blade. His left hand held his knife but, even so, he was barely holding off his opponent.

I tossed my remaining knife across to my right hand and pulled my arm back for a second throw. As I did so, William yelled my name, his eyes focused on something behind me. I ignored him and carried through with the movement.

This time my aim was off slightly, and I missed the man's shoulder. But the blade buried itself in his right arm instead, and he dropped his weapon. As soon as I saw he was down, and the prince was safe, I turned to face my previous assailant.

His face had gone white, and he knelt, his hands clutching at a knife hilt protruding from his left thigh. I spun back around. William's left hand was now empty. Our eyes met, his reflecting back the same strange exhilaration I felt. We made an effective team.

I didn't have time to waste, however. Stopping only to draw the two knives strapped to my back, I raced through the doorway after my agent.

The three lanterns in the hut had been brighter than the meagre moonlight, so it took my eyes a moment to adjust. My agent, limping slightly, had made it half way to the palace. He glanced back over his shoulder and sagged in relief when he saw me.

He had hesitated too soon, however. Two more men rounded a large bush and gave a yell at the sight of us all. They weren't sentries so had presumably been on their way to join the off-duty guards in the hut. One rushed forward and grabbed my agent. He tried to wrestle free, but his arms were still secured behind his back.

The other ran full tilt toward William and me.

"I've got this one," said William, stepping forward, his eyes trained on the man, and his sword held out in front of him.

I nodded, even though he wasn't watching me, and took off toward the two struggling figures. I swung wide to avoid the charging guard. My knives felt solid and dependable in my hands, and the sight of the injuries on my agent filled me with wrath.

I narrowed my eyes as I ran, focusing in on my target. As I approached them, my blade slashed downward, all my effort on precision. My agent's hands flew free. He swung his arms around to grapple with his opponent, while I raced around behind them.

Flipping my knife, I brought the hilt down on the attacker's head with all the force I could muster. He crumpled.

Behind us William and the lone remaining guard dueled, their swords glinting in the moonlight. I held my breath, but William lunged forward, combining skill and strength to easily best his opponent. Within moments the man was both disarmed and disabled.

William didn't pause for breath but ran hard toward us. Without bothering to ask permission, he grabbed my injured agent and slung him over his shoulder. We both raced toward the palace, afraid of being caught by any sentries who might have heard the fighting.

Once we had slipped inside, we wound our way back to the practice hall. My nerves sang as we walked. My agent was alive and safe, and I had finally gotten the action I craved. My eyes seemed irresistibly drawn toward William. He had fought well, and he now carried another grown man with seeming ease. I tried not to remember the way his muscles had looked when he fought without a shirt.

I told myself it was the elation and shared camaraderie of battle that made my mind lose focus in such an unacceptable way. That moment when our eyes had met in the hut had been spine-tingling.

With the door closed safely behind us, William carefully lowered the man to the ground.

"I knew you would come for me, Aurora." His voice was gruff, weathered by years of service to the guards. "I didn't tell them a thing."

"I never doubted you for a moment."

He could barely see out of the black eye, and he clutched at the leg he had been favoring earlier. A rush of gratitude for his loyalty swept over me, but I knew he didn't want sympathy. He was a hardened soldier facing his battle leader, not a subject looking for the compassion of a princess.

"What happened?"

He delivered his lines as if giving a routine report after sentry duty. "A small contingent of the mercs aren't happy with the forced inactivity. Most are perfectly happy to collect a purse for no extra work, but these ones are a little too fond of violence and throwing their weight around."

William shook his head in disgust, but the man's focus was on me.

"They've done it before. Decided someone looks suspicious and taken them off for 'questioning'. They didn't seem overly interested in getting answers, though. The sport was enough for them, I think. I don't know what I did to attract their attention, but they didn't seem to have any real information against me."

"Lanover appreciates your service and sacrifice."

The man's smile seemed strangely triumphant. "It was worth every moment."

I raised my brows.

"A couple of those men have been around since the beginning. And when they're in that hut, and in their cups…" He wrinkled his nose in scorn. "Well, they talk pretty freely."

I crouched down beside him. "Tell me everything you heard."

I hadn't dared to dream that the night could have such a successful outcome. Not only had we retrieved my agent, but he had come with a treasure trove of information.

We had parted ways at the practice hall, William agreeing to help him to a palace doctor. They had agreed on a story between them. William would claim he had been unable to sleep and had decided to take a walk through the moonlight. He had found the guard injured in the garden, the victim of several of his fellow guards who had lost money to him in a gambling match the night before.

Unfortunately, it meant he would likely face some form of discipline once he was deemed fit to return to the guards.

Gambling was forbidden among those stationed at the palace. I had apologized to my agent, but he had shrugged it off.

My heart swelled with pride. Aurora's achievements would be impossible without men and women like this one.

The next night I received even better news. The agent who had tipped me off about the hut had heard the story we were putting out and had used his initiative to take it even further.

The six guards we had injured had reported to the military medics with all sorts of wild stories about an attack on the palace. Of course, they hadn't bothered to align their stories, so it had been easy enough to convince the sergeants to disbelieve them. It helped that most of the loyal Lanoverian officers had been looking for an excuse to get rid of the troublemakers for some time.

My agent had used the guise of a feud with one of the injured guards to convince several of his comrades to join him in a convenient lie. Each of the guards in question had run afoul of the troublemakers at some point and were eager to be a part of bringing them down.

They claimed they had come upon the men attacking their fellow guard over their lost money and had attempted to defend the victim. The men had turned on them, and they had all been forced to fight for their own lives. Several of them even went so far as to give themselves small cuts and bruises to back up the story.

By the time the report reached me, the troublemakers had already been discharged from the ranks of the guard and transferred to a cell in the city to await trial. The city magistrates were notorious for their slow pace, and I hoped I would have the opportunity to expose the rebellion before my agent was called upon to perjure himself.

In the meantime, both of my agents were being hailed as heroes among their comrades. The arrested men had been universally despised. Even the other mercenaries had lived in fear of being singled out by them as a 'traitor'. Their new-found status could only lead my men to better information.

～

Every day improved my picture of the shape of the rebellion. Ercole, the visible leader, had slowly been building his mercenary army, hiding them within the ranks of the regular guard. The rebellion had been fomenting for some time; however the increase in activity suggested preparations for the final attack. But I knew Ercole was only an intermediary, and still any information on my aunt, the true leader, eluded me.

As Princess Celeste, I could demand answers from my parents. They clearly knew more about my aunt's history than they were sharing. But the curse would never allow such a thing. And Aurora couldn't seem to discover anything through less direct routes.

I had started keeping a written record of all the details of the rebellion, ready to present to the duchess as soon as she returned. We had received word that she had started back home, but Arcadia lay between Northhelm and Lanover, and the journey was long. And meanwhile a rebellion that my father knew nothing about grew in his own palace.

I had considered having one of my agents approach him or one of his advisors. But the information I had gathered had grown far too large. No one would believe it to be the observations of a single suspicious servant. My agent would be arrested and questioned, and my father's resources would be bent toward uncovering my network instead of the rebels.

I carried the record on my person at all times, day and night, and several times I found myself standing outside my father's office when I knew he was occupied elsewhere. I could easily leave the papers on his desk…

But I always turned away. With no idea where it had come

from, would my father believe the testimony of a mysterious report? Or would he take the accusations to his long-standing quartermaster, Ercole, with a demand for an explanation? All my efforts could be undone.

And worse. If he challenged the rebel alone, who knew what the outcome would be? I felt confident the rebels awaited their leader's presence. While she remained trapped on her island, we had time. But if their guilt was exposed? And Ercole found himself alone with the king at the time? He might be tempted to move the timeline forward.

Fear had flashed through me at the idea. That night my agents had received new orders. Protecting the palace supplies and any new shipments now took second priority to protecting my family. Thankfully, neither my parents nor my siblings seemed to have noticed the series of servants who now trailed them around the palace and the city. My agents had strict instructions. My family were never to be left alone with anyone known to be a rebel.

So far, my people had reported no activity, but the fear did not diminish. I couldn't risk leaving my notes for my father to find.

Eventually I made contact with one of my agents among the palace messengers.

"I need you to leave tonight. Take one of the horses from the stables and ride as fast as you can. Find the duchess and give her this."

I handed over a water-proofed leather pouch containing a copy of all my notes and a plea for the duchess to hurry. "Make sure you put it in no hands but hers. Tell her people you've come with a message from the king. They'll let you through."

I handed over a much smaller pouch that jingled as it changed hands. "Change horses as often as you need to and spare yourself no comfort on the journey if it might help you to travel faster."

The girl turned to leave without a single question, but I

stopped her with my hand on her arm. "I know this sudden desertion will cost you your position, and that's before taking the horse. But I swear that I will protect you from the consequences."

She nodded once and left.

I watched her all the way down the corridor until she disappeared from sight. It was the only honor I could give her.

# CHAPTER 13

$\mathscr{I}$ knew that even riding at full pace, the messenger would take days to reach the duchess, and the duchess would take even longer to return. But I still had to restrain myself from looking for their arrival each day.

The activity of the palace had turned toward the newlyweds' planned sailing trip. Father had granted them the use of the royal yacht, a vessel as big as any of the navy frigates, so Rafe had decided on a lengthy voyage. Together he and Marie oversaw the preparation of supplies and planned a route.

William was to accompany them, and I already felt the occasional pang of loneliness at the thought of his departure. Celine still avoided me, and William provided my one source of entertainment during the day. He enjoyed laughing, and I enjoyed making him laugh. Even if I had to disguise my witticisms as foolish and naïve comments.

My fear that he would be turned away by my stupidity had yet to be realized. His attentions had certainly decreased slightly, but I found a sort of satisfaction in that since I attributed the change to his growing relationship with Aurora.

Given his presence during my debriefing of the captured

agent, William now knew more about the shape of the rebellion than anyone, except for me. He had become my confidant in the absence of the duchess. He had even offered to take our information to the king, but I had forbidden it.

He would be even more suspect than one of my regular agents. Where had he gotten the information on this supposed rebellion? A spy network? A Northhelmian one?

Lanover would need all of its resources to fight the danger within—stirring up trouble between the kingdoms was the last thing I wanted.

William had pleaded with me twice now to reveal my identity. Each time I had simply turned and walked away, cutting short our rendezvous for the evening. After the second time, he stopped asking.

And, despite our late hours, he never seemed tired or showed any inclination for his bed. I suspected he would have stayed with me all night if I would let him.

"Oh. It's you." Celine's voice interrupted my memories.

She had come around a corner, wandering through the gardens apparently aimlessly. I cast around in my mind for a curse-approved topic that might interest her enough to stay and talk to me and came up blank.

"Isn't this flower lovely?" I held up a large pink blossom that I had been absentmindedly twirling between my fingers. I already had a frangipani in my hair, taken from my breakfast tray, but I hadn't been able to resist plucking the large, fragrant flower anyway.

She glanced at it and then away without commenting.

I tried again. "I went into the city yesterday to visit that new seamstress you discovered."

"She's not my seamstress, since Mother won't even let me wear the dress she made." She narrowed her eyes. "And thanks for inviting me, by the way. I would have liked a ride yesterday."

I looked back down at the flower, hoping she wouldn't see the guilt in my eyes. Rafe, Marie, William, and I had all gone, but I hadn't invited Celine. I hadn't wanted to endure her sullenness the whole way.

She slumped down beside me on the bench. Her demeanor suggested she was only sitting because moving on would have required too much energy.

"I know none of you want me around. I'm not stupid."

"Oh Celine..." I reached out to grasp her hand, but she pulled it out of my reach.

"I don't know why I'm even telling you. You wouldn't understand." She kicked her legs out and looked at me sideways. "If Cordelia were here, she'd tell me off for saying that. She'd say it wasn't your fault." She was silent for another moment before bursting out, "But that's the problem! Cordelia isn't here." She shook her head. "Sometimes I wish I was cursed, too, so I didn't have to notice how boring it is around here."

She sounded so sad but also so young and foolish. What did she know of loneliness or of curses?

I placed my hand over her balled up fist and looked her in the eye. "This will pass Celine. It's not as bad as it seems right now. Adventures will come your way. You won't be so young forever."

The curse limited me to the trite words, but I hoped something in my expression would give her a hint that I truly did know what I was talking about.

It didn't work.

"Ugh, who are you? Uncle Horace?"

I pulled my hand back, disappointed I'd so obviously failed.

Celine gave a reluctant laugh, reaching over to pull a leaf off a nearby bush. "Sorry. That was a bit too far. No one should ever be compared to Uncle Horace." She gave an exaggerated shudder, and I giggled.

"He is a little..." I wrinkled my nose.

Celine held up her hand. "Say no more. I don't think I could cope with a Lettie description of Uncle Horace right now."

I giggled again. She had used my nickname, so maybe I had made some sort of impression after all.

She looked down at the leaf in her hand, carefully smoothing it out. "Do things seem a bit strange around here lately to you?"

I sat up straighter, eyeing her warily. What had she noticed? I needed to tread carefully.

"Strange?"

She looked up briefly and then back down at the leaf, scrunching it up in her hand. "Never mind. I don't know why I asked you anyway. Things could get a lot stranger before you would notice anything."

I widened my eyes. "What do you mean?"

"Exactly." She jumped to her feet. "It's probably nothing anyway. Just this sailing trip."

I didn't need to hear the tone in her voice when she said the last two words to know how jealous she felt. Even I felt it this time. I tried not to let myself imagine standing next to William at the railing of a ship, feeling the breeze in my hair and watching the endless blue-green of the waves.

I should know better. I wasn't fourteen, and I was needed here. The duchess would arrive at some point and then who knew what would happen?

~

"I've decided to accompany you, Rafe dear."

My mother's words produced a choking fit in my brother who had unfortunately just taken a mouthful of soup.

"A…Accompany us, Mother?"

"On the royal yacht. It has been far too long since I've been sailing."

Rafe looked helplessly at Marie and then back at our mother. "You want to accompany Marie and me on our wedding tour of the islands?"

"Certainly." She sipped another spoonful of soup. "Along with Prince William, of course. It seems only right that our family be represented on the voyage as well. I wouldn't want us to seem lax in any way."

"N...no, of course not."

For once, Celine actually attempted to restrain her emotion. But I could see her whole body shaking from the silent fits of laughter. Rafe narrowed his eyes at her, and years of silent sibling communication made it easy for me to interpret the look. *Just wait until it's your turn, and Mother does something equally outrageous.*

"How lovely," said Marie, and I gave her an admiring smile. She had been well-trained.

"Viktoria? What is this?" Horace sounded far from impressed. "Aren't you a little old to be gallivanting around with the young ones?"

"Certainly not." My mother seemed entirely undisturbed at the slight on her age. "It is high time one of us inspected the outermost regions of the kingdom, and Leonardo can't be spared at the moment. A perfectly unexceptional extension to the purpose of the trip."

The smallest of looks passed between my parents. Interesting. Something else was going on here. I wished for the hundredth time this week that I was free to have an open conversation with my parents.

My mother continued to sing the praises of ocean voyages and to list all the parts of the kingdom she was "just longing to see".

Most of the family ignored her, and Uncle Horace maintained a steady stream of mutterings about the foolishness of jaunting around the kingdom at my parents' age. I couldn't resist rolling my eyes. Thankfully no one noticed, so the curse left me alone.

You would think my mother was in her dotage from the way my uncle carried on.

"I can see my duty is clear," he announced, gaining the attention of everyone in the room. "If Viktoria is going, and Leonardo cannot, then I must go too."

"You, Horace?" My mother's obvious surprise didn't prevent her taking another mouthful of soup.

"Certainly me. Who else is to ensure you are treated with the respect you deserve? Not these heedless things." He glared at us all indiscriminately.

Celine snickered. "This is the first time I've been glad I'm not going," she whispered, her words clearly audible to the whole table.

She pretended not to notice the look Uncle Horace directed her way.

Rafe looked around at the rest of us. "Anyone else? Frederic, Cassian? Feel like coming along?"

Both of our brothers looked suitably revolted at the idea. I had to admit that the idyllic image of me standing in a boat had dimmed somewhat. Even a glittering green island, surrounded by a long stretch of pale golden sand, lost something of its appeal when viewed in the company of my mother, my uncle, and two newlyweds.

I glanced sympathetically toward William. That unpalatable role would fall to him. He appeared to have fully grasped the situation, pushing the rest of his soup away.

"What about you, Princess?" he asked. "Feel like joining us for a sail?" Unlike Rafe, his eyes gleamed with sincerity.

Even given the recent additions to the passenger list, a large part of me wished I could say yes. I shook my head. "Oh no, I get sea sick, remember?"

He glanced toward Celine. "I thought your sister said you didn't?"

"Oh." I looked between the two of them. "I must have forgotten. Perhaps it's carriage sick that I'm thinking of."

Celine groaned. "You don't get carriage sick, either, Celeste."

"Oh." I adopted an expression of serious concentration. "I know what it is. The ocean scares me." I smiled around at them all, as if proud of my excellent memory.

"Scares you?" Rafe frowned at me. "Why?"

"Well, it's so big. And wet. And did I mention big?"

"You did mention that, yes," said William, clearly trying to keep a straight face. "You will be sorely missed."

"Not by us," muttered Rafe.

$\mathcal{T}$wo days later, I waved goodbye as the whole party and a ridiculous mound of luggage moved away from the palace toward the harbor. William had spent the whole morning in the garden with me and had assured me that he would think of me every day.

"I am quite sure that we will encounter nothing as beautiful as what we are leaving behind." He lightly touched the frangipani tucked in my hair. "I hope you'll miss me."

"Of course. I shall miss you all."

He looked like he wanted to say more and, as he walked away, he paused and looked back. "I won't be idle while I'm gone, Princess. I shall search for a way to break your curse."

"How kind." I smiled gently at him, careful to show no great enthusiasm. "Thank you."

He pressed his lips together and then hurried to join the rest of the traveling party.

Celine was noticeably absent from the farewell, but I could hardly blame her. I hoped her disappointment at being left behind wouldn't destroy the small amount of ground I had gained with her recently.

I waved a final farewell and returned to the palace. I wandered, my mind dwelling on the departing group, and on the duchess, who should be hurrying toward the capital by now. For all my skills, I had never learned to wait well. And lately it felt like I did nothing else.

Without conscious thought, my feet directed me to Celine's chambers. Misery loves company, I suppose. The rooms were empty.

I rocked back and forth, trying to think where she might be. William and I had strolled through most of the gardens and seen no sign of her. I headed toward the library.

Thirty minutes later I began to feel alarmed. The palace might be large, but I knew it well.

I saw Rosie and called to her.

"Yes, Your Highness?"

"Have you seen Princess Celine anywhere, Rosie?"

"Why, yes, Your Highness. She retired to her chambers before the traveling party left. She said she had a headache and didn't want to be disturbed all day." She hesitated, her brow furrowed, and then added, "She looked that sad, poor thing, it's no wonder she has the headache."

Panic gripped me. "Are you sure, Rosie?" I kept my voice light.

"Certainly, Your Highness. She asked me to let His Majesty know not to expect her at the evening meal." She sighed. "Hopefully she'll be feeling a little more cheerful tomorrow."

"Oh, of course. I will check on her there, then."

I hurried toward Celine's rooms, my mind whirring. I flung open the door and checked everywhere, including her wardrobe. The large space looked disordered in a way I had never seen before. Usually Celine took pride in it.

A closer examination revealed several missing items of clothing, along with a large leather bag.

Oh no. I groaned and sank onto a conveniently placed chair. Apparently Celine had decided to find her own adventure. And it couldn't have happened at a worse time. With the rebel numbers growing, and their activity increasing, Celine had put herself in danger by setting off alone.

If the wrong person recognized her…

I blamed myself, at least partially. I should have made more of an effort to connect with her. Perhaps then she wouldn't have done something so foolish.

The scene in the gardeners' hut rushed into my mind, only this time the figure on the floor wore my sister's face. I shivered. I had to do something. And immediately.

I didn't have time to transform into Aurora. And the sun still held its place high in the sky, anyway. Whatever I did would have to be done as Celeste.

My feet began to move before my mind had finished making the decision. They led me to the stables. "My horse," I called to a passing groom. He gave me a funny look but obeyed, probably not wanting to challenge a princess.

I shifted from foot to foot as I watched him work. I felt sure I could have done it faster, but Princess Celeste didn't saddle her own horse. Not since the curse, anyway.

"There you are, Your…"

I snatched the reins from his hands and led the horse over to a mounting block. He watched me in surprise, as I settled in the saddle and moved away.

I ignored him, holding myself to a walk with extreme difficulty. As soon as I had safely traversed the steepest part of the road from the palace, I urged the horse to a faster gait.

Celine could have headed in any direction, but I trusted she had retained some sense. Surely she knew better than to go off adventuring alone. Hopefully she had headed for the royal yacht.

The tension coiled inside me increased as I wound my way through the city. I longed to push the mare into a gallop, but the other people filling the streets made such a move far too dangerous.

Part of me wanted to accost the people I passed, asking if any of them had seen Celine. But I couldn't afford the time. If Celine wasn't at the yacht, I would stop at every shop and home on the way back looking for word of her.

I clamped down on my imagination firmly since it only seemed able to supply me with increasingly fatalistic scenarios. Celine would be fine. She had indulged in a fit of youthful rebellion, as had many a young person before her. She would be fine, as all of them had been fine.

Except for the ones who hadn't been. No. I urged my horse slightly faster and focused on the harbor ahead.

I swung down when I reached the entrance to the docks and entered on foot, leading my mount by the reins. I didn't want to miss noticing something important. The royal yacht had a dedicated docking bay at the far end. I walked toward it, surprised at how quiet the whole dock seemed. It normally teemed with activity.

When I neared the yacht, a lone worker called out. "You can't go over there, miss. They're preparing for a royal departure."

I turned around, and he started. "My apologies, Your Highness. I didn't recognize you."

I approached him. "Have you seen my sister, sir?" I thought quickly. "She came to see the others off, but I have a message for her."

He scratched his head. "I can't say that I have, Your Highness. And I've been working here since this morning, save for a couple of short breaks." He eyed me sideways, but I ignored him. His work habits were the farthest thing from my mind.

"That whole section has been off limits since first thing this morning. Except for those sailing on the yacht, of course."

Many years ago, my father had named the royal vessel *Viktoria* after his young bride, but the people seemed to feel it would be disrespectful to call it by name and invariably referred to it as the yacht.

I handed him my reins. "Could you watch my horse for me please? I won't be long." I hoped I was telling the truth, and that I would be returning with my sister by my side.

He didn't question my request or even look surprised. No one in the city expected much sense from me. Instead they all shared a sort of sympathetic affection for their Sleeping Princess. As if I were a puppy or a small child.

I strode quickly toward the *Viktoria,* trying to identify the figures on deck. A small handful of sailors moved around, preparing the ship to sail. Where had the rest of the crew and passengers gone? If I had been one of them, I would have been watching the action on deck.

I hesitated. Should I make my way up the gangplank and accost one of them? I bit my lip. I didn't want to inform the sailors that my sister was missing. The fewer who knew the better. But the ship would have to be searched.

I still hoped to bring her back quietly and without a fuss. But if she wasn't here, then my father would have to send out search parties. And Celine wouldn't like the consequences when they found her. I had to at least attempt to shield her. I owed her that much.

I stepped forward, lifting my skirts in preparation for crossing onto the ship, when an odd flash of color caught my eye. I let the material fall and turned in a slow circle, scanning the open dock.

There. I saw it again, behind a pile of barrels covered by an old net. The whole area reeked of fish, and I scrunched up my nose as I headed over to investigate.

I trod softly, hope filling my heart. Rounding the barrels, I gasped in relief.

She crouched behind the barrier, her eyes peering between a small gap.

"Celine!"

She jumped, losing her balance and falling onto her rear. "Celeste! What are you doing here?"

"Saving you from a lot of trouble." I put my hands on my hips. "What were you thinking, Celine?"

She eyed me angrily. "How did you know I was here?"

I stared at her, the faint stirrings of a headache telling me I had been stupid. I should have thought of an answer on the ride over.

"I went to have another look at that new dress of yours. I wanted to compare its material to the one the seamstress made for me. I saw all the missing items and rushed straight here."

Celine narrowed her eyes. "But how did you know to come here?"

I waved my hands around vaguely. "I didn't. I just started riding. And then I thought maybe Rafe and William could help. And Marie. I thought one of them might have a good idea..."

I let myself trail off as if I hadn't had a plan at all but had merely run to my brother. Apparently my performance had been convincing because the pain in my head faded away.

"Great," she said. "The one time your irrational thought patterns actually lead you to the right place."

My relief at finding her receded into confusion. "But Celine, what are you doing here? Behind the barrels, I mean." I pinched my nose closed. "It smells terrible."

She grimaced. "I left well before the others. I was supposed to arrive first and stowaway with plenty of time to spare. Only I forgot that I wouldn't be able to bring a horse. And it took the longest time to get here on foot."

"I thought you didn't want to go, now that Mother and Uncle Horace are part of the voyage."

"I didn't want anyone guessing my plan. And it's not entirely untrue. They do make the prospect less appealing. It's still preferable to being left behind with you, though." She glanced at me again. "No offense."

"I'm sorry it didn't work out." I wasn't. But it seemed better to try to lure her back to the palace with sympathy. "But don't you think being at the palace with me would be preferable to hanging around with an old, fishy net?"

"I'm not going back." Her eyes had returned to the ship. "I've been waiting for the rest of them to go below deck. Mother invited all the passengers and the officers to the state cabin for a celebratory drink to christen the voyage."

"There are still sailors on deck, though."

Celine still didn't look at me. "Do you remember Tom?"

"Tom?"

"You know, the cabin boy from when Father used to take us on trips as children. We were the same age and the best of friends."

"Oh yes, I do remember you and some partner-in-crime getting up to all sorts of mischief. Don't tell me he's still part of the crew."

She nodded. "He's a lieutenant now. And he's promised me that none of the sailors will try to stop me. That's how I was going to get on board originally. And he's the one who told me about the tradition of a christening drink. 'Just in case,' he said. I didn't think I'd need the information, so it's a good thing he's more thorough than I am."

"Celine…" I couldn't help some uneasiness creeping into my voice. "Surely you realize I can't let you stowaway on that ship."

She stood up finally and faced me.

"Please, Celeste! Is it really too much to ask for a little adventure? Our mother will be there, for goodness sake."

I winced. "If it were up to me, you know you could go on all the adventures you please. But Father will be so angry. I couldn't possibly."

Celine sighed. "I was afraid you would say that."

Her hand swept out from behind her back, a blur of wood

catching my eye. With anyone else, I would have blocked the move in time. But she was my baby sister, and she had taken me completely by surprise.

Darkness consumed me.

# CHAPTER 15

*A*n unpleasant pulling sensation and the sound of voices dragged me toward consciousness. But my head hurt so badly I didn't dare open my eyes. I had experienced headaches like this before, during the first year of the curse, and I knew that light would make it worse.

I kept them tightly shut and tried to remember what I had done to bring on such a violent reaction. My sluggish mind refused to cooperate.

Eventually my body settled into stillness, and the sound faded. The light behind my eyelids had also dimmed, however, so I risked cracking them open. The dark of my surroundings gave no hint of my location. Was I in my bed?

No, the surface beneath me felt hard and...wet?

Sudden memory returned, and I tried to sit up fast. My head swirled, and when two hands pressed me back down, I let them.

Slowly I reopened my eyes and focused on the face above me. Celine. I groaned. "What have you done? Where are we?"

"We're in the hold. But only for now. Once the ship is out to sea, the wind won't make it easy for them to return. And you know Mother. She doesn't approve of too much exertion. She'll let us stay."

So many thoughts began to rush through my mind that I knew I needed to keep my mouth shut or risk uttering the wrong thing. My head still ached too much to make thinking easy. Slowly I raised my hand to feel the spot where most of the pain seemed to emanate from. A round lump had already formed under my hair.

"Sorry, Lettie." Celine sounded genuinely contrite. "I've never used a cudgel before. It made such a horrid sound, I thought I'd killed you!"

I groaned again. "Celine! I don't want to go to sea. I need to go back to the palace. Why in the kingdoms did you bring me down here? *How* did you bring me down here?"

"It wasn't easy. I had to drag you."

That would explain the uncomfortable sensations before I returned to full consciousness.

"Tom wouldn't help me, either. He said he couldn't possibly assist in the abduction of a princess." I could hear the smile in her voice. "He did carry my bag for me, though."

An overwhelming urge to hit her swept over me. I suppressed it. "But, why?"

"Well, I originally planned to leave you on the docks. Only then I thought I'd killed you. And after I worked out you were still alive, I realized I couldn't just abandon you while you were unconscious. Anything could have happened to you."

"I think anything did happen to me. It certainly feels like it." The pain in my head had subsided enough for me to start registering all the other places that hurt. I imagined Celine dragging me up the gangplank and down the hold stairs all on her own and winced. It would take a long time for all the bruises to heal. "Celine, I insist you let me off this ship!"

"I'm really sorry, Lettie, I can't do that."

I took a breath to call for help, and she clapped a hand over my mouth. I bit it, and she yelped.

"Lettie!" She gave me a wounded look and cradled the hand against her chest. I narrowed my eyes at her.

Slowly I pushed myself up to a sitting position. She watched me warily but kept her distance. I tried to stand but fell to one side, off balance. I clenched my teeth, willing my body to return to functionality.

And then the ship tipped in the other direction. Oh. So it hadn't been me. The ship had already sailed, and we had hit the first of the waves.

I didn't bother trying to push myself back up this time. If it was already too late, I wanted to give my head more of a chance to settle first.

I tried to think through the consequences of Celine's rash actions. I had made no provisions for leaving. My network would be leaderless. How long would it take them to realize I was missing? I didn't contact each of them every night, so it might take them a while to realize no one had heard from me. Especially since most of them knew only one or two of the others.

I trusted them to continue with their assignments in my absence. But they would be concerned. They might even do something rash in an attempt to find me. And if they discovered anything new, who would they report it to?

I trembled with relief that I had possessed the forethought to send a copy of all my notes to the duchess. She would be at the palace soon enough and could finally inform my father of the rebellion. Hopefully my agents would know to go to her.

Of course, she would be equally concerned to discover me absent. And what of my father and brothers? What would they think when they discovered both Celine and I had disappeared?

I traced back over the events of the day and remembered my horse. Hopefully the dock worker would take him back to the palace and report our conversation. From there, it wouldn't take much intelligence to work out both Celine and I were on the yacht.

Another horror reared its head. Princess Celeste and Aurora both mysteriously vanished on the same day. If even one person saw through the coincidence...

My head pulsed with a new surge of pain, and I didn't know if it was the curse sending a warning or my fear heightening the pain from the bludgeoning. My only consolation was the continued absence of word on my aunt. If she escaped her prison, I felt sure the news would reach me.

As long as she stayed safely behind her wall of thorns, the kingdom remained safe for another day. Perhaps I would even have time to return before she found a way to escape.

I wiggled around until I found the most comfortable position, leaning against a bundle of unidentified material. I didn't worry about staining my dress. I couldn't examine it properly in the low light, but I felt fairly certain it would be unsalvageable.

My eyes fell on a large lump. Celine's bag. Since this was all her fault, she would be splitting her dresses with me. Thank goodness she had already had her growth spurt. Of course, I would have to scavenge something suitable for Aurora.

The thought of abandoning my secondary persona for the length of the voyage didn't even cross my mind. We would be sailing for weeks. I would go crazy if I was stuck as Celeste that whole time.

Of course William would be a problem. He could hardly avoid questioning Aurora's presence on the ship.

Strangely enough, I didn't consider avoiding him, any more than I had considered remaining Celeste. He had become such a fixture of my life as both Celeste and Aurora that I couldn't imagine having him in only one.

"I'll check if it's down here. I'm sure I saw it carried on board." Uncle Horace called the words upward as he began to descend the ladder into the hold. We couldn't hear the reply, if there was one, but we heard him muttering to himself as his feet found the floor.

Celine and I met each other's eyes in shared horror. For a moment, all our differences were forgotten. Uncle Horace was the last person either of us would have chosen to discover our presence.

He turned around and peered into the gloom, still grumbling away. At first his eyes passed over us, and hope stirred. Perhaps he wouldn't see us in the darkness. Neither of us had even taken a breath yet.

But then his gaze swung back toward us, his mutterings silenced. It had just taken his brain a moment to catch up with what his eyes had seen.

His whole body seemed to swell, and for a fascinated moment I forgot all my aches and pains and wondered if it was possible for a person to explode from rage. His eyes traveled back and forth between us and then settled on my sister.

"CELINE!"

She actually trembled and, despite my anger at her, I slid my arm around her shoulders. She was still my baby sister.

Uncle Horace opened and closed his mouth several times but seemed unable to think of the right words. Eventually he turned and climbed back up the ladder, leaving us quaking and giggling in equal measures.

That was how the rest of them found us, Rafe and William leading the group who piled down the ladder. My mother merely stuck her head over the opening to peer down at us and sigh.

I came out of the confused jumble of explanations intact, of course. Even if I hadn't been so obviously a victim, no one believed me capable of masterminding such a plan. Or of having the desire to do so.

To maintain the charade, and with a distant hope that they might actually turn the ship around, I had a mild fit of hysterics when William helped me up on deck and I saw the ocean swells spread in a glittering carpet around the ship. Inside, however, my heart soared, and I drank in the salt scent on the breeze.

Celine's predictions proved entirely true. Now that we were here, our mother decreed that we could stay. Celine wasn't even to be punished. Mother promised all sorts of dire consequences upon our return but stopped short at enforcing any of them on board ship. I suspected it had something to do with her state cabin being the only place on the ship with room for me and Celine to sleep. Keeping Celine confined to her quarters would punish more than just my sister. I appreciated my mother's restraint.

I ruthlessly raided Celine's luggage and chose the nicer half of her gowns for myself. Celine, still reeling from the sternest lecture she'd ever received from her favorite brother, didn't even attempt to protest. It probably helped that the lump on my head radiated pain which caused me to flinch whenever I made a sudden movement. And every time I flinched, she looked guilty.

Marie even volunteered some of her own dresses, and I took them gratefully. I had to spend my first full day on board taking up all the hems, but at least the curse considered sewing an unexceptional activity. When it came to clothes, I had full rein. I was even allowed to be grumpy and authoritative and order my sisters around.

The chore of hemming didn't feel in the least onerous when performed on the deck of such an immaculate sailing vessel. The elite sailors who crewed the royal yacht kept the wood scrubbed clean and the deck spick and span. The wind prevented the bright sun from becoming too hot, and I never tired of watching the foaming water race past.

Even the oldest veterans of the crew seemed to enjoy the clear weather, stopping often to admire the pod of dolphins using our bow wave for surf practice. I put the first completed dress down and leaned over the railing, stretching my hand out as far as it could go. My fingers hung in the air, a long way from touching the water, or the sleek, gray bodies, but I couldn't help myself. A girl could dream.

A strong arm slipped around my waist and pulled me gently back. "Woah there, Princess. We wouldn't want you going over the side."

An unexpected shiver ran through me at William's touch. His arm lingered after I tried to pull back, so I glanced up into his face. It was closer than I had expected, and I couldn't read the expression in his eyes.

"I thought you were scared of the sea, Princess." The softness of his voice maintained the illusion of a private moment, despite the sailors moving around us.

I couldn't help the slightest of indrawn breaths. Was he testing me? I needed to think of a suitable answer, but my mind had scrambled. I tried to remind myself that the sun shone brightly, and I wore a dress. I was Celeste not Aurora in this moment, and I needed to fight to keep my eyes from matching the intensity in his.

Why hadn't I noticed how tightly Celine's borrowed dress squeezed my midriff? Was it a curse sensation, warning me not to allow any cracks in my performance? Or was William's arm responsible for the effect all on its own?

"Dolphins." I said the first word that came into my mind.

"Dolphins?" He let me go and stepped back, his voice returned to normal.

I turned back to the railing, nodding with slightly desperate enthusiasm. "Yes, aren't they beautiful?" I pointed toward them and then gasped in not-entirely-assumed delight when one leaped from the water.

"Almost too beautiful." His voice had dropped again, and I glanced over my shoulder. He wasn't watching the waves.

I pressed on, afraid of what the change in his manner might mean. "I heard a story once about a girl who fell off a ship." I shuddered. "But it turned out all right because some dolphins rescued her. Now that I know the dolphins are guarding our journey, I don't feel afraid anymore."

"I'm glad to hear it." William stepped forward to join me at the rail. "I've always loved the ocean, myself. I'm greatly looking forward to seeing these islands of yours."

We chatted about the upcoming voyage in our usual friendly manner, and I forced my body to relax against the side of the ship. But inside the tension remained.

When Rafe eventually called William away, I watched him go, my happy expression betraying nothing of the turmoil within. Why did I feel as if I had been weighed and found wanting? Tested in some way I didn't understand.

I tried to take a deep breath, but the tight band around my middle had yet to release. For years I had fooled everyone around me with relative ease. I had even come to an uneasy acceptance of my situation.

And now this prince had come along and destroyed all my equilibrium. He blurred my boundaries in dangerous ways. I would have to tread more warily than ever. This unexpected voyage could prove my undoing in more ways than one. And if I fell, who would stand between my aunt and the destruction of my family?

# CHAPTER 16

*I*stretched, feeling rough material scrape against my skin. I missed my usual clothes. I had managed to scrounge an outfit from the cargo hold, but the quality left a lot to be desired. At least I had found a piece of decent material to use as a scarf to cover my head.

I took a deep breath of the salt-filled air and wished I stood up on deck. I could easily imagine the moon and the stars and the feel of the wind on my face. Unfortunately, even at night, sailors on watch also populated the deck. If I wanted to exercise unseen, the cargo hold was my only option.

I gazed through the gloom around me and decided to use my surroundings as a challenge. The royal yacht wasn't a cargo vessel, so the hold wasn't packed full. The large storage space had only been included in the original design because royals generally didn't like being limited when it came to their luggage.

Shaking out my limbs, I began to run through the confined space. Picking up speed, I leaped over several crates, imagining enemies right behind me. I pushed off a large roll of material and leaped onto the top of a barrel. I paused there for a moment, keeping my balance as the ship pitched and rolled.

I smiled, alone in the dark. I had found the perfect place for honing my sea legs. I propelled myself off the barrel and continued twice around the large hold, jumping off and over obstacles whenever I had the chance. Once I misjudged a leap when the ship hit a large wave and landed hard on my rear. I winced. Yet another bruise to add to the ones already turning purple and yellow.

I forced myself back up and kept going. Most of the luggage and supplies in the hold had been strapped against the sides, leaving an open space in the middle. As I moved into the open, rounding a particularly large stack of crates, I whipped out one of my hidden knives, bringing it up in a blocking move against an imaginary opponent.

To my shock, the blade met resistance with the clang of metal striking metal. I fell back and drew a second knife, settling into a crouch as I re-centered myself. The physical response came instinctively before my mind understood what I saw.

A low, familiar laugh made my taut muscles relax. A second later, they tightened again as a knife swung toward me. I blocked, maneuvering myself around and fully into the open.

William pulled back and then attacked again, the laugh still reflected on his face. "You have no idea how pleased I am to see you here."

"You have a strange way of communicating pleasure." I blocked another lunge, proud that my voice betrayed no breathlessness despite my recent exertion.

"I've been wanting to try my skills against yours ever since I saw you fight in that gardeners' hut." He shook his head. "And here you are, clearly lacking an opponent."

"Well, hello to you, too." I lunged forward with a feint and then a sharp jab, but he pulled back out of reach just in time. William was taller and stronger than me, so I had to move with extra speed to make up for it. I wasn't sure how long I could maintain the pace.

As soon as my breath became labored, and a drop of sweat ran down my face under my scarf, I pulled back, lifting my hands in surrender.

William raised an eyebrow at me, but I shrugged.

"This isn't a game to me, Princeling. I never practice to the point of exhaustion. Real danger could strike at any time, and I might find myself without sufficient reserves."

William gave a small bow. "Consider me corrected. Wise advice in these perilous times."

I carefully returned my knives to their places and watched as William did the same.

"So, tell me, Oh Wise Aurora, why I have the very great pleasure of your company aboard this ship. I must confess to some surprise. I thought you were busy in the capital putting down a rebellion."

"I have my reasons."

He waited, and I debated how much I should say.

"I have a certain…interest…in the islands that I didn't wish to delegate."

William's quiet exhale suggested he understood my unspoken words. "I didn't realize the itinerary included Banishment Island."

"It doesn't at the moment. But do you doubt me?"

"Never." The admiration in his eyes made me grin ruefully beneath my scarf. Now I just needed to figure out a way to follow through with it.

Especially since it wasn't entirely a cover story. I'd had time to think about it and realized I could work this trip to my advantage. I intended to take the fight to my aunt, exactly as I had hinted.

William beat me to the hold the next night and joined my exercises without comment. His leaps could clear the crates and barrels more easily than mine, but I was more sure on my feet. The next night I was expecting him, and he didn't disappoint.

As we finished our third circuit, he cut in front of me, reaching our original starting point two steps ahead.

"I win." He grinned over his shoulder at me.

"Boys." I rolled my eyes. "I didn't realize it was a race."

"It's always a race."

"I'll remember that next time."

"Do." He leaned against a tall barrel, his gaze turning calculating. "So, I've been doing some thinking."

"Sounds dangerous." I was still trying to think of a way to reroute our trip, so I wasn't paying him much attention.

"There aren't too many females on this ship."

My eyes flashed to his, all other thoughts forgotten.

"The way I figure it, there are two possibilities. One is that you spend the day in hiding somewhere. In which case your options are limited." His eyes flicked around the hold. "The other is that you spend your day in plain sight. And there aren't too many women on board among the sailors and soldiers. The number goes up a little when you include the queen's attendants, of course, but not by much."

"Stop." I held out a hand to halt his words, my eyes locked on his. "I'm only going to say this once. If you ever try to find me outside of this…" I gestured around us without breaking eye contact. "If you ever even attempt to identify me, that will be the last time you ever see me. I will be gone, and I won't look back. And I will know if you try."

Something flashed in his eyes, and the strength of my desire to understand his emotions surprised me. How much did William care if he never saw Aurora again?

For a long moment, we stared at each other.

Was my imagination responsible for the fear and longing I saw reflected back at me?

He pushed himself off the barrel, keeping his gaze on mine,

and stepped forward, closing the distance between us. I resisted the impulse to step backward, unwilling to look weak.

One of his hands wrapped around my upper arm, and he almost whispered my name. "Aurora."

I drew a ragged breath, waiting to hear what he would say. But the next words weren't his.

"Aurora? So this is where you keep sneaking off to—or should I say *who*? I've always wanted to meet the mysterious Aurora." The all-too familiar voice smashed the tension like a hammer blow.

The infamous spymaster, more shadow than woman, never gasped. But it took all my self-control to hold one in. I turned slowly, knowing that my performance needed to be flawless. The decision had been made for me—Celine was being introduced to Aurora.

For a long moment the three of us stood still, sizing each other up. Then Celine cried, "Yes!" and punched the air with her fist. Her triumphant crowing caught me by surprise.

"Excuse me?" I put extra depth into my Aurora voice.

Celine shook her head, still chuckling to herself. "Something strange has been going on at the palace. I got a little worried that all the action might be happening there, and this might turn out to be nothing more than a boring sailing trip. But if Aurora chose to come along, then I made the right decision. The excitement will be here."

I suppressed a wry smile. If only she knew—choice had nothing to do with it.

William glanced between us, clearly too wary to say anything. I pondered my next move. I hadn't realized Celine knew about Aurora. But she had obviously heard of her, and she had also recognized something strange was going on at the palace. She was more aware than I had given her credit for.

I bowed low. "I am honored by your esteem, Your Highness."

William turned a surprised expression on me. I had never

shown him half as much respect. But he wasn't Lanoverian, and I didn't want Celine to get the wrong impression from his presence. "I hope you have heard that my loyalty lies with the royal family and with Lanover."

"Oh, of course." Celine waved her hand, as if physically dismissing any possible doubt. "You are the one who guards us and watches over us. I know that well enough."

I blinked. "Forgive me, Your Highness. I didn't know any of your family knew of me at all."

She sat down on a conveniently sized bundle and looked at me, the smile still tugging at her lips. "None of the rest of them do, I'm pretty sure. I considered telling them, but..." She shrugged. "None of them listen to me or take me seriously, so why should I tell them what they're too busy to find out for themselves?"

She bit her lip as if she knew how petulant she sounded. After a moment, she shook herself. "You can learn a lot from the servants, if you're bored enough to listen. Cordelia would be proud of me. She was always the observant one when we were children."

She turned her gaze on William. "But I don't know what you're doing here, Prince William. What connection could you possibly have to Aurora?"

"No connection but the veriest chance. I am nothing but one of her many admirers."

Celine raised an eyebrow. "Does my sister know that?"

My eyes flew to her face at the dry words before I remembered that she didn't know my true identity. I bit my lip. I would have to tread more carefully than ever. I couldn't afford to let my guard down.

William shifted uncomfortably and didn't reply. I took pity on him and changed the subject.

"Why did you desire to meet me, Your Highness?"

"Are you joking?" Celine stared at me with wide eyes. "You're everything I wish I could be. Your life must be filled with excitement."

"You'd be surprised." My mind ran over the endless hours I spent training and waiting and watching. And that was before I even counted the time I spent as Celeste.

Celine's expression suggested she didn't believe me, and I reminded myself she was only fourteen. "You said something strange was going on at the palace…"

She nodded, bouncing a little on her improvised seat. "The servants and the guards were following me around. Everywhere I went." Her tone turned defensive. "You might not believe me, but it's true."

William turned dancing eyes toward me. "Oh, she believes you."

I took a deep breath. The prince needed to learn when to keep his mouth shut.

Celine looked between the two of us. "Wait! Was that you?" She wrinkled her nose. "But why in the kingdoms would you want to have me followed?"

"For your protection, of course, Your Highness."

"My protection?" She narrowed her eyes. "And why would I need extra protection? I've never been followed before."

I had definitely been underestimating her. I held her gaze, keeping my own strong and steady. When the silence had stretched out between us, she shook her head. "All right, you don't have to tell me. But if you give me a chance, I'll show you I can be trusted."

I smiled beneath my scarf, proud of her for not trying to use her royal status to order my cooperation. "And how would you suggest I do that?"

She shrugged. "Let me train with you. That's what you've been doing, right? I was watching you for a while." She seemed proud rather than embarrassed of her spying. "And I heard what you said to Prince William, too. I won't try to find you or anything, I swear."

I nodded slowly, and then my eyes swung to William.

He sighed, seeming to know what I was waiting for. "It seems you're leaving me no choice but to make the same promise. Despite the temptation, I won't try to find you when you don't want to be found."

I withheld my own sigh, not wanting either of them to know how nervous I had been. I glanced between them and then recognized the true source of my relief. I didn't feel so alone.

Several of my agents had been instructed to make sure they were included in the traveling party, but somehow not a single one of them had made it onto the royal yacht. And that despite the full crew of sailors and the company of guards my uncle had insisted my father send along for his and my mother's protection. I noted my father had sent the smallest of the companies attached to the palace, but they still numbered over eighty men.

And yet it only took me the first day to realize that none of my people were among them. And I had never had either the necessity or the opportunity to recruit any of the crew of the *Viktoria*. Their absence concerned me, but I could do nothing about it.

I had been all alone on this ship, but now I had a team of three. My normal band of agents had been with me for so long that I had forgotten what it was like to operate without support. A foreign prince and a fourteen-year-old princess were hardly the agents a normal spymaster would choose, but they were exactly the people I wanted standing at my back.

"Well then," I said, letting my pleasure color my voice. "Welcome aboard."

# CHAPTER 17

*C*eline had never possessed the discipline or the will to stick to a steady exercise regime, so she struggled to keep up with us when we trained. But she never complained, no matter how many times she lost her balance and fell. And every night she pushed herself harder.

Around Aurora, the old Celine returned. And I realized how much I had missed her. Clearly I had been wrong to exclude her for so long. I wasn't the only one constrained by circumstances outside my control and in desperate need of an outlet.

William accepted her inclusion with good grace, even if his eyes did sometimes linger on me a little wistfully, as if he missed our time alone. He treated her as a younger sister, and she embraced the relationship in a way she had never done with Frederic or Cassian.

I had to take extra care when transferring between my two personas now that Celine was sneaking out of the state cabin at night as well. I was more grateful than ever that the beds each had a privacy screen. I walked a tightrope, and I knew it.

Since I spent my nights cooped up below decks, I endeavored

to spend as much of the day as possible in the open air. Most of the other royals seemed to feel the same way, with the exception of my uncle who preferred to avoid us all by holing up in his cabin.

Rafe and Marie kept largely to themselves, and I tried to respect their privacy as much as I could. They had already been forced to bring half of their family along on their wedding tour.

We enjoyed almost perfect weather, the boat flying along on the planned route. We passed several islands, but Rafe had decided to sail straight to our southernmost port and then stop off at some of the larger isles on the way home. Even from a distance the islands looked magnificent, however. And, thankfully, the curse allowed me to enjoy them openly.

William and Celine's shared secret produced a new camaraderie, and spending time with them reminded me of what it had been like between me and my siblings before the curse and before Rafe and Cordelia had left Lanover. Celine was a great deal more fun on board ship than she had been lately at the palace, and I once again regretted holding myself back from her.

As we traveled, William read aloud from a travel guide he had found at the palace, and Celine interjected with scathing and hilarious commentary. I giggled often and added my own observations whenever I thought the curse would let me get away with it, which was much less often than I would have liked.

"Is that the smallest island we've seen?" William asked, standing at the rail and gazing across the waves.

Celine nodded. "That's Inverne."

I jumped up from my seat on a large coil of rope and leaned out over the edge. Inverne was my favorite island, and I had been looking forward to passing it. The bright aqua of the water as it approached the island almost took my breath away. I squinted, trying to make out fish and coral below the surface.

The white sand reflected the sun, broken only by a few small, dark spots which I knew from experience to be giant turtles. The emerald green foliage rising from the beach looked cool and inviting.

I sighed, letting a little wistfulness creep into the sound. The curse hadn't touched my love of the small tropical paradise. Celine patted my hand comfortingly.

"We can ask Rafe to let us stop on the way back. I'm sure Marie would love to visit Inverne."

I smiled at her. "I'm sure anyone would."

William pulled out his book, and Celine groaned. "Can't Inverne, at least, remain untouched by that monstrosity?"

William ignored her and began to read in a lofty tone. "The small island of Inverne is the smallest of the inhabited Lanoverian islands." He broke off to look back out over the water. "People live there?"

"Of course they do! Look at it. Who wouldn't want to live there?"

"Umm, me." Celine shook her head at me. "It's nice to visit, but can you imagine how boring it would be to be stuck there all the time with only a handful of other families?"

"Sounds idyllic," I murmured under my breath, but I had to admit I would probably go crazy after a while.

"I suppose it would depend who the other inhabitants were," said William, his eyes sliding sideways to rest on me. I pretended not to notice.

He looked back down at the book, but Celine snatched it from his hands. "Absolutely not," she said. "The question of living aside, Inverne is a paradise to visit, and I won't have it spoiled by a dry list of its imports, exports, trade patterns, demographics and historical significance to Lanover."

William tried to wrest the guide back from her, but she clambered up onto the coil of rope and held the book over the railing.

I laughed. "Celine, don't!"

She ignored me. "No more." She looked at William. "No more of this book for the rest of the week, or I drop it over."

"What about the rest of the day?"

"The week, or it goes over."

I was fairly certain William only read the book in the first place because it annoyed Celine so much, but I didn't like to ruin his fun by suggesting that to her. I stepped up onto the rope and snatched the book from her hand.

"Hey! Celeste!" Celine pouted at me.

"All books must be respected."

"Even boring ones?" She quirked an eyebrow at me.

"Especially boring ones," I said firmly. "What else do they have going for them, after all? Their status must be respected, if nothing else." I handed the book back to William. "A bit like Uncle Horace."

"Lettie!" Laughter exploded from Celine. "You say the most outrageous things." She sighed, collapsing onto the rope. "I think he would actually explode in apoplectic rage if he heard me say half the things you do. You get away with everything."

"Do I?" I looked at her innocently.

"You should leave your sister alone." Our mother glided over to us, the picture of serenity despite the hot day.

"You should tell her to leave Uncle Horace alone," said Celine.

"Your uncle doesn't need my protection, but I'm glad to hear you so quick to defend him."

Celine made a face.

"In fact, here he comes now."

Celine jumped up and looked around. "Where?"

Our mother sank into the spot Celine had just vacated and then smiled calmly at her daughter. "I can't see him now. Perhaps I was mistaken after all."

"Mother!" Celine rolled her eyes and threw herself down onto the deck. "I guess I can't blame Lettie when it's so obvious where she got it from."

William watched us all, slowly shaking his head.

I smiled at him. "A little different from Northhelm?"

He met my eyes. "You have no idea."

A warning twinge in my stomach told me I'd been a little too astute. I forced my smile brighter. "It's always cold in Northhelm, isn't it? Nothing like this." I waved around me. "Do you even have sailing ships there?"

William looked a little taken aback, visibly reassessing my earlier comment.

Celine sighed. "Really, Lettie? *Of course* they have ships. Ships can sail in the cold as easily as the heat." She turned to face our mother. "We were talking about Inverne. Is it on the schedule for our return?"

I tried not to look too attentive, but I had been hoping to turn the conversation to our return voyage. I still needed to somehow convince my family to detour past Banishment Island.

"You would have to ask Rafe about that, dear. All I know is that he won't consider stopping before Largo."

"Largo? Is that another island?" William asked.

Celine shook her head. "No, it's our southernmost port. We'll turn around there and come back north."

"Goodness!" I looked around at them all with wide eyes. "Largo. I hope the captain knows what he's doing. I don't know if the dolphins could rescue us all."

"Dolphins?" Celine looked at me as if I were mad.

"Her fear of the sea has been lifted because she places her trust in the dolphins to rescue her if she should happen to fall in." William delivered the line with a straight face, but Celine laughed anyway.

"Can you imagine getting a ride on a dolphin?" She gazed over the side. "It almost makes me want to 'fall' in."

"Celine don't you dare," said our mother before turning to me. "Our captain is the very best, Celeste dear." She patted my knee. "But what makes you so concerned?"

"Largo is so far south, it must be near...and Father said... submerged rocks...and reefs..." I hit my aim of incoherent perfectly, and Celine looked confused. Understanding sprung into William's eyes, however, and I guessed Banishment Island had already been on his mind as well.

My mother also seemed to follow my train of thought. "There's no need to be afraid, my dear. We'll pick up one of the captains who knows the area in Largo."

"Wait, what? What area?" Celine frowned, trying to catch up.

"I have decided to make a slight diversion." Our mother spoke as if she was merely suggesting we embark on a stroll around the deck. "We will be stopping off to attempt to make contact with your aunt."

Celine's shriek nearly covered William's small indrawn breath. I only wished I had the freedom to make either expression of astonishment.

Despite the restraint of his reaction, William couldn't hide the awe on his face. He clearly thought Aurora had worked her hidden influence. But I knew the truth. I could take no credit for this announcement.

I sat back and watched the curious questions pour from Celine's mouth. Somehow, our mother avoided answering any of them directly without ever actually refusing to respond. By the time she left us, I had reached an inescapable conclusion.

I wasn't the only one with a hidden agenda on this ship. And I wasn't the only one with an interest in my aunt and that island.

~

"I am once again humbled in your presence." William gave an exaggerated bow to match his statement.

I still had no idea why my mother wanted to make contact with my aunt but, since I had no intention of admitting as much to William, I graciously accepted his compliment before continuing to warm up.

"Huh?" Celine looked back and forth between us. "Why do I always feel like I'm missing something?"

"It's because you're so young and insignificant." William tweaked her nose. "We're always talking about important stuff and then saying, 'let's not tell Celine since she's such a baby.'"

Celine glared at him. "Not funny, William."

"Really?" He sat down to stretch before grinning over at her. "I thought it was hilarious."

She picked up a small lump of unidentified something that had fallen from one of the cargo bundles and threw it at him. It made an unpleasant squelching noise when it hit, and she laughed triumphantly.

"Why, you..." William started to push himself onto his feet, when I interposed myself between them.

"Come on, you two. Stop bickering. What am I supposed to be, your mother?"

Celine snorted. "Hardly. You can't be more than, what... twenty-one?" The gleam of curiosity in her eye betrayed the casual tone. And William was just as bad. His attempt to look uninterested in my answer failed badly.

I rolled my eyes. "Nice try. If you two are so distracted today, I'm going to win easily." I took off without waiting for a response and smiled at the sound of them scrambling to catch up.

We were half way round our second circuit when an unexpected sound caught my attention. I slid to a halt, listening hard. My hand snapped up, signaling the others to stop. When I recognized the sound of someone coming through the hatch into the cargo hold, I gestured for them to hide themselves.

Halfway to my own hiding spot I remembered William and Celine weren't my agents. I looked back, afraid I would see them standing in confusion in the middle of the hold. But William had already disappeared, and I could only see the swish of Celine's skirts as they disappeared around a pile of small barrels.

I found a position between several large crates, my back pressed up against the side of the ship. The footsteps of two people reached the bottom of the ladder.

"We're not supposed to be down here." The man sounded uneasy.

"Well we're acting on the major's orders and I, for one, don't plan on going against him. Do you?"

The first man only grunted before following the second one in my general direction. I held my breath as they passed mere steps away from me. The shadowy outline of their forms confirmed they were guards.

They wrestled open a crate and pulled out a rectangular box. From the little I could see in the darkness, it looked different from the storage containers around us. More like the expensive receptacle for a valued item or weapon.

"What is it?" The voice of the uneasy guard echoed my own curiosity.

"How would I know? All I know is that the major originally wanted it packed down here, but now he's changed his mind. Thinks it will be safer in his cabin."

"Safer from who?"

"I already told you, that's all I know. Probably those good-for-nothing sailors. Wouldn't surprise me if they rummaged around down here whenever the fancy took them."

I frowned at his words. Guards and sailors didn't traditionally get along, but the sailors on the royal yacht seemed like the peak of the trade as far as discipline and reliability went.

The two men clomped their way back to the ladder and then up and out of the hold. I waited two full counts of a hundred before emerging from my nook. William and Celine followed my lead.

"Well, that was…odd." William rubbed the back of his neck, his gaze fixed on the now-empty ladder.

"There's something odd about all those guards." Celine wrinkled her nose.

I frowned, giving her my full attention. She had noticed my agents following her back at the palace, after all. If she said something was off now, I was all ears.

# CHAPTER 18

"What do you mean?" I asked.

"I've been talking to Tom."

Ah, her lieutenant friend. I nodded in understanding. They already assumed Aurora knew everything that went on, so I didn't need to act dumb. Plus, I was too busy feeling proud. From the sound of things, my little sister was a natural. Already she was using her connections, keeping her ear to the ground and developing her own contacts.

"Who's Tom?" William wasn't quite as well-informed.

"He's a lieutenant, and an old friend. He used to be the cabin boy when we were children."

William gave her an easily interpreted look, but I wasn't worried. I'd initially wondered if she was romantically interested in her old friend, only two years her senior, but I'd been watching her closely during the day, and she didn't show that sort of preference for him. I'd seen enough of her brief infatuations to know what they looked like.

"Everyone knows sailors and guards don't get along." The scepticism was thick in William's voice.

"Of course not. I know that." Her defensive response came a

little too quickly, reminding me she was only fourteen. "But this is different. He said all the sailors are on edge about having so many soldiers on board."

I sighed. Perhaps the sailors saw it as a slight on their ability to watch over the royal family. Usually the king himself only brought fifty guards with him.

Celine shrugged. "It isn't anything overt. He said that none of the sailors know any of the guards, and none of them are at all sociable with the sailors. They act a bit strangely."

"Definitely something to keep our eye on," I said. "And good work talking to Tom." Celine visibly swelled with pride. "Keep it up, and let us know what you hear. For now, I want to know what was inside that box."

"It looked like a sword box to me," said William.

"A sword box?" Celine made a face. "Who would keep a sword in a box?"

William shrugged. "It's not that uncommon for ceremonial or ornamental weapons. Family heirlooms and the like."

"All right, but why would the major bring his heirloom sword on board with him?" asked Celine.

"That is, indeed, the question." I tapped my leg as I thought, and William and Celine both waited silently for my conclusion. "The major likes to make surprise visits to his men on night watch. To check that they've remained alert."

William and Celine exchanged looks but didn't ask how I knew that.

"None of the cabins on ship are locked. We'll wait until he leaves and then go find out exactly what's in that box."

"All of us?" The breathy excitement in Celine's voice made me question my plan to take her along.

"I don't think we should all go." Apparently William agreed with me. "I think you should stay behind, Aurora."

Wait, what? "Excuse me?" I injected as much frost into my voice as the humid air of the hold would allow.

He ignored my tone. "If the major discovers Prince William and Princess Celine in his cabin, what exactly can he do about it?" His look said that he knew I knew he was right. "If the major discovers you, on the other hand…"

I let out a slow breath, turning his words over in my mind. As much as I hated to admit it, he did have a point. This ship wasn't my usual territory—the cabin had only one exit, and there was nowhere to run. What *would* happen if I was discovered?

But at the same time, I had already been reminded once tonight that William and Celine weren't my agents. I couldn't trust that they wouldn't miss something or leave behind some trace of their intrusion.

After a long pause, I shook my head. "It's not ideal, but I have to be there. We'll just have to make sure we aren't caught."

William looked worried, but I didn't give him any time to think about it, leading the way toward the ladder. Celine followed eagerly, not willing to speak up and risk us changing our minds about taking her along.

Moving through the upper decks required extreme caution, so our progress toward the major's cabin was necessarily slow. And once we arrived there, it was no easy feat to find places for each of us to wait out of sight. By the time we had accomplished all of that, the guards delivering the box had long gone.

Thankfully, since a cramp had begun to form in my leg, we didn't have to wait more than half an hour before the major emerged. I couldn't even see his cabin from my vantage point, but I did see him go past as he left.

Creeping forward, I soon felt the others at my back. As expected, the door opened easily. The tiny cabin on the other side had to be the smallest on the ship. The major probably considered himself fortunate to have a cabin at all, considering how many royals were on board.

A second's glance revealed the bare surface of the small desk, so my eyes moved first to the chest at the foot of the bed and then to the tiny wardrobe. The chest, built into the wall like the bed, didn't appear to have a lock.

William moved toward it, so I stopped him with a hand to his arm. He froze beneath my touch, looking down first at my fingers and then up into my eyes. I forced my mind to stay focused and not to respond to the uncertainty in his face. Especially since I could feel Celine's curious gaze on us.

"Be careful," I whispered. "Take the time to look at how everything is positioned before you touch anything. The major will expect the waves to disrupt his possessions slightly, but we don't want to leave anything different enough to make him suspicious."

He nodded, so I let him go, turning toward the narrow wardrobe. I had barely opened the doors when a low cry from William made me spin back around. He held the box from the hold in his hands.

"Well, that was easy." Celine sounded disappointed. "Maybe it's not important, after all."

I shook my head. Easy was good. Much better than the alternative.

"Open it." I needed to know the contents before I decided if this was merely a scouting mission, or if it was an extraction.

William opened the box and, sure enough, an elegant sword lay inside on a bed of red satin. We all drew close to examine it. Even in the faint moonlight from the single porthole, the metal of the blade gleamed. My fingers itched to pick it up and test its balance.

I could tell from William's expression that the simple leather of the hilt didn't fool him any more than it fooled me. He held an expensive and valuable weapon.

Celine looked less impressed. "It's just a sword." She grabbed the box from William and carried it over to the porthole to get a better look. "Maybe there's something written on it or something."

I took one step toward her before I heard quiet voices outside the cabin door. For the briefest moment, the three of us stared at each other. Then William's eyes moved from the sword box in Celine's hands to the wardrobe. My thoughts followed his gaze. Celine and our prize would just fit inside the narrow space.

Strong hands lifted me off my feet and two wooden doors shut in my face. I swallowed a gasp. It had all happened too quickly to follow. In the few available seconds, William had acted to protect me rather than the sword. I wanted to curse his protectiveness, but a moment's reflection reminded me of the danger of my being caught. Gratitude washed over me as the cabin door opened and a startled exclamation rang out.

I stiffened. The voice didn't belong to the major. But I did recognize it.

# CHAPTER 19

*I* peered through the small gap between the wardrobe doors. Sure enough, Uncle Horace stood just inside the cabin, gaping at William and Celine. The major stood behind him, his eyes traveling from his open chest to the box still in Celine's hands. He raised both eyebrows but said nothing. William had been right; a major could do little against a prince and princess.

My uncle, on the other hand, had no such compunction. "What is the meaning of this?"

Celine seemed torn between terror and defiance. She and our uncle had never gotten along. When she didn't say anything, William drew himself up and took the box from her hands, closing the lid over the sword. "We witnessed this item being stolen from the hold. We are merely reclaiming it." His expression dared either of them to question him.

An admiring grin crept across my face. His golden hair caught the moonlight, and he looked confident and powerful, every inch the prince. I could see why Cordelia had written so much praise of him in her letters home after she had first arrived in Northhelm.

Uncle Horace looked surprised, but after a moment of assessing William, he seemed to deflate a little. "Well, no harm done, then. The sword is actually mine, and I requested the major to retrieve it from the hold for me. I had become concerned that the box might be damaged down there. It is a... valuable item."

I could see the reluctance in William's face as he handed the box over to my uncle. But what could he do?

Their brief interaction had apparently provided enough time for Celine to recover her confidence. "Why did you bring an old sword with you, Uncle Horace? It seems a bit strange to me." She stared at him, her expression demanding an answer.

Uncle Horace chuckled a little nervously. "This isn't just an old sword, my dear."

Celine winced visibly at the title, and I suppressed a chuckle. Nothing riled Celine like Uncle Horace's disdain and condescension.

"It's a beautiful weapon." William watched my uncle closely.

"That it is, that it is." He patted the box and then looked between them. "But I must confess to still being confused. What exactly were the two of you doing roaming the ship together in the middle of the night?"

Despite the lack of direct accusation, William stiffened and looked offended. If my sister hadn't been so young, I would have understood my uncle's natural conclusion. But he should have known better than to think William would ever get involved with a girl who was only fourteen.

Celine looked equally offended, but in response to William's affront. I could only hope she wouldn't be upset with him for long.

Slowly William forced himself to return to a state of calm. "I would be happy to explain it to you, of course." He let his eyes linger meaningfully on the major. "Perhaps we could adjourn the conversation to your cabin, or mine, if you prefer."

"Oh." Uncle Horace glanced back at the major, seemingly having forgotten his presence.

I understood William's motivation. He wanted to clear the room so I could make my escape. But something about the situation wasn't adding up, and I refused to be cut out of the proceedings. I could handle Uncle Horace.

I took a deep breath and stepped out of the wardrobe. The major gasped and fell back. Everyone else turned startled faces in my direction. William pressed his lips together into a tight line and glared at me.

I focused on my uncle. "Your Highness, I second the suggestion of retiring to your cabin. At the very least we will all have a little more room to breathe."

He shook himself and looked around the confined space with bulging eyes. "There's no one else concealed in here, is there? Because I don't know if I can take any more surprises tonight. I'm not as young as I used to be." No one replied since no other hiding places remained. He turned back to me. "I'm amazed and confused but, now that you mention it, it is a little tight in here." His eyes swung toward Celine. "Of course, I would be a great deal more amazed if I hadn't found my reprehensible niece involved. She has a penchant for stirring up trouble."

Celine glared at him, both hands curling into fists at her sides. I pushed down my own anger at his words and repeated my suggestion that we move the conversation.

"Oh, very well. If that is what it takes to get answers, I am willing enough to play the host." He gestured for us all to follow him out of the cabin. "I even have a rather fine brandy we can sample." He directed his words toward William, who maintained an impressive diplomat's face of polite interest. Celine could learn a lot from him.

The major made as if to follow us, but William gave him such a haughty look that he stopped. My uncle glanced over his shoulder. "Oh, yes, Harrison, you stay here. No need to accompany us.

I can't imagine I'll come to any harm in the presence of my niece and my nephew's brother-in-law. Despite the presence of a mysterious stranger among us." He chuckled, apparently finding himself humorous. No one else laughed, but the major reluctantly stepped back into his cabin.

My uncle kept up a quiet stream of small talk directed at William as we made our way across the ship to his larger cabin. William replied as briefly as possible, but Uncle Horace didn't seem to mind.

He ushered us all into his cabin and suggested we take seats around the small table while he found several glasses and the brandy bottle. Only William accepted a glass, and I noticed he didn't drink anything.

"So," said my uncle, once he had also taken a seat, "are you planning to remove that scarf now?"

"No."

He frowned. "I'm a prince, you know. I could have you arrested for insubordination."

"You could try." I kept my voice even. "And since I am loyal to the Lanoverian royal family, having to resist you would cause me great distress. I hope you won't attempt it."

"Well, then." He narrowed his eyes at me.

"We aren't here to discuss her face." William swirled the drink in his glass. "We're here to find out the significance of that sword."

"Are we now?" My uncle transferred his attention to the prince. "I thought we were going to find out why you were wandering the ship in the company of my young niece." His gaze flitted briefly back to me. "And apparently a mysterious young woman of unknown origin."

I didn't like what I saw lurking in his face. He might not try anything now, when we easily outnumbered him, and he wanted answers. But I suspected the guards would be receiving orders to search for me after this. I growled inaudibly. I might need to curtail my time spent as Aurora for the rest of the voyage.

I cleared my throat. "My origin isn't unknown. I work with the Duchess of Sessily. I assist her in keeping our kingdom safe. I have no nefarious intentions, but my work is best done from the shadows."

William nodded his support of my assertion. "I had many dealings with the duchess in Northhelm. She is greatly concerned for the well-being of Lanover."

I bit back a smile. A diplomat's answer, not a word of which was untrue.

Uncle Horace looked between us several times before narrowing his eyes in Celine's direction. "I admit I was curious about a prince of Northhelm's involvement. But it seems a little clearer now. What young prince could resist the request to assist such an intriguing young woman? Your involvement, Celine, seems entirely unnecessary, however."

Celine glared at him. She sat ramrod straight, touching as little of the furniture as possible. "Why shouldn't I be involved? I care for our kingdom as much as anyone."

Our uncle eyed her off for another several seconds before deciding to let it go. "About that..." He took a sip of his brandy. "Exactly what sort of risks to our kingdom does the shrewd duchess foresee on this journey?"

"What sort of risks do you foresee? Why insist on so many guards?" I leaned forward. "Why has the queen announced a new stop on our itinerary?"

The sword might belong to Uncle Horace. And he might have requested the major to have it retrieved for him. But why had they been exchanging it in the middle of the night? I had attributed Uncle Horace's presence on the voyage, and his insistence on so many guards, to his usual concerns over the prestige and safety of the royal family. What had I missed?

Uncle Horace took a deep breath and then steepled his hands

together, resting his elbows on the table and his chin on his fingers.

"It is true that I encouraged Viktoria to make such a stop. She was easily persuadable, however." He glanced at Celine. "I think your questions the other night had an impact. I think my brother and his wife would like to check on our banished sister."

My blood surged as usual at the mention of my aunt. Something of my passion must have leaked out of my eyes because my uncle fixed his gaze on me, and something in his manner changed.

"Ah," he said softly. "I see you're not a fan of my fair sister."

"My loyalty doesn't extend to anyone who would commit infanticide. Let alone against a royal child." I tried to keep my voice level but didn't entirely succeed.

"Well, then." My uncle leaned back in his chair and surveyed us all for a full minute. "Perhaps it was more than chance that brought us together tonight."

We remained silent, waiting for him to explain.

He leaned forward abruptly, a new, more fevered, light coming into his eyes. "I hand-picked the guards aboard this ship. They, and their major, are loyal to me."

I exchanged an uneasy glance with William. Tom had been right about the guards.

Uncle Horace noticed the change in my manner. "I should say, loyal to Lanover. And willing to make whatever sacrifices are necessary for its well-being."

What in the kingdoms was that supposed to mean? My nerves hummed, on high alert. The night had taken an entirely unexpected turn.

"My brother is blinded by his love and compassion," my uncle continued. "He cannot see our sister for the true traitor that she is. While she lives, she is a danger to our entire kingdom. And now she has created a magical barrier to shield herself from the world. What is she doing back there? That is the question we should be asking ourselves." He took a deep breath. "That, and how can she be stopped? Permanently."

I stared at him, my pulse roaring so loudly it obscured my hearing. All these years I had scorned my uncle. And now it turned out that he was the only one of my family who recognized the danger. Who understood the risk my aunt posed to us all. Had he been the one to order the Largoan captains to attempt to penetrate the hedge?

"You mean to storm the hedge? You realize there will be a price to pay for going against the king."

"If my brother found himself unable to follow through with the law and execute his sister after she attempted to kill his own child, I feel confident he will forgive his brother for doing what he could not. I will use my position and influence to shield my soldiers as much as possible. But, as I said, they are ready to make the necessary sacrifice for the good of our people. As am I, if it comes to it."

I leaned back in my chair as I tried to process his revelation. I struggled to think clearly, however. Finally, after all these years, someone intended to do what needed to be done.

I forced myself to breathe and to appear unconcerned. I had just been thinking that Aurora needed to disappear for a while, and now I didn't need to fear the outcome of that absence. I could relax. I could sit back and let my uncle and his soldiers crush the head of a rebellion they didn't even know about.

The thought sparked a frantic churning in my stomach. For three years I had honed myself and my network. I refused to take a sideline now. I told myself weakly it had nothing to do with personal revenge, but the hatred burning in my chest told me otherwise. And I didn't care. I deserved revenge. And I wanted to be present to see justice carried out.

I considered the ways I could force my uncle's hand, make him agree to include us. Then I paused. "Why are you telling us this?"

"We're all interested in the same thing—the good of Lanover. And it seems to me that our interests might align."

"You mean you want us to help you?" I carefully kept any hint of satisfaction or pleasure from my voice. "You have a whole company of guards. What do you want from us?"

"I told you earlier that this is no ordinary sword." He patted the box which he had laid on the table. "It is, in fact, a godmother item."

Celine gasped. I suspected it was the first time she had ever seen one. I had encountered our godmother several times in my years as Aurora and had even managed to acquire an item from her to send with my sister Cordelia to Northhelm to help her with the unrest there.

Somehow, knowing that such an elegant and simple item came from the godmothers didn't surprise me. They preferred quality to ostentation.

"What does it do?" William seemed almost as intrigued as Celine, if slightly warier. What history did he have with godmother items?

"It can break through any barrier, when employed by the right wielder."

I narrowed my eyes. Now we were getting to the heart of it. "And who is the right wielder?"

My uncle shrugged. "That is what I don't know. But somehow I doubt it's any of my guards. I will try it myself, of course, but elderly bachelors aren't usually the heroes of tales or the wielders of magical objects. Young adventuring princes and mysterious maidens on the other hand…"

His words made sense, but years of natural antipathy made me loath to trust him. "If you really want an alliance, then give the sword to Prince William as a gesture of good faith. He is the most natural candidate. And no one would question his posses-sion of a valuable sword if they stumbled upon it."

Uncle Horace looked at us each carefully. He frowned when

his eyes rested on Celine, and she glared straight back. She said nothing, however, and I resolved to congratulate her later on her improved self-control.

"Very well," he said at last. He pushed the box toward William. "Guard it well. I will ensure that we arrive at the island in the late afternoon, ensuring we will need to make camp for the night before proceeding. Meet me at the hedge at dawn, before the rest of our party wakes. Each of us shall have our chance to test the sword. With the safety of our kingdom at stake, I trust that one of us will prove worthy."

With the sword safely in our possession, none of us could leave fast enough. We convened in a shadowy corner for a quick farewell. I feared that my uncle would alert the guards immediately, and I already faced the delay of waiting for Celine to return to our cabin before I could escape to safety myself.

"I don't like this," Celine whispered. "I don't like it at all. Allying with Uncle Horace!" Her voice dropped even further. "Being party to an assassination."

"It isn't an assassination," I said, not bothering to soften my cold tone. "It is the legal punishment for a crime that she openly committed. You asked us to trust you. Now you have to trust me. Your uncle is a means to an end, a temporary ally. We don't have to like him, we just have to work with him for as long as our interests align."

"Aurora, I'm not sure about this…" The discomfort in William's tone fanned my anger into open flame.

"This is not open for debate. You are both either with me or against me. Even now Prince Horace may be alerting his guards to search the ship for me. I cannot remain out in the open discussing this with either of you."

William's eyes widened, and he looked quickly from left to right. "We stand with you, of course. You should go."

I took two steps away and then looked back at them.

He gestured for me to hurry. "Don't worry, I'll guard the sword."

I shook my head. "No, it's not that. Don't come to the hold again tomorrow night. In fact, don't come again at all unless you hear from me. I need to lie low after this."

I took another step away, but a hand gripped my arm, pulling me to a stop. William had closed the distance between us and, when I turned, his face hovered just above mine.

"How are we supposed to contact you?"

"You don't." I fought to keep my voice steady, but the pressure of his hand ignited a fire that raced up my arm. It warred with the energy that had flooded me since my uncle had outlined his plan.

"How will we know if you're safe? You can't just disappear!"

I forced myself to look into his blue eyes without flinching. "Of course I can. I'm the spymaster, that's what I do."

I wrenched myself from his grip and disappeared down the passageway.

# CHAPTER 20

William's interference had given me the opportunity to escape to our cabin before Celine arrived, and for that I was grateful. I lay beneath the covers, fully clothed, until her breathing indicated she had fallen asleep. Then I carefully undressed.

My heart still pounded, despite the long period of inactivity, as I carefully hid my disguise beneath my mattress. And I couldn't discern the cause. The thought of seeing justice filled me with elation, but the idea of confronting my aunt produced such an intense wave of nausea that it reminded me of the first year of the curse.

The burn of the mixed emotions seemed to consume me. And yet, every time I closed my eyes in an attempt to sleep, it was William's face I saw. I could still feel the imprint of his hand, gripping my arm, and see the heated intensity of his gaze.

Celine shifted in her sleep, and the sensation of sickness hit again. I had been hardened by years spent in a double life. But what business did I have exposing my young sister to the execution of one of her own family members? I instantly resolved to forbid her to accompany us. If only I could be sure she would obey.

I tossed and turned for most of the night before falling into fevered dreams.

The morning brought a forced calm. But playing the empty-headed Celeste proved unusually difficult when I knew that the nights would bring no escape. When the wind picked up, I felt nothing but relief. The sooner we arrived in Largo, the better.

William and Celine both spent the day in a subdued state. They attempted to joke as usual, but all their efforts fell flat. Their obvious uncertainty drove me to take one final risk.

That night I waited until Celine fell asleep. It happened so quickly that I suspected she was exhausted from keeping pace with me. She probably felt secretly relieved to have our night-time training canceled. I donned my disguise and crept out into the main part of the ship.

I moved with extra caution, which meant it took a painfully long time to reach my uncle's cabin. If he left it, I would take the opportunity to search his belongings. I didn't like to intrude on a family member in such a way, particularly one I didn't like. After all, only the direst necessity would ever force me to do such a thing to my parents or siblings. But I feared that Celine and my dislike of our uncle made it too easy to leap to an unfair judgment.

But my sense of loyalty to William and Celine overruled my concerns. They followed me and trusted me, and I didn't want to let them down. I would do whatever it took to show them we were making the right decision.

I waited outside his cabin for three hours. Eventually my unrest from the night before caught up with me. Even I had my limits.

My head had drooped for the third time when a sharp hiss startled me into wakefulness.

"There! I'm sure I saw something move."

In my sleepy state, I reacted instinctively, turning toward the voice of the guard. For a suspended moment we stared at each other, both too shocked to move. Then he shattered the stillness.

"It's her! The one the major warned us about. Quick!"

I turned and ran for my life.

Despite the gloom, I knew the corridor well, and my many practice circuits of the cargo hold helped me stay steady on my feet. My pursuers both stumbled over a coil of rope that I had effortlessly cleared. The higher swells that had accompanied the increased wind served me well now.

I put on an extra spurt of speed, trying to put some distance between us. When I reached the door of the state cabin, I needed to be out of their sight.

I slowed my headlong pace as I reached for the door handle, glancing under my arm for any glimpse of the guards. I could hear them, but they had yet to round the corner. I wrenched the door open and flung myself inside, forcing my arm to move slowly so that I could close the door soundlessly.

As soon as the latch caught, I slipped behind my screen and under my covers. Ripping the scarf from my head, I fanned my hair across the pillow and turned to face the wall. My pounding pulse sounded deafening in the quiet, and my wide eyes stared at the wooden wall that anchored my bunk.

I didn't think they would suspect me of having entered the state cabin. And I didn't think they would dare check, either. But, just in case, I held myself still. Seconds later feet thundered past the door, not even slowing.

I rolled onto my back and took a deep breath, willing my heart to relax. The soft breathing of my mother and sister seemed impossibly incongruous. I had to remind myself how quiet the entire episode had been despite the drumming in my ears.

I pulled my clothes off under the covers and realized that I truly couldn't venture out as Aurora again. I could only hope the wind picked up even more and drove us into Largo without rest.

~

Sitting on deck the next morning, I stared at the dark clouds scudding behind the ship. Perhaps I should have been more circumspect with my wishes. My skirts whipped around me, dancing first one way and then another, so that I had to hold them down.

Sailors scurried around the deck, far more than I had seen out at one time before, trimming sails and lashing down anything that could move.

I sat, letting their frantic motions calm my scattered emotions. What did it say about me that it took such chaos for me to find a moment of inner calm?

"Princess!" A sudden crack of thunder nearly drowned out William's voice. He held out his arm to me. "The captain has ordered all passengers below deck. The storm will break any minute."

As he spoke the last word, a large drop of rain landed on his outstretched elbow.

"Oh!" I exclaimed, leaping to my feet. "We're going to get wet."

I gripped him hard, staggering far more than necessary as we made our way off the deck. He tucked me against his side, and I smiled, my face turned down against the increasing number of rain drops. If he only knew it, I was actually the steadier of the two of us. But I still leaned into his offered protection. And it wasn't thoughts of my cover that motivated me.

William delivered me to the door of the state cabin and warned me to put away anything that wasn't attached to the floor. "The captain said late storms like this one can be rough. But not rough enough to put us in any danger. If you stay safe in your bunk, you won't come to any harm."

I smiled my thanks and slipped inside.

"Celeste! There you are." Celine pounced on me. "A storm.

Isn't it terrifying?" She looked more thrilled than afraid, so I enthusiastically agreed.

"We shall be through it soon enough, I'm sure, my dears." Our mother sat calmly at the table, apparently unperturbed by the violent rocking of the ship.

"William said we need not be afraid. But, Mother, he said we would be safest in our bunks." My mother rarely engaged in physical activity of any sort. I would much prefer to see her safely lying down.

"You two are no fun. Where's your sense of danger?" Celine lurched across to one of our portholes to peer out at the storm. "Oh, look! Did you see that?"

I crossed over to join her, making sure to stumble a little. I shivered. "Lightning. I hope it doesn't strike the ship."

"If it does, I'm sure it can do no great damage." My mother's calm truly was imperturbable. "Not when the wood is so wet from this rain."

I didn't entirely share her confidence, but I did believe in the skill of the captain and our crew, and their knowledge of the seas. We would ride through the storm safely.

The lurching of the floor made any activity untenable, and the driving rain soon made it impossible to see anything out of the portholes. Even Celine gave up and decided to attempt a nap.

I couldn't remember the last time I had passed an undisturbed night, so I quickly followed suit. Our mother encouraged us both into our bunks but remained sitting at the table herself.

At first I feared I could never sleep with the storm tossing me around the bunk so wildly, but then I opened my eyes again to the certain knowledge that time had passed. The ship rocked and surged even more violently than when I had fallen asleep, and the wind roared outside the hull. I pulled the blankets tighter around my chin, wishing I could block it all out and return to slumber.

Usually, when I lay awake in my bunk, I listened to the sound of my mother's and sister's breathing, waiting for an opportunity to slip out of the cabin. But this time I could hear nothing over the sound of the wind and the waves beating against the ship. The absence felt unnatural so, after a minute, I decided to get up and check on them. I couldn't seem to resettle without the sound of their peaceful sleep.

I stood up and an unexpected wave thrust me against my screen. I caught myself before I knocked it entirely over. When a wave tipped me in the right direction, I let myself slide out to grip the edge of the table. My mother no longer sat there, so I had two bunks to check.

I slowly moved to Celine and gazed down at her sleeping form. Her arm hung off the edge of the bunk, swaying with the movement of the ship. I waited for a lull between waves and lifted it gently back up, tucking it beneath her blankets.

I watched her peaceful face and my first thrill of fear hit. She looked so unconcerned in sleep, that my own anxiety rose up as if to balance her lack. I shook off the foolish feeling and continued to my mother's bunk.

The rush of terror at the sight of her untouched bedding overwhelmed the pale worry I had felt next to Celine. I grasped the privacy screen and scanned the cabin. But I already knew she wasn't there—the space just wasn't that big.

I looked up at the boards over my head, picturing the deck above. Unconcerned didn't equal foolish. My mother would never have ventured up top. Perhaps she had merely gone to check on Rafe.

My stomach settled. Yes. That made sense. Without forming the thought, my body traveled toward the door, moving in rhythm with the tossing of the ship. I would join them. There could be no harm in that.

An empty corridor greeted me, free of the usual obstacles. The sailors had done their job well. With no one in sight, I moved with confidence, finding the beat of the storm. I reached Rafe and Marie's cabin without difficulty and knocked. I knew they couldn't hear me over the storm, but skipping the convention felt wrong.

I pushed the door open, almost falling inside. The newlyweds occupied a much smaller space than the state cabin and, even in the midst of my fear, I winced. They should have been alone on this voyage, occupying the state cabin themselves.

A visual sweep of the room confirmed my mother's absence. And my family's unnatural ability to sleep. Rafe lay with his back to the room, cradling his sleeping wife between his body and the wall of the ship. His arms looked both strong and gentle, and I had to push away an unwanted image of William holding me in such a manner.

The thought of my mother soon drove away such foolish daydreams. If she hadn't come to Rafe, where could she possibly have gone?

I returned to the corridor and nearly collided with two sailors rushing past. Clinging onto one of their arms, I tried to shout above the storm. "Have you seen my mother? The queen? Where is she?"

He frowned at me, gesturing toward his ears and raising his other arm helplessly. "You need to return to your cabin, Your Highness. And I'm needed up on deck."

I couldn't hear his words and had to read them on his lips instead. He gently pushed me off and then bolted away. I followed, no set plan in mind.

He held the door to the deck open for the briefest possible time, but a wall of water still gushed through, half soaking me. My body shook at the shock of cold while I tried to formulate a strategy.

A coil of rope had rested next to this door every other day of our voyage. Where had it been put now? I stumbled along the passageway until I managed to find a storage alcove. I chose the longest length I could find and tied it tightly around my waist.

Taking a deep breath, I opened the door and stepped outside.

I gasped and spluttered as freezing water instantly soaked the rest of me. For a moment I forgot it was still daytime. The gray clouds and heavy rain completely obscured my vision, darkening the sky.

I struggled to pull the door closed behind me, not letting go of it until my other hand had found the iron ring attached to the outside wall next to the doorway. I fumbled, the cold and wet making my fingers clumsy, but eventually managed to tie the loose end of my rope to the ring. Several other ropes were already secured there. Should I follow one? It might lead me to my mother.

A flash of lightning briefly illuminated the deck before me. Several sailors moved across it, but the brief glimpse was too short for me to see what they were doing. The peal of thunder followed on the heels of the lightning. We were in the heart of the storm.

The density of the rain gave the sensation of swimming across the deck rather than walking. Part of my mind screamed at my foolishness, but I couldn't go back to our cabin and wait quietly, hoping for the best.

When a second streak of lightning lit up the sky, I peered around, trying to take in as much of the scene as I could. I stood on the port side of the deck and could see no sign of my mother. The accompanying thunder rang out so loudly and so quickly that I started. My feet already struggled to grip the soaking deck, and my violent movement unbalanced me. The ship hit a huge wave and I fell, sliding across the deck.

My heart sank into my stomach at the awful sensation, and I reached wildly for something to catch hold of. Every moment I anticipated the violent tug of the rope around my waist. My old bruises had finally faded, but I would soon have far worse ones.

When the snap didn't come, a new fear rushed through me. How well had I tied my knot? The deck rushed under me, the edge approaching fast.

# CHAPTER 21

One hand hit something hard, and I grasped it with all my might, just as the ship pitched in the other direction. I used the momentum to swing my body around, wrapping my arm tightly around the wooden post.

Clinging on with all my strength, I gasped in great breaths, the rain spattering into my eyes and open mouth unheeded.

What was I doing? I would achieve nothing like this but my own death. I struggled back to my feet, still clinging to the anchoring pole. I couldn't immediately recall its usual purpose, but I had never been so grateful for a piece of wood in my life.

The wind rushed at me, ripping at my clothing and tearing at my skin. My whole body shuddered spasmodically, but the movement barely registered. Another fork of lightning gave me a glimpse into the storm. My rope had become tangled, and I forced myself to move back the way I had come, carefully freeing it as I went.

The brief light also revealed a ladder, and I moved toward it. Gripping the rungs with numb hands proved unexpectedly difficult, and I ended up wrapping my entire arm around each one, inching slowly upward. Now, when the ship lurched sideways, I feared free falling into the water with nothing but my rope to save me. But I needed a higher vantage point before the next flash.

When it came, I was ready. On the other side of the deck, a figure huddled against a wall. Unlike the occasional sailor I had glimpsed, this person didn't move, and although the rain made vision difficult, I thought I saw purple. My mother had been wearing purple.

Gratefully I reversed my upward climb, soon reaching the marginally more secure footing of the deck. A new sense of urgency drove me. I had been out here for mere minutes, and I already struggled to feel my hands. How long had my mother been out here? Would the next wave be enough to shake loose her current grip?

I doubted she had a safety rope, which would have involved either tying a secure knot on her own or finding a sailor to help her. Neither of which were likely possibilities. But, whatever her danger, a fall would destroy all my progress, so I forced myself to move slowly.

When the sky next lit up, I knew which direction to look. My mother clung to a small bench, her body curled around it, her face tucked down.

I reached her before the next flash. Gripping her shoulders, I tried to draw her to her feet. She resisted. I didn't even bother attempting to speak to her. I didn't think I could scream my words loudly enough.

Instead I continued to tug against her until she finally let go and uncurled herself. The sky whitened, the first sheet lightning since I had come on deck. In the strange illumination, her eyes looked glassy and wild, and her lips moved although I couldn't make out any sound.

I wished I had thought to bring a second rope. Without one, the journey back would be dangerous. I pulled some of the slack rope toward me and wrapped it several times around my mother, standing on tiptoe to loop it over her head. Then I positioned myself behind her, my arms wrapped around her waist, and propelled her forward.

She no longer resisted me, but neither did she help. I had to balance us both. Each step strained me to my limits. My eyes remained fixed on our goal as another brilliant blaze of lightning split the sky. The door beckoned, nearly within reach, but it was the porthole to one side of it that caught my attention. Was that a face? Had someone seen our predicament? My thoughts distracted me enough that the next wave caught me off guard. I had no strength left to fight it, so I could only be glad that it tipped us in the right direction, sliding across the slick planks.

We both slammed against the door, and it swung open. We fell through, and I twisted and slammed it shut. The ship still rocked and the storm screamed against the wood, but the absence of the wind and rain made the dark passageway feel blessedly calm and warm.

I lay for a moment next to my mother, taking deep breaths and letting my violent shudders subside. We had made it. We were both alive.

A flutter of movement made me push myself up. But when I looked down the corridor, no one was in sight. I shook my head. Another hallucination then, like the face in the porthole, brought on by the after-effects of the lightning. I would probably be seeing things for hours as my anxiety drained away. I forced my trembling fingers to untie the knot around my waist. The water-logged rope made the task difficult, but I eventually managed it.

I gently lifted my mother up. Her lips pressed tightly together now, but the fevered look remained in her eyes. She seemed to stare right through me, giving no sign of recognition.

My heart rate, which had only just begun to slow, picked up again. Her skin felt clammy to the touch, and she was no doubt in shock. I needed to get her dry and warm.

Abandoning the rope in the passageway, I led her toward our

cabin. Pushing open the door, I pulled her inside and called for Celine.

"Celine! Celine! Oh no! Oh no!"

"Wh-What?" Celine's groggy voice sounded from her bed.

"Oh Celine, it's Mother!" I burst into tears. They came incredibly easily, my body coming down from high alert with a crash. Usually, when I needed to cry as Celeste, I had to think of my favorite horse who had died when I was twelve.

Celine's head shot out from her screen, and she screeched at the sight of us. "Celeste! Mother! What in the kingdoms happened to you?"

"I don't know." My teeth chattered so hard, I could barely form the words. "The door to the deck was open. And Mother was lying just inside it."

I led my mother toward her bunk, the occasional shudder still interrupting my movements.

"But you're both soaking wet!"

"There was water everywhere. It kept pouring in the doorway. Something seems to be wrong with her."

I hadn't even been able to wipe my face, since I had yet to encounter anything dry, and the only reason I could feel the tears still running down my cheeks was their warmth against my skin. Celine thrust a blanket into my hands, but I wrapped it around Mother.

Celine half slid across the room and returned with a second dry blanket. She pushed our mother down to sit on her bunk and then turned to me. She didn't offer me the blanket.

"Get your dress off, quickly."

"What?" I frowned, feigning confusion.

"Do it, now. You need to get dry."

"Oh." I worked as fast as my fumbling fingers would allow, dropping the garments onto the floor and kicking them away from me. Celine then wrapped me gently in the blissful warmth of the blanket. She gave me only a moment to enjoy it before she began to vigorously rub my shoulders through the material.

"Dry yourself off and get into something warm."

I obeyed, casting anxious glances back at my mother, still huddled on the bed. As soon as I was clothed again, Celine and I managed to undress our mother and force her into a dry shift. Tucking her into bed and piling on all the blankets I could find, I turned worried eyes on Celine.

My sister already had her hand on the door. "I'm going to find the ship's doctor. She's delirious and much too hot."

I didn't want to let her go, but I had no choice. The curse prevented me from arguing that I was more capable of fetching help than her.

I sat on the bunk next to my mother and waited. I didn't regret any part of my actions, but I feared what would happen when my mother returned to health. Would she remember what had happened and who had saved her? What consequence would the curse exact if she did?

As my mind wandered, remembering the series of terrifying experiences, I recalled the face at the porthole. It had seemed so vivid, not at all like the tricks of the mind that produced such strange luminescence in the wake of lightning.

And the flicker of movement in the corridor had come some time after the lightning. Had someone been in the passageway, peering out into the storm? If so, why had they fled instead of offering us aid? And, even more importantly, had they seen what I had done?

~

Celine tucked me into bed as soon as she returned and refused to allow me to get back up again. She brushed away my gratitude, claiming she was merely trying to avoid ending up responsible for two sick relatives.

By morning, the storm had faded into nothing, and the sea lapped calmly against the sides of the ship. I woke to a gentle rocking instead of a violent shaking and was informed that my mother had already significantly improved. The doctor had diagnosed shock and a fever, brought on by a prolonged cold soaking. He had found a small bump on her head but still expected her to be completely recovered within a couple of days.

Rafe and Marie visited as soon as they heard of her illness and then left to carry the good news of her improvement to William. Uncle Horace attempted to come in as well, but Celine refused him entry, claiming she did so under doctor's orders. He was forced to bluster and complain from the doorway, demanding an explanation of what had happened to the queen.

Celine merely shrugged. "She isn't lucid yet. And the doctor said she might not remember even when she is. Celeste found her lying just inside the doorway, so I suspect she found the door open, attempted to close it, and fell. Who knows how long she was there? Thank goodness Celeste has no sense whatsoever and decided to go wandering below decks in the middle of a storm."

I was too grateful for her reasonable interpretation of events to even twitch at her unflattering portrayal of my role.

When our uncle finally left, I frowned at her, however. "The doctor didn't say anything about keeping Uncle Horace out."

She grinned, unrepentant. "He said to keep a calm and quiet atmosphere which means the same thing."

I shook my head but couldn't resist smiling back at her. The sea had calmed, and the sun once again shone through our portholes. And the doctor said Mother would soon be well. The world seemed an entirely different place from just a few hours before.

For three full days, Celine and I barely left the cabin, devoting our full attention to seeing our mother restored to full health. After the final, long day, the three of us sat around the table together, my mother appearing well and entirely unruffled by her experience.

Celine had been unusually quiet the whole day, and I was surprised she didn't seem more pleased with our mother's progress. Clearly something was on her mind.

"Mother, I have to ask you something." Her words proved my suspicions right.

"Certainly, my dear. I only hope it is not about the mysterious happenings during the storm. It would sadden me to disappoint you. You know I can't remember a thing about it."

Celine drummed her fingers on the table. "It is about what happened in the storm—sort of. Not about your accident, though. About afterward."

I picked up a piece of embroidery. It was easier to hide my true interest in a conversation if my hands were occupied.

Celine's fingers tapped faster. "You were delirious for much of the night, talking in your sleep." She flashed a glance at me. "Lettie was sleeping. She didn't hear."

I peeked at my mother's face, and my fingers stilled. She looked paler than I had ever seen her, and her hand trembled where it rested on her lap.

Celine continued. "There's something you're not telling us. About Aunt Melisande. I think it's time you told us the truth. I...I *need* to know the truth."

# CHAPTER 22

*B*ile rose in my throat at the mention of my aunt, a mix of fear and anger and desperate curiosity. What secrets had my parents been concealing from me?

But my own emotions didn't blind me to Celine's response. I knew what fueled her anxiety, and my heart ached with pity. I hated that I was the one who had put her in this situation.

Our mother looked back and forth between us. "Oh girls." She folded and unfolded her hands, twisting them together in her lap in a nervous gesture I had never seen her make before.

Neither of us responded and, after a long moment of silence, she spoke again.

"It all happened so long ago. I only wish I could forget it but, of course, I cannot." A shadow lurked in her eyes as she looked at me. The living reminder. "And, truly, I should not wish to. Some things should not be forgotten. People should not be forgotten."

My embroidery lay forgotten in my lap. People? What people? Surely she didn't mean my aunt?

"Before either of you girls were born, your aunt married a minor noble from Arcadia. He had no great riches or position, but your aunt loved him so fiercely that she convinced your grandparents to allow the match. At first, she was blissfully happy. But slowly her joy faded." Our mother's hands stilled, squeezing together so tightly I feared she would cut off her circulation.

"No child came to them, though your aunt desperately wanted one. She loved your brother Frederic when he came, but I could see she found it more difficult to smile when the twins arrived. Such an excess for me, when she had nothing. When I became pregnant with Rafe, I was almost too afraid to tell her. But, of course, such things cannot be hidden for long."

She drew a deep breath. "Everything changed when I became pregnant with you, Celeste. For several days I fretted about telling her, until I noticed how radiant she had become. The smile never left her face, though she started missing meals. I knew, then, what had happened, of course. I could not have been more delighted.

"I told her my news, and she responded with her own happy announcement. Her baby was due two months before mine, and she had just been preparing to tell us the news. Our shared joy transformed both of our pregnancies. I delighted in you, Celeste, like I had not let myself delight in Rafe. Your aunt and I spent hours together, sewing for our new babies and imagining the mischief you would get up to together." Several tears leaked down my mother's face, but she didn't stop to wipe them away.

"After waiting so long, Melisande was very careful. She didn't leave the palace, and she never overexerted herself. She often scolded me for my own careless ways. But after so many pregnancies, I couldn't bear to be too confined."

I clutched at my embroidery until my knuckles turned white. I couldn't imagine my aunt as a loving, joyful young mother. It made no sense.

"When her time came, she had a healthy baby girl. We both hoped then that you would be a girl as well. Two cousins who would be closer than sisters.

"Your aunt asked if her daughter could share the nursery with our own children. But with four young ones and another on the way, our two poor nursemaids were already overworked. Leonardo and I refused, but we helped her set up a nursery of her own.

"One week after the birth, her husband went out riding and was thrown from his horse. He broke his neck instantly."

Celine gasped and covered her mouth with a shaking hand. I sat as still as a statue and reminded myself I had no reason to pity my aunt.

Our mother ignored us both—she seemed to have lost herself in the memories. "Your aunt took it badly, of course, how could she not? Not that she screamed or cried after the first horrific day. Instead, she poured herself into her baby with an intensity that frightened me. It wasn't healthy. I could tell, even then. But what could I say? She had just lost her husband.

"At first she wouldn't let the baby leave her side. But, eventually, the grief and the demands of a newborn took their toll. Your father and I forced her to leave her baby with her nursemaid for a few hours, so she could get some sleep. We didn't mean…How could we have known?" A small, hiccuping sob broke the words.

After a pause, she continued. "But the nursemaid fell asleep. And, somehow, we'll never know how, one of the candles started a fire. It was the middle of the night. It took a while for anyone to realize what had happened. A guard smelled the smoke, and an alarm was raised in time to stop the fire spreading to the rest of the palace. But when it was safe to enter the room, we found it was too late for the nursemaid." She shook. "And too late for your baby cousin. The smoke had gotten to them—the baby in her crib, and the nursemaid in a rocking chair beside her."

Our mother looked between us wildly, her eyes bright with tears. I didn't think it was us she saw. "There was nothing we could do! When I remember your aunt's face after she broke through the crowd and saw the scene..." A full sob racked her body, and she cried quietly for a full minute.

At last she regained enough control to continue speaking. Neither Celine nor I had made a sound. "She screamed so loudly, and for so long, I thought we should all go mad with her. She screamed that it was all our fault. For refusing to let her daughter into our nursery. For choosing an irresponsible nursemaid. For sending her to bed.

"And then the morning came and brought with it silence. And I realized that the quiet was worse. She became like stone, with no emotion at all. How could I even attempt to comfort her, huge still with my own baby? The stress brought on my labor pains, and you were born three weeks early, Celeste."

Her voice dropped to a whisper. "A little girl, just like we hoped." She cleared her throat. "You were so perfect, and I felt so terribly guilty to have you safe in my arms. Five! I had five children while my sister-in-law had nothing. And, with her husband gone, not even the hope of another child.

"When she came to see you, she made no more accusations. Just a single request. That your father issue a royal edict: no one in the entire kingdom was ever to speak of her husband or daughter again. The baby had yet to be Christened, so she hadn't even been officially named.

"As mad as the request seemed, when faced with her pain, we agreed. As far as I know, this is the first time anyone has spoken of either of them in nineteen years."

I forced my eyes away from my mother's face, unable to bear the emotions reflected there. Silent tears streamed down Celine's face. I looked into my lap.

"I didn't know what to say to Melisande after that. We didn't want to remind her of her loss, so we avoided her. And kept all of you children away, too. But, of course, we had to have you Christened. It felt cruel to ask her to come and join a celebration for my fifth healthy child. So we didn't invite her.

"She turned up, anyway, of course. Along with the whole court and far more godmothers than was usual. Everyone seemed desperate to celebrate life in the face of such a horrible loss, but it must have seemed so pointed to poor Melisande. And you both know what happened after that. But now you know why. Her grief had turned to anger and bitterness and resentment. She had twisted into a different person.

"But she was still Leonardo's sister, and we had loved her, and her poor, dead baby. We couldn't execute her, no matter what she'd done.

"So we banished her instead, sending her somewhere far away, where she couldn't hurt our children. I couldn't bear to even think of her and fought every day to suppress the memories. Eventually it worked. And the stresses of seven children turned out to be less onerous than I had anticipated. I had lived through the kind of tragedy that puts everything else into perspective. By the time the curse hit, my grief had faded. It pained me to see even the limited effects of the curse, and I have thought many times on the wrong Melisande did us."

She paused, and a different expression crossed her face. "You are both young, my dears, and I hope you treasure it. But with age comes wisdom, at least in some small measure. For more than three years now I have dwelt with this and considered it in my heart. And I see, now, that I was at least partially to blame as well.

"Melisande asked us not to speak of her loss, but that did not mean she wanted to be alone. In her rawest grief she blamed us, certainly, but that did not necessarily reflect her ongoing opinion. And yet we abandoned her. We had told ourselves we did it for her. But now that almost two decades have passed, I have looked into my heart and seen the truth. I did it for myself. Because I could not bear the feelings of guilt and grief. I chose to protect myself first and I left her alone in her grief, far worse than anything I faced."

She heaved a deep sigh. "Oh, girls. It is not always a pretty sight to examine our own deepest motivations. Remember that, if you can, next time you find yourself convinced of your own innocence."

I frowned. I didn't need to examine my heart. The facts were clear and undisputed. I had been the innocent victim before I could walk or talk.

Celine moved her chair closer and took our mother's hand. "What an awful, awful thing. But why are we going to find her? Why now?"

"Because of you, Celine."

"Me?"

"You asked what had happened to her, and I realized it was the very question that burned in my own heart."

I tried to smile, but it came out as a grimace. So William had ultimately been right. It had been the machinations of Aurora that had brought us to this point after all.

Mother turned to gaze out the nearest porthole. "And here was your brother about to embark on a voyage to the islands. The coincidence seemed more than opportune. After all these years, it is time that Melisande and I spoke again. We don't know if we can break through the hedge, of course, or what we'll find on the other side if we do. But I am determined to try.

"Your father would have preferred to come as well, but he cannot be spared from the capital right now. Just as we could not risk traveling to Cordelia's wedding."

"Why?" Celine's voice sounded weak and fragile, as if she were afraid of any more revelations. I had been right not to burden her with information about the rebellion.

"Nothing for you to worry about." But something shaded our mother's eyes. How much of the rebellion had they managed to uncover on their own? I hoped the duchess had arrived in the capital by now, and that she and my father were working to annihilate the diseased branches, while I attacked the root.

Except my righteous certainty had wavered. Bringing justice against a violent madwoman, enraged to the point of murder by a petty slight was one thing. But bringing it against a bereaved young wife and mother, driven to the point of madness by grief? The crime had not changed, and yet too much else had changed.

Stabbing pains in my stomach reminded me that I sat in full view of others. And yet still I couldn't maintain any sort of detachment from my mother's story. If my pain was any indication, the raging storm played out plainly across my face.

She had wronged me, had attempted to kill me for no other crime than being alive. But I would have been inhuman not to be affected by her story. Could I really stand by now and watch her killed?

My old emotions still roiled—I could not forget them entirely. But now new ones had joined the mix, and I was horribly afraid I would not be able to contain the explosive mix.

Then I remembered that I was not going to Banishment Island because of my curse. I went to put down a rebellion. Whatever the excuse for my aunt's past crimes, there could be no justification for her current ones.

I stood up, letting my embroidery fall to the floor, and retreated to the privacy of my bed without a word. It was the only safe thing for me to do.

But my head pounded and my stomach cramped all night, giving me little rest. How much of it was the curse, and how much my own unbridled emotions?

The restless tossing from Celine's bunk, and the quiet sobs from my mother, told me I wasn't the only one unable to sleep. The tragedy might have increased my mother's natural composure all these years, but even she couldn't outrun the grief forever.

CHAPTER 23

When we woke the next morning, all three of us acted as if the day before had not occurred. I suspected that they, like me, simply didn't know what to say. Thankfully we could finally emerge from the cabin, although that meant facing our uncle at last.

"No, Horace, I'm afraid I don't remember a thing, and no amount of questioning by you is going to change that. I have a vague idea that I may have decided to leave the cabin to check with the captain and ascertain if the ship was in any sort of danger. I must have taken a wrong turn or something."

My mother listened to him complain for another minute before interrupting. "Personally, I'm pleased to have no recollection of it. It sounds like quite an unpleasant experience."

He gaped at her, finally silenced.

"Really I think it would be best if we put this whole thing behind us. Oh, look." She pointed over the edge of the ship. "Dolphins, and one of them has a calf."

Uncle Horace shook his head, meeting William's eye with a significant look. "A company of guards, and apparently not one of them was able to stop the queen of Lanover from ending up in harm's way." He walked away still shaking his head. William watched him go with a speculative expression.

I turned my own gaze to the dolphins, uttering empty admiration for my mother's benefit. My uncle shared my suspicions even though he only knew half the story. How had she ended up on deck in the middle of a storm with a bump on her head? None of my agents had made it on board—had one of my aunt's?

Largo truly couldn't come quickly enough.

It helped that the storm had driven us well ahead of schedule, so we sailed into Largo Bay that afternoon. But the crew needed to undertake some minor repairs, adding an extra night to the one we had planned to spend here.

At the evening meal, the passengers all buzzed about getting off the ship the next morning. With a full day at our disposal, all sorts of activities and excursions were discussed. Rafe had always loved Largo and kept telling Marie how much she would love it, too. He also told the rest of us, in no uncertain terms, that we weren't welcome to join them for the day.

He received some humorous teasing over the pronouncement, but no one really blamed him. William seemed to take it as permission to break off from the group and said he would be leaving first thing in the morning to do some exploring on his own.

Sure enough, he was gone before I announced I would remain on board to rest. With William and Rafe both absent, no one protested. Celine did throw me an incredulous look, but she couldn't seem to muster the energy to argue about it.

I waved them all off and found a seat on deck, watching the coming and going of other ships in the harbor. I figured I should give them at least an hour's head start.

When the allotted time had passed, I stood up and walked down the gangplank. Largo had a deep-water port, and the royal yacht had received the premium berth at the quay. A couple of the sailors glanced my way, but with no officers or royals around, no one questioned me.

I hurried through the port city, attracting stares, as I always did. A small shop advertising a range of pre-made clothing caught my eye, and I ducked inside. Twenty minutes later I emerged as Aurora.

The southernmost city in the Four Kingdoms hovered between the jungle, the desert, and the sea. Its unique position offered adventure and freedom, and had enticed a diverse community. Bright colors and exotic outfits filled the streets, and pale-skinned northerners were almost as common a sight as the darker-skinned locals.

This transplanted northern community provided me with a unique opportunity. Many of them, to protect their fragile skin from the hot sun, had adopted the garments favored by the small communities of traders who traveled the fringes of the Great Desert.

These voluminous robes came with a head covering that left nothing but the eyes exposed. Men and women alike wore them, usually during the hottest parts of the day, so I easily slipped through the crowd unnoticed.

I held my head high as I walked through the streets. Sunlight had never produced such a heady effect in me before. But then I had never ventured out as Aurora during the day before, either.

Eventually I found the right door and knocked three times.

Two hours later, I stepped back out into the street. I had originally planned to return straight to the ship, but I couldn't bring myself to do it. Instead my feet carried me toward the huge marketplace that formed the center of the city. I watched people stream around me and matched my gait to theirs. Largoans moved slightly differently from those who dwelt in the capital, and I enjoyed trying to make myself blend seamlessly into their midst.

I passed Rafe and Marie wandering through the market, but they didn't give me a second glance. My usual nights spent as Aurora were nothing compared to this freedom.

My nose took over the directions, drawing me toward a food stall offering succulent skewers of meat. The long line of locals suggested they tasted as good as they smelled.

I moved toward the end of the queue but stopped halfway. Apparently I wasn't the only one from the ship whose stomach had started grumbling.

I sidled up to William. "Princeling. Fancy meeting you here."

He jumped, turning toward me with such a stream of emotions chasing across his face that I could barely identify half of them.

"Aurora." It was more a breath than a word.

He grabbed my arm and towed me away from the line into a more secluded spot. When we stopped, he looked me up and down, apparently rendered speechless.

I widened my eyes. "Why so silent, Princeling? Don't tell me you truly did want a day to yourself?"

His wide smile spread across his face. "I may have hoped for certain company to find me. I couldn't help worrying, though. I haven't seen you for days."

He bit his lip, and the hand on my arm tightened convulsively. I swallowed and tried not to look at his lips.

"Well, here we are, out enjoying a day in the city. Are you planning to get back in that line and buy me a skewer?" I glanced back toward the stall. "Or two or three?"

"What? Don't tell me we have the afternoon off! No secret mission? No sneaking or hiding?"

I chuckled. "I dare say I could find somewhere for us to trespass if you're that hooked on the thrill."

"Absolutely not!" He pulled me back toward the line with as much enthusiasm as he had previously dragged me away.

We were soon wandering the marketplace, a skewer in each hand. William led the way, and I followed, casting him sideways glances through my lashes. When he caught me looking, I blushed beneath my head covering.

As Aurora, I was used to taking the front, always one stride ahead. It had been more than three years since I had engaged in any sort of social activity without the curse looming over me. I had forgotten what it felt like.

He found a spot for us to sit beneath a shady tree, and we ate. Awkwardly, in my case, as I tried to work around the head covering. William pointed out various people passing by, and I told him about the different groups who populated Lanover. He seemed particularly fascinated by the nomadic desert traders, whose style I had borrowed.

"They're an offshoot of the traveling merchants and are bound by the rules and treaties of the merchant council. They don't like to stray too far from the desert, though, so if a council of caravans is called, they usually only send a couple of representatives."

William leaned back and looked at the large tree above us. "It's hard to believe we could be anywhere near a desert when we're surrounded by so much green."

"Well, it's not that near, really. Largo is just the closest connection they have to the sea and, subsequently, their biggest trading city. It's the farthest they like to venture from their usual territory. Their mounts don't do well in this climate."

William turned his fascinated gaze on a group of traders standing some distance away. "I still can't quite believe they travel the deserts on those…creatures."

I smiled as I looked at the camel and imagined seeing one for the first time. "They are a bit…"

"Ugly?"

I laughed. "Yes, that too."

"And I can't imagine they're very comfortable. Look at those humps!"

"They're suited to the desert, though, and that's the most important thing."

William's eyes lost their focus. "Vast hills of sand. It's difficult to imagine such a thing. I would love to see it one day."

I opened my mouth to tell him I would take him there, and then remembered that I could do no such thing. Today was a once off aberration. I didn't live in Largo. During the day I was Princess Celeste, the Sleeping Princess, bound by a curse since infancy.

The sudden anger and hatred made the meat churn in my stomach. Except now, after my mother's revelations, the familiar emotions filled me with confusion. I stood up, trying to distract myself. I refused to spoil this unprecedented opportunity. I would put all thoughts of my aunt aside for one afternoon.

William stood beside me, unable to see my expression beneath my covering. He turned his grin on me, and the darkness melted away. "Ready to go?" He held out his arm.

I took a deep breath and offered my hand. "Lead away."

Two hours later, I collapsed against a tree, laughing too hard to stay upright without assistance. "No, really?" More laughter. "You didn't!"

He tried to look modest and failed. "I have a sort of natural charm."

I laughed even harder.

"I can show you if you like." He moved closer, trapping me against the tree, one arm on either side of my head. His eyes laughed down into mine, but my own laughter died away. We had wandered into a public garden near the marketplace, and no one else was in view.

My breath caught in my throat at his nearness, and for the second time today, I struggled not to focus on his lips.

He matched the change in my mood, the light of laughter in his eyes transforming into a different sort of glow. I wanted to forget, for a moment, that I was Celeste or Aurora and melt against his chest. I wanted to feel his arms wrap tight around me, like they had that night in the corridors of the palace when we hid in plain sight.

I wanted to be just a girl, laughing with the boy I loved. *Wait.* The world faded. *Loved?* Did I love William? My heart pounded as I considered the question.

"Aurora." He leaned so close, he filled my vision. His eyes burned into mine as he pulled me against him, and the fire leaped from his eyes to the spot where his hands rested on my back.

Despite the strength in his muscles, the tiniest tremble rippled through him in response to the contact between us. I knew, without a doubt, that if it hadn't been for the thin piece of material covering my mouth, he would be kissing me already. And I would be letting him.

For a moment I toyed with the idea of unwrapping the headpiece and letting his lips meet mine. Would his kiss be enough? Could it break the spell?

"Are you ever going to let me see your face?" His soft words crashed into my dreams with destructive force.

William didn't love me. He had just said as much. He couldn't love me without seeing my face. I remembered the appreciative gleam he had so often directed toward me as Celeste. This prince was just like all the others—captivated by beauty.

I pushed him away from me with so much force that he staggered back. His shock echoed between us.

"I'm sorry, Aurora." I hated the desperation in his voice. "I know you said not to ask about you. But I have to know. Will you ever choose to show me?"

I looked at him and wished my heart wasn't breaking. I thought I was stronger than this. I straightened my spine. "No. I'm a spymaster not a lovesick maiden. This afternoon was a mistake."

He shook his head and reached for me, but I stepped away. "The situation has changed with Banishment Island."

He pulled back, confusion on his face at my abrupt change of subject.

"We'll be there tomorrow afternoon, and I need to know if you're still with me."

"Aurora, of course." I feared that the fire in his eyes would leap the distance between us, no matter how many steps back I took. "I will not desert you, no matter what."

I wished I could believe his words. Believe that his loyalty would remain, regardless of what hid beneath my mask. "Good. Meet me three hours after midnight then, at the hedge. Bring the sword."

His face asked the question his mouth didn't bother to form.

"And don't mention anything to Prince Horace. The situation is more...complicated than I realized, and I don't know how far he can be trusted. It is possible that the princess might deserve a second chance—if she's repentant."

"What do you mean?" He tried to step toward me again, prompting me to move further away.

"Just be there."

The thought of the next day brought back the churning queasiness. I imagined meeting my aunt and then stilled, gripped by a startling revelation. I forced myself to meet William's dangerous gaze. "And promise me that no matter what happens you'll try to take down that hedge. That even if I miss the rendezvous, you'll fight your way to the princess. I'll catch up, if necessary."

"What do you mean?" I could see the concern pushing him to close the distance between us, but he'd learned his lesson and remained where he was, unnaturally still.

"Promise me."

He took a deep breath. "Very well. I promise."

I turned and fled toward the marketplace, hoping he wouldn't try to follow.

# CHAPTER 24

*D*espite my time with William, I still beat everyone else back to the ship. I stopped at the same little shop, changing back into my original dress and collecting my other purchases. I walked back on board as Celeste, a bundle of shopping in my arms. Once again, no one questioned me.

My new acquisitions included my desert outfit; it was much more comfortable than my makeshift disguise from the ship. And I had bought another unusual ensemble as a last-minute addition. The pair of pants belled out in soft folds of material before cinching around my ankles. When I stood still, they almost resembled a dress, but they gave me greater freedom of movement than any skirt.

I would need them soon, thanks to the startling realization that had hit me as I spoke to William. I couldn't confront my aunt as Aurora. I needed to truly meet her face-to-face, and I needed her to know who I was. Which meant I needed to meet her as Celeste.

That had been the thought that had made me extract the promise from William. Somehow I was going to have to convince him to attack that hedge with Celeste by his side instead of Aurora.

I greeted them all at the evening meal, wearing one of my newly purchased dresses. Celine and Marie both plied me with questions, and I admitted to having left the ship briefly on a shopping expedition.

"On your own?" Celine sounded horrified.

I turned large, confused eyes on her. "Of course. Why ever not?"

"How did you know where to go?"

"Oh." I waved my hand vaguely through the air. "I just asked until I found someone who could direct me. People are always so helpful." I beamed around the table.

"I'll be they are," said Rafe with a sigh. "You should probably take one of us with you next time you go out, Lettie."

"All right, if you wish it."

Celine rolled her eyes and shook her head before launching into an enthusiastic rendition of the many sights I had missed. I nodded and smiled and sighed when expected and tried not to meet William's eyes.

As soon as the meal had finished, I escaped up onto deck, breathing in the salty air and gazing up at the stars. They looked peaceful and removed. If only I felt the same way. My two personas had become so entangled, I might never be able to return to my old life.

When I felt a warm presence at my back, I didn't need to turn around to see who it was. Would I always feel this attuned to his presence? Would I ever be free of the chaos he had wrought on my life?

William stepped up beside me and leaned against the rail. I kept my eyes on the stars.

"It's beautiful out here at night," I said.

"Beauty." He gave a single shake of his head and a rough laugh.

"Sunlight or starlight, it makes no difference. I have never seen such beauty." He hadn't once lifted his head to look at the sky.

I knew I should turn to him and innocently question his meaning. But I couldn't bring myself to do it. My hands tightened on the railing. If only I could make myself immune to his opinion of me. If only I could laugh it off like I did with all the men at court.

"You are the most beautiful woman I have ever seen, Princess. Sometimes it hurts me to look at you."

"I do not wish to cause you pain." The soft words were the only truth I could utter. The only certainty I could find in my heart.

How many times had I been told I looked enchanting in the moonlight? Too many to count. And yet never had I heard the words said with such sincerity. And never had it pained me so to hear them.

Only hours before he had spoken to Aurora with the same intensity. Was a beautiful face all it took to make him forget that connection?

Both halves of me responded to him with frightening ease. And each time, the other half pulled me back. Nothing but the truest love could save me. And once again William had proved that my beauty would always be the most important thing about me. I could not escape it.

Two tears escaped my eyes and slid down my cheeks. A gentle finger reached up to catch them. "And I do not wish to make you cry. What have I said to upset you, Princess?"

I shook my head, mutely, unable to come up with a single reply that the curse would allow. Instead I picked up my skirts and ran for my cabin.

He didn't try to catch me, and I sternly told my heart to be glad. There was nothing I could say to him.

~

A new pilot had joined us at Largo. None of us had met him before, but the two hours I had spent with my agent in the city had reassured me of the newcomer's integrity. I didn't have many agents outside the capital, but a handful of them had moved over the years, and I had kept track of their whereabouts in case of such a need.

"The Largoan captains who carry the crown's trust are without equal in skill or loyalty," he had said. "I would trust any of them as willingly with your life as with my own." Two years hadn't dulled his devotion to me.

True to my uncle's promise, the local sailor delivered us safely into Banishment Island's largest harbor in the late afternoon. The island looked even smaller than Inverne.

"I think they need to update that guide book," William muttered at my side. I ruthlessly suppressed a smile. I didn't need a reminder of how closely our thinking aligned. Not when I already had to fight so hard to resist him.

Even though I knew what to expect, the sight of the island still shocked me. A deep sandy beach gave way to rough dirt and a spattering of ground cover. But right where the trees should have begun, a tall, thick hedge erupted from the earth.

No one looking at it could possibly think it natural. Stretching away in a jagged line in both directions, I knew that it circled the entire island. My mother had requested a full report from the Largoan sailor, and we had all been present for her questioning. So I knew that the thick thorns prevented anyone from climbing over the hedge, and the wood possessed an unnatural resistance to ax or fire.

A small stream slipped beneath the branches and down to meet the sea without leaving an opening big enough for a person to exploit. It would provide us with fresh water, however.

A heated discussion between the captain and my uncle had resulted in a reluctant agreement. The crew and the soldiers would use the last few hours of daylight to unload the necessary supplies from the ship. The actual attempt on the hedge would wait until the next morning.

My mother made no attempt to move the timeline forward, and I suspected she had reached the limit of her plan. She had no idea how to breach the magical barrier. The ship's two longboats made countless trips back and forth while I watched from the deck. No one suggested I step onshore until the camp had been properly established.

I didn't mind since the curse would have prevented me from exploring anyway. As long as I was in place by nightfall, nothing else mattered.

A number of tents for the royals and officers soon appeared toward the back of the beach, well past the high tide mark. But the crew worked inefficiently, many of them breaking off their work to glance at the unnatural greenery and mutter to themselves. The captain's face reflected the uneasiness—but directed toward the sailors rather than the hedge. Once camp had been established, he ordered a bonfire and extra rations.

Good humor quickly returned after that, and I only hoped they wouldn't stay up telling tall tales of the sea until late into the night. I excused myself early, knowing I needed to get some sleep. As impossible as it seemed, I would have to force my body to rest. I had no idea what waited on the other side of the hedge, and I needed to be operating at full capacity.

Sure enough, hours later, my eyes sprung open in the darkness. I didn't need to see the time to know I had woken on cue. I had always possessed that skill. Nothing but the gentle sound of the waves greeted me, signaling a sleeping camp. Still, I would need to avoid the sentries.

I slipped out of bed and dressed quickly, careful not to disturb my mother or sister. I donned my new pants and a slim fitting shirt and vest. Creeping out of the tent, the cool night breeze brushed against my face. I felt naked without my scarf. Almost as strange as wandering the streets as Aurora during the day.

An unfortunately placed sentry forced me to detour through the camp, picking a painfully slow path among the tents and the many men who slept out in the open. I had almost reached an unguarded stretch of beach when a sharp hiss made me freeze.

A large tent blocked the moonlight from hitting me, and I shrank back against the canvas.

"Aurora? Is that you?" I recognized the voice, but my surge of fear didn't fade away. I couldn't let Celine see my face.

"Stay where you are," I whispered back. She stood several steps away with the full moon shining directly on her face. I hoped the light would make it harder for her to see my features in the shadows.

"Oh, thank goodness, it is you. I can't see you properly though, I'll just come…"

"No!" I cut her off. "What are you doing out here?"

She looked hurt. "Making sure you and William don't sneak off without me, of course. I'm a part of this, too, whatever it turns out to be. And there's something I need to tell you about my aunt."

"I already know."

Her obvious surprise and confusion alerted me to my mistake. I would need to come up with some sort of cover story to explain my knowledge. But I didn't have time now. I had told William to go on without me, so I couldn't be late.

"That's why I'm doing this," I said. "William and I are going to try to break through now, to find the princess before Prince Horace and the guards arrive. He seems intent on dealing out justice, and I want the chance to talk to her first."

"Without me?"

I hated the hurt on her face. "I don't know what we'll find in there, Your Highness."

"I'm not a child!"

"I know you're not. And that's why I need you to stay."

My answer surprised her enough that she didn't immediately

argue. I pressed my advantage. "Something mysterious is going on here. Something magical. If we succeed in breaking through the hedge, the prince and I are going straight for the princess. But we don't know what's waiting for us on the other side. We don't know what we might unleash. We need someone here who knows where we've gone. Someone who's ready to rouse and defend the camp."

I took a deep breath and hoped she recognized the sincerity in my voice. "I underestimated you for far too long, Your Highness. I'm not asking you to stay here for your safety. I'm asking you to stay for everyone else's."

As I said the words, I knew they were true. And I realized I was getting sloppy. I should have thought of the danger to the others before now. I had nearly left the entire camp sleeping and helpless, as well as going to face an unknown adversary without backup. I needed to get my head back into shape. I needed to be the spymaster for a little longer. I couldn't afford mistakes.

Celine straightened. "You can count on me, Aurora. And if you're not back by dawn, I'm sending every single one of the guards after you."

I smiled although she couldn't see it. "You do that." I was pretty sure they'd be coming after us at dawn no matter what. "Now go, quickly. I don't want to risk attracting anyone's attention to this side of the camp."

Celine saluted and melted away, disappearing among the tents. I lingered for a moment, pride and relief distracting me. Then I took a deep breath and stepped out onto the sand.

## CHAPTER 25

*M*y first sight of the hedge had clearly shown my mistake. It was one thing for Uncle Horace to tell us to meet him at the hedge. A large group of guards would be hard to miss, and we wouldn't have needed to avoid the sentries since they would have been with us.

One man, on the other hand, was a completely different story. I had been forced to leave a note in William's tent. I hoped it hadn't been too cryptic, but I couldn't risk being more explicit. Of course, even if he was waiting in the right spot, I still had to convince him to allow Princess Celeste to tag along on his adventure.

The full moon cast strong light across the beach, but it also threw the hedge into strange shadow. The branches shifted and rustled disproportionally to the light breeze. The sand sank beneath my feet, and I lengthened my stride, trying to cover the ground more quickly.

The beach curved slightly, and I clambered over an outcropping of rock, my boots slipping on the wet surface.

"Who's there?" William's whisper carried easily through the still night.

"Oh!" The curse turned my startled exclamation into a soft gasp. I lifted my head, my stomach fluttering with either nerves or the beginnings of a curse cramp.

"Princess?" He moved as if to sheath the naked sword in his hand before remembering he didn't have a scabbard for it. "What in the kingdoms are you doing here?"

I pressed my hand to my chest and took several audible breaths. "I thought you were a bear."

"A bear? Really?" He turned his head first one way and then the other to observe the short span of coastline.

I bit my lip. Was his expression scathing or contemptuous? A bear had been a bit much, even for Celeste. I shivered. "Everyone is saying that hedge is magic. That anything could be here. And I've heard that bears are scary."

He relaxed slightly. "They're fairly terrifying, yes. But I think I can safely assure you that whatever else we meet on this island, we're not going to meet a bear." He shifted his weight, trying to glance surreptitiously over my shoulder.

"Oh, good." I focused on his sword. "And you'll be here to protect me anyway. I don't feel afraid now that I've found you."

"Were you looking for me?"

"Of course! What else would I be doing out here?"

He closed the short distance between us and took one of my hands in his. "Why were you looking for me, Princess?"

"Apparently you're on your way to meet my aunt."

That caught his attention. He dropped my hand, and his eyes narrowed as he examined my face in the dull light. "And how did you know that?"

"Celine told me."

His eyebrows shot up. "And where is Celine?"

I shook my head and rubbed my arms. "I don't know. She told me she'd been commanded to stay in camp—to protect it." I wrinkled my nose. "But she wouldn't tell me by who."

"And this mysterious personage wanted her to send you in her place?"

I hesitated. "I don't know that I'd say in her place, exactly..." I frowned. "I'm not even sure why Celine would be here, to be honest. She's a child." I looked up at him accusingly. "I hope you haven't been leading her into danger—she doesn't know any better." Thank goodness Celine couldn't hear my words.

"She's a bright girl, none of you give her enough credit."

On second thought, Celine would love being here right now.

"Well, she said if anyone was going to speak to our aunt, it should be me." I straightened. "And I agree with her. I'm not entirely oblivious, you know. I know I'm under a curse, and I think I have the right to look my aunt in the eye and ask her why."

I held his gaze steadily while a sharp pain began to blossom behind my right eye. If he didn't capitulate soon, I would be incapacitated. Surely he recognized my claim, whatever he thought of my intellect.

He sighed and broke eye contact. The pain began to fade away.

"Perhaps this is what she meant by talking to the princess first." He spoke quietly to himself, and I pretended not to understand. "I don't like this."

"I'm not worried, I know you'll protect me."

He chuckled without humor. "That's what concerns me."

Instead of responding, I turned my gaze back on his sword. We needed to get moving. Our head start on Uncle Horace was disappearing by the minute. "Is that for the bears?"

"There aren't any..." He ran his hand through his hair. "It's for the hedge."

I laughed softly. "A sword? For a hedge? What a silly idea."

"It's from the godmothers."

"Oh!" I let my eyes widen. Silence descended. "Are you going to use it?"

214

"I don't actually know if it will work. It needs the right wielder." He looked over my shoulder again.

"Well, there's only one way to find out. Why don't you try it? I'll be right here, hiding behind you."

"Thanks." I hid a smile at his dry tone. "That's reassuring."

He stepped forward, however, the hilt gripped strongly in his hand. At the last moment, he paused and threw me a charming smile. "How about a mark of favor from the princess before I attempt this mighty deed? A kiss would work."

I giggled. "That was a good try."

He shrugged. "I had nothing to lose." He hesitated again. "Do you think there's some special method I need to use?"

"Well…I've never used a godmother item before. But I heard you're supposed to swing a sword. You know, in general."

He snorted. "That is the general way, yes."

"Maybe try that, then."

He looked at me for a moment, trying to work out if I was joking. Then he shrugged and, clasping the sword in both arms, swung it wide.

The blade hit the closest branches and kept going, cutting through a broad swath of hedge. He fell back a step and stared down at the blade.

"That was…easy." He looked over at me.

Was it foolish to be disappointed? I'd been expecting something more spectacular. Like maybe the whole hedge crumbling into dust. Or some shooting stars, at the very least. Of course, this way was a lot less likely to attract attention.

I peered at the dent his swipe had made on the greenery in front of us. The sword had cut a clear arc, everything it touched cleanly severed in two. Even the leaves. The hedge was thick, though, and there was still no sign of the other side. Several of the thorns measured as long as my forearm. "I guess you're the right wielder."

"Step back." He gestured behind him. "And follow me."

I moved into line, and he swung again, quickly establishing a rhythm. As we moved slowly forward, he took the time to clear out the hedge to our left and right as well, forming a wide tunnel through the green. I didn't try to hurry him. I didn't like the look of those thorns one bit.

At one point I looked over my shoulder at the now distant beach. I imagined the hedge closing up behind us, the thorns reaching for us like hungry teeth. I shivered and moved a half step closer to William.

"I think it's thinning out up ahead." The hedge deadened the sound, so he had no need to whisper. He did anyway, and I replied in kind.

"Oh, thank goodness. I think I just saw one of the thorns move."

"I really hope you're joking."

I giggled. "Of course I was. Oh! Wait! Did you see that?"

"Princess!" The warning had clearly been delivered through gritted teeth.

Distracted, he stumbled as his next swing cut through into open air. I crashed against him, and we both tumbled out the other side of the hedge. He twisted at the last moment and tossed the sword clear of us.

"Oof." I landed on top of him.

He grunted and gripped me against him, preventing me from bouncing off and onto the ground. When we had both steadied, he slowly let go. I told my body to move. Nothing happened.

I spoke more sternly to myself and managed to push myself up off his chest. I glanced down into his eyes while I did it and then quickly looked away. That had been a bad idea. I reminded myself who waited for us inside this hedge, and my mind instantly detached from William's handsome face and muscular chest.

I straightened. Something landed against the side of my head, hard. Something else whacked my face. I threw up my hands, but the deluge kept coming, buffeting and scratching me as I tried to fight my way free.

A scream ripped through the air. It hadn't come from me.

# PART III
# ISLAND OF THORNS

# CHAPTER 26

The piercing screech hadn't sounded like William, but a new level of panic set in anyway. I put both arms up to protect my face and took off running. After ten steps, the attack lightened. I could see the small, individual black bodies and wings slapping against me now. I altered my route, curving back toward where I had left William.

He had also clambered to his feet and rushed forward to meet me. By the time we connected, the last of the bats had disappeared. I ran straight into his arms without thinking.

He held me tightly. "Are you all right?"

I drew a shuddering breath, putting every last feeling of terror on display, despite the fact that my mind had returned to a state of calm. I didn't need a new headache right now, so I needed to look overset.

William clasped me tightly, and his warmth seeped through me, quelling the last of my shaking. I told myself I only let him hold me because of the curse.

"What in the kingdoms was that?"

A second screech rang out, as grating as the first had been. My pulse spiked, and we both spun to face the jungle before us. "And that!"

"There!" William pointed into the canopy.

I tried to follow his finger but must have been too slow. "What? I didn't see anything."

"A monkey." He let me go and stooped to retrieve his sword. "Just a monkey."

I peered back into the trees but couldn't see anything in the dark. "Are they dangerous?" I looked down at a long scratch on my arm and grimaced.

William followed my eyes. "You're hurt!"

"I can't feel it at all," I hurried to reassure him. It was already going to take us long enough to make any progress due to my Celeste act. I didn't want him coddling me more than necessary. "I just hope those bats don't attack again. Or the monkeys."

William frowned. "The monkey looked like a small one from what I could see. I would have said we were safe enough from them…but then I would have said we were entirely safe from bats. I've never heard of them swooping someone like that." He lifted his sword and faced into the jungle. "We knew this place wasn't entirely natural—I guess we just got a reminder."

He didn't move, so I prompted him. "Do you know where we're going?"

"Not exactly." He looked back toward the tunnel through the hedge.

Since I knew that waiting for Aurora wouldn't do us any good, I edged around him and wandered over to the start of the trees. "Maybe we should follow the path."

He joined me. Vines and leaves had started to encroach, but it had clearly once been a dirt path leading down to the beach. I guess it hadn't gotten much traffic since the hedge had gone up.

"Princess Melisande must have a home somewhere on this island. Perhaps this path leads there. I can't think what other purpose it could have."

I strode two steps down the path before the prince's arm pulled me to a halt. At the same moment a sharp pain shot through my stomach. I clenched my teeth. I had forgotten the role I had to play. I couldn't let that happen.

I allowed William to pull me behind him. "I think I should go first, Princess."

"Please do." I shivered. "I think I might have seen a monkey."

The pain faded as we set off into the jungle, me cowering safely behind William. He glanced once more over his shoulder toward the hedge before we were fully swallowed up by the jungle. I pretended not to notice.

A surprising amount of moonlight made it through the canopy, perhaps because it wasn't as dense as I had expected. Less light filtered through than on the open beach, however, and my eyes needed time to adjust. Safely out of William's eyeshot, I put extra effort into scanning our path carefully, watching for signs of danger or anything that might lead us to my aunt.

Sailing in, the island had looked small, but on foot it seemed to go on forever. We trudged along the overgrown path in silence. How far behind us would our uncle and the guards be? Far enough to give us a chance to talk to my aunt first, but not too far, I hoped. Whatever she had to say, I couldn't risk the kingdom. And I didn't want to put William at risk.

He moved confidently through the darkness, his sword gripped lightly in front of him. Had I made a mistake dragging him into this? I trusted him so implicitly at this point, that I sometimes forgot he wasn't Lanoverian. If this went badly, our kingdom would be in an even worse position than before.

In several places, large ferns had grown across the path, almost completely obscuring it. No more screeches sounded from the monkeys, but a constant undercurrent of flutters, chirps, clicks, and rustles reminded me that the jungle lived around us.

Every time I heard a whoosh, I couldn't help flinching slightly.

The bats' attack might have turned out to be relatively harmless, but it hadn't felt like it at the time. I let the twitches continue in case William was monitoring me.

After over an hour of walking, William called a break. The ground had been mostly flat, so I had to fake some breathlessness. In reality, I felt far from tired yet. I wanted to push on, but I made myself sit on a fallen log beside him.

My eyes had finally adjusted to the new lighting, and the jungle seemed to come to life around me. I couldn't relax, remaining on high alert, ready for any possible danger.

William laid the sword down beside him. "You're doing well, Princess."

"I often walk around the gardens at home. This is just like that, except darker." I smiled. "Perhaps when we return it will be light, and I'll have the chance to admire the flowers."

"Perhaps I can find some for you now." He reached into the foliage behind the log, but his eyes seemed to have caught on my face, and he wasn't paying attention to his questing hand.

My stomach seized. I had spent enough time in the southern jungles as a child to know you never put your hand somewhere you couldn't see. Far too many poisonous things lived here. I opened my mouth, but my brain stalled over how to deliver the warning in a curse-approved manner.

A slither of movement flashed in the corner of my eye, and I couldn't delay any longer. I lurched forward, throwing myself against his chest, and his hand pulled back to catch me.

He clasped me against him, making no move to push me back upright. Another flicker from behind us showed a snake, sliding off into the underbrush. I sighed in relief at the averted catastrophe and felt William's indrawn breath in response.

Looking into his eyes, I saw danger. I knew how I looked in the moonlight, and I had just thrown myself into his arms unprovoked. I bit my lip, wondering how to extricate myself gracefully, and his eyes flicked down to my mouth. Another mistake. It didn't help that he could feel my heart beating as fast as his own.

I squeezed my eyes shut and buried my face in his chest. I managed to produce a dry sob. "I'm so glad you're here. I could never do this without you."

A quiver ran through him, and he patted my back. "No, I imagine not. But what has brought this on?" When I didn't answer immediately, he added, "Not that I mind in the least, of course."

I manufactured another heaving sob. "Those bats. I suddenly remembered them all around me, and…"

He patted my back again and waited until I pushed myself off him.

I smiled, injecting a small tremor into the expression. "Shall we keep going?"

"If you need longer to rest…" William once again looked back the way we had come.

I shook my head. "Oh, no. I feel much better now, thank you." I projected a brighter smile this time and stood up.

He reluctantly followed. Enough time had passed that I could see a faint lightening in the jungle around us. Would all of the guards be preparing to mobilize in preparation for their dawn meeting? Or had my uncle only intended to take a small unit with us? Either way, it would take them a while to realize that William was gone and not just oversleeping in his tent.

We had been walking for long enough that I started to wonder if we had passed the midway point of the island and were heading toward the opposite beach. The path looked no more well-traveled than it had previously, and small prickles of doubt began to creep in. Perhaps this old trail didn't lead to my aunt at all.

I examined the path itself and our surroundings more closely as we walked. Some distance further along, I noticed a slight break in the foliage. As we approached it, I slowed, examining the ground. Another path appeared, intersecting with ours. I paused between strides to stare down the new trail. Did it look more defined? Less invaded by green?

William hadn't noticed my pause, and I had already received enough warnings from the curse that night not to call out my findings. I flung myself forward onto the ground, a sharp cry falling from my lips. He spun around, sword at the ready, but could see no danger. Stepping back, he knelt at my side. I rolled over and half sat up, clutching at one of my ankles.

"I'm sorry." I squeezed out a tear. "I tripped."

He shook his head, brushing away my apology, but I noticed frustration lurking in the line of his brow. He had been expecting a partner, not a burden, on this trip. He had one, of course, he just didn't know it.

I pointed to the side of our path, toward where the other trail broke off. "I think I can see a large branch over there. If you get it for me, I might be able to use it as a sort of crutch."

He looked sceptical but followed my directions anyway and started rummaging through the underbrush. "I'm afraid I can't see anything that would be tall enough...Hey!"

"You found one?"

"No, but I've found something else. Another path."

"A path?"

"Yes. Stay there for a minute." He straightened and took off down the new trail at a much faster pace than we had been traveling previously. He disappeared from sight from my lowered vantage point, but I soon heard the sounds of his return.

"I think this path looks more established. We should try it." His enthusiastic voice broke off when he saw me still sitting on the ground. "Oh. Your ankle."

"It's feeling better already. Perhaps it isn't sprained after all."

"Let's hope not."

I reached my hands up toward him, intending for him to

assist me to my feet. Instead he leaned down and scooped me into his arms.

"I'll carry you for a while." He started down the new path before I could protest. For a moment I worried he would end up skewering me with his sword. But he successfully juggled us somehow, and I had to admit his arms felt comfortable around me.

We moved at a faster pace than on the previous path—he had been holding himself back before, an indication of his perception of Celeste's capacity. I still didn't know what we would face if we found my aunt, however, so I soon insisted he let me walk. He needed to conserve his strength.

He set me down gingerly, and I made a show of testing my foot, before beaming up at him. "Not twisted at all. What a fortunate thing."

He shook his head slightly, his eyes narrowing. "Indeed." He didn't complain, however, and I wondered what had truly motivated him to carry me. I had to confess to having dreamed about it once or twice myself.

It soon became apparent that we had made the right decision. The path grew more and more defined. And, after a while, we even saw the occasional distinct footprint showing in the dirt. My nerves intensified. What awaited us? Would my aunt attack us on sight? Was she alone, or had she somehow accumulated a rebel guard? I did a mental count of the knives I had hidden on my person. I hoped I wouldn't have to use them, though. Not as Celeste.

Dawn broke as we stepped out into a large clearing. The increased light clearly illuminated a large pool, what appeared to be a small, cultivated garden, and a large stone house.

I blinked twice. My aunt could not have built such a habitation on her own. William nudged me and pointed to the chimney. A small waft of smoke drifted out. My eyes flew back to the doorway. Someone was home.

He raised both eyebrows, gesturing for me to retreat to the protection of the jungle. I shook my head. After a moment he sighed and started toward the house. I trailed behind, fighting the itch in my palms that told me to draw one of my knives.

A storm as big as the one we had weathered on the *Viktoria* erupted in my stomach. If the evening meal hadn't been so long ago, I feared I would have lost it. How many times over the years had I imagined confronting my aunt? What would she be like after so much time alone? My usual confidence seemed to have crumbled under the eruption of a lifetime of anger and hatred and confusion. But the burn that had replaced it pushed me forward just as surely.

When we reached the wooden door, William checked that I was close behind him. When I nodded encouragingly, he lifted the latch and flung it open, entering the house blade first.

# CHAPTER 27

The door crashed against the inside wall with a loud bang, and a blur rushed toward us, chattering loudly. William, caught off guard, swung toward it with his sword.

"No!" The scream made him halt, just as the small animal corrected its course and streaked away from us. Swinging across the furniture, the monkey jumped onto the shoulders of a middle-aged woman standing next to a small fireplace and attempted to hide in her hair.

She held a ladle in her hand, a small pot hanging over the flames in front of her. Clearly we had interrupted her breakfast preparations. In her simple garb, she looked like any other island dweller. Only her bearing and her beauty gave any hint of royal lineage.

She stroked the animal clinging to her neck absentmindedly, her wide eyes fixed on William. "I always knew someone would come eventually." Her gaze slid to his naked blade. "I didn't expect it to be a northerner, though. How do you come to be in possession of the Sword of Lanover?"

"Excuse me?" William seemed completely thrown off balance. "The what?"

She raised her eyebrows in polite incredulity. "You don't know the weapon you carry? You did use it to breach the hedge, did you not?"

William shifted his weight from one foot to the other and didn't answer.

She sighed. "The Sword of Lanover is an heirloom of the Lanoverian royal family. Gifted to us generations ago by the godmothers." So that was how Uncle Horace had come to have it. Although my mother didn't seem to have been aware of its presence on board the ship...

When William still said nothing, the woman continued. "Able to cut through any substance or barrier when wielded by a bearer who is pure of heart and full of truth. I suppose I should be grateful for such a noble executioner."

William found his voice at last. "I'm no executioner, Your Highness."

"No?" She looked slightly incredulous. "What other purpose could you have here?"

"I am an escort, nothing more. For someone who wishes to speak with you."

"Who could possibly wish to speak with me?"

William stepped forward and to the side, revealing me standing in the doorway.

My aunt's curious expression changed to wonder and then shock. She gasped loudly and staggered backward, collapsing into a chair.

"Celeste," she whispered. "You're so beautiful. Even more beautiful than I imagined." Tears streamed down her face entirely unheeded, as she clutched both hands to her chest. "I never thought I would get to see you again, but I've imagined what you must be like so many times. My imagination could not conjure such a vision, however. And you're so grown up!" For some reason this last thought seemed to tip her over the edge, and she buried her face in her hands and wept with great, shuddering sobs.

William visibly swallowed, looking at me helplessly. In any other situation I would have smiled at his ineptitude. He had no more idea what to do with a crying stranger than any of my brothers would have.

But I was as paralyzed as him. I had imagined so many variations of this scene—but none of them had ever looked like this.

For two whole minutes the three of us remained in awkward stillness. Eventually my aunt's sobs slowed and then stopped altogether. She looked up at us, wonder still transforming her face when her gaze fell on me.

"If my godmother had appeared and asked me what I would most like to do before I died, I would have said to have the opportunity to speak to you. And here you are." She shook her head.

I shifted uncomfortably as William had done in my spot minutes earlier. It felt jarring to think of my aunt having her own godmother. But, of course, she was a princess and had once had a Christening of her own.

Had I entered some sort of alternate world? I hadn't come here to fulfill my aunt's dreams. This woman wanted me dead— had always wanted me dead. Could this be a strange attempt to lull us into a false sense of security?

I remembered her expression when William had stepped aside to reveal me. She had no reason to expect me and had clearly been taken by surprise. If this was a plot, she was incredibly fast thinking as well as an amazing actress. I didn't believe it. But what did that mean?

My aunt stood and crossed back over to her pot. "You must tell me your story, of course. But first, can I offer you some breakfast? We can talk while we eat."

Neither of us said anything, but she doled out three bowls of porridge anyway. When she sat and still neither of us moved, she looked up enquiringly. William glanced over at me, clearly waiting for me to take the lead, so I moved forward. None of it felt real. Perhaps I had strayed into a dream?

I sat at the table but made no attempt to eat. The storm still raged in my stomach, and I wasn't sure it would stay down. William, on the other hand, took my acquiescence as permission to tuck in hungrily. Although I noticed he placed the sword down in easy reach.

My aunt looked between the two of us, her gaze lingering on my untouched bowl, but said nothing. After several bites, she laid her spoon down on the table. "Godmother told me that I would have my chance for redemption, but I never imagined she meant it so literally."

My mind churned, but I didn't dare reveal any of it externally; I didn't think I could take any more activity in my stomach. Which meant keeping my face blank. I had no approved emotions for this moment.

Her godmother visited her? Here on the island? I looked around the small, tidy home. I could see a half-finished sewing project and a makeshift broom leaning against the wall. The visions of a rebel leader faded further and further from my mind. Every indication suggested Melisande was exactly who she was supposed to be—an exiled princess living alone on a small island.

But the rebels had been interested in her. They had sent someone to investigate her records in the palace. A vague unease stirred in the back of my mind. Had I made a terrible mistake?

"I should have guessed it, though," said Melisande. "The Sword of Lanover was the logical tool to break through the hedge. And who better to wield it than my innocent victim?"

A surge of bile rose up in my throat as I remembered her earlier words. *...when wielded by a bearer who is pure of heart and full of truth.* An unpleasant tingling broke out across my scalp. Without William we would still have been stuck on the other side of the hedge. I could never have successfully wielded the sword. I had exulted at the thought of seeing this woman killed. There was nothing pure about my heart.

For years I had let myself be consumed by hate. And I had thought it was all right because she deserved it. But it wasn't her crime that prevented me from wielding that sword. Her guilt was irrelevant. It didn't matter if she deserved the hatred, because I was the one being consumed by it.

For so long I had lived under a shadow. And I had believed the curse and my activities as Aurora to be responsible. Now I recognized the true source of the shadow. All these years I had been waiting for someone else to lift it from me when I had always been the only one capable of freeing myself.

I sat there unable to speak—even after everything, I was still constrained by the limitations of the curse. And for all her surprising welcome, I had yet to hear my aunt apologize for the murder she had tried to commit. And yet, the thought of the curse reminded me of my godmother's words all those years ago —about the lessons I still had to learn. I suspected I had finally discovered her meaning.

I was finished letting the wrong my aunt had committed against me define my life. I would relinquish all desire for revenge so that I could finally be free.

A darkness I hadn't even recognized lifted from my heart. I breathed deeply and wondered why the air tasted so much sweeter.

My aunt watched my blank face curiously. "Is she always like this?" she asked William.

He grimaced, nodded and then hesitated. "Mostly."

What had that meant? I wished I could stand up and walk away from the whole situation. My new-found forgiveness hadn't come with trust, and I suddenly wanted nothing but to escape. I didn't want to hear her story or to feel sorry for her. The anger and hatred were gone, but I wasn't ready to replace them with liking.

Melisande sighed, her face darkening. William looked between us a little helplessly, clearly unsure what to do next. "Perhaps you should tell us your story," he said at last.

"Certainly, if you wish it." She looked out of the window for a moment, her eyes unfocused. "I assume you know what happened before my banishment. I do not know if the request I made immediately following your birth, Celeste, was honored or not. Perhaps you don't know that my husband and child died in the weeks before you were born."

My face remained impassive, but William looked shocked and confused.

"This house had been built many years ago for people such as myself. I was delivered here with the promise that I would never leave. And I did not want to. For a while I barely moved. I had been left supplies, and I did no more than was required to keep me alive. And then, one day, as I staggered out for fresh water, I saw a beautiful flower. The deepest, most vivid red I had ever seen. And the darkness lifted, just the tiniest fraction.

"Most days after that got a little better. Some days I slid backward again, but then the next day I would creep forward toward the light. This little guy found me." She patted the monkey who still clung to her shoulder. "He was barely more than a baby and had lost his mother somehow. Having his company made a big difference. But full awareness brought with it a terrible burden. The memory of what I had done." Her eyes locked on me. "I considered ending it all, but I couldn't bring myself to do it. I knew I didn't deserve peace."

"I am truly sorry for what I did to you, Celeste. I would make any sacrifice now to free you. For years now, I have thought of you every day. Imagined you growing and changing. Pictured you as you laughed and cried. You see, my daughter would have been your age if she had lived.

"For a short time, my grief drove me to the edge of desperation. My anger overwhelmed me to the point where I couldn't bear the resentment I felt toward your parents for having you and your siblings when I had nothing. I thought that your existence was a pain I could not bear. An unfairness against my own dead daughter.

"But I realized a long time ago now that it was precisely the opposite. A bit of my daughter lives on in you, her cousin. Your life could have given me a small glimpse into what her life would have been. You are my living connection to her—until one day I pass into the next realm and see her again in truth."

Several more tears ran unheeded down her cheeks. "And I let my grief and anger nearly destroy you. I let it drive me to murder."

I couldn't prevent the heat rising in my face. All these years I had never once imagined looking at my aunt and seeing myself reflected back. Yet I had nearly let my hatred and anger drive me to murder, too. It was a sobering realization.

Not that I regretted the years she had spent in banishment. She had committed a great wrong, and her punishment had been just. But she was obviously repentant and, with the hatred gone from my heart, I found I wished no further suffering on her.

Any lingering doubt as to her role in the rebellion had disappeared. This woman had neither the will nor the resources to lead such an uprising. The same tickling at the back of my mind distracted me again. I was missing something, if only I could think what it was.

In the meantime, I needed to make some sort of response. Eventually my silence would become more jarring than my forbidden emotion. I found my voice and a thought innocuous enough to voice. "My mother told me my cousin had yet to be Christened. That she hadn't been given a name. Did you choose one for her?"

My aunt looked surprised, then her face softened. "I called her Briar Rose—a name as bittersweet as her short life."

William cleared his throat. "It's a beautiful name."

I wanted to reach across the table and hug him for making an effort in such an uncomfortable, tension-laden situation.

"How extremely touching," said a voice from the doorway.

All three of us looked up, startled. We had been too wrapped up in the intensity of the moment to hear the sound of a new arrival.

Uncle Horace stood in the doorway, a group of guards at his back. His sister gazed at him coldly, no sign of greeting in her face for her younger brother. "Horace. I should have guessed as much."

He barked a laugh. "You always were a little too knowing, Melisande."

I glanced between the two of them, the niggle in the back of my mind flaring up into a terrible realization. I had always prided myself on my intelligence, and as Aurora I had worked tirelessly to hone my skills. And yet I had let my hatred drive me to the wrong conclusion. I had let it blind me to the truth.

I had vowed to protect my kingdom, and then I had walked straight into my uncle's hands.

# CHAPTER 28

*W*hile my aunt and uncle locked eyes, William slowly slid the sword off the table and hid it in his lap. The godmother item would give us a small advantage in a fight, but I didn't know how many guards my uncle had brought with him. We needed more information.

"Uncle Horace! What are you doing here?" I gave him my best court smile.

He rolled his eyes and glanced at William. "I can't imagine what possessed you to bring her along. And where are the other two?"

He looked around the small single-roomed home as if he expected Celine and Aurora to leap out of a cupboard. "Ah well, it makes no difference in the end. The guards I left back at the beach know they have two princesses to take care of. It doesn't much matter which two of you it is."

A chill froze me to my seat. Celine and Marie. Would Celine see them coming? Would she be ready for them?

I wanted to jump up and run for the beach. But, as hard as it was, I had to put my trust in Celine. It would take all of my wits to get William and myself out of this alive.

"Horace!" Melisande's horrified gasp didn't seem to faze her brother in the slightest. "It's one thing to come after me. But our nieces and nephews?" She shook her head. "I knew you had changed—ever since your visit to the other kingdoms when we were young. But I told myself you would never stoop so low. And that was all so long ago now. I don't understand!"

"I am not an impatient man. I do not like to leave things to chance. I thought at first I could convince our brother of the error of his ways. But I see now that he will never listen." He shot a poisonous look in my direction. "And his children are no better. So for a long time now I have been gathering my strength, ensuring that everything was in place for one decisive move."

I had always known that Uncle Horace didn't like us younger ones much, but I had never seen such a look of hatred in his eye. Clearly he had been holding back all these years. Even his apparent soft spot for Frederic and Cassian must have been a mask.

"I acted rashly, seizing an apparent opportunity, only once," he continued, "and it failed me." He shook his head. "I thought I could trust to a storm to do my work for me, and it could have led to my complete undoing. A reminder that nothing must be left to chance."

A storm? My mother's near death now made sense. My uncle must have found her searching for the captain and hit her over the head, dumping her outside and trusting to the storm to do the rest. Naturally he wouldn't have wanted to risk his own skin by stepping onto the deck. Fury rose inside me.

I looked carefully at each person in the room and then pinned my confused gaze on Uncle Horace. "I'm sorry, Uncle. I don't understand…"

He barked a short laugh. "Of course you don't." He looked at Melisande. "And my brother couldn't even do what needed to be done then, either. It would have saved me a great deal of bother, if only he had dealt with you as you deserved."

Melisande arched a graceful eyebrow. "What threat have I been to you, brother, sequestered here on my island?"

"Threat?" Another laugh. "No threat. Just a loose thread. And I don't like loose threads."

Understanding dawned on Melisande's face, and she nodded.

"You cannot think the kingdom will let you get away with mass murdering the royal family!" William's voice remained steady, his eyes holding my uncle's.

"I am doing this for the kingdom!" My uncle's angry words sounded slightly unhinged. I could see that attempting to reason with him would achieve nothing—he believed in his cause to the exclusion of all reason.

"King Josef of Rangmere taught me a lot," he continued. "The people need to be governed by a strong hand and a tight rein. My brother is a fool, and Lanover suffers under his rule. Our kingdom is capable of greatness, if he would but see it and act." He shook his head. "But it is too late for that. It is clear he will not so act, and a new ruler is needed."

How had I been so blind? With all my resources and contacts, I had still not recognized the truth. I had allowed my obsession with my aunt to taint every conclusion, unable to see what was right in front of me.

William spoke the words the curse prevented me from uttering. "And King Josef was murdered in his sleep by a member of his own family. I would hardly take him as a role model."

My uncle regarded him coldly. "You are young and blinded by beauty, or you wouldn't be courting my foolish niece." His eyes skimmed over me, clearly discounting me entirely.

I held my breath as I considered whether I could turn his disdain to my advantage. William continued to argue with him, but I no longer focused on their words. A window gave me a limited view outside the front door. I estimated at least twenty guards milled around out there.

I couldn't imagine my uncle would have brought too many

more than that. He came expecting to face four people, and the guards he had left at the beach would need to carry out their murders in the face of the entire crew of the *Viktoria*.

I had to force my mind away from the beach. I couldn't help them now, and thinking of them might get us killed.

William stood, his chair tipping backward, the sword in his hand. "You will touch either of these women only over my dead body."

My uncle regarded him coolly. "Yes, I have resigned myself to that necessity. Your parents will naturally be heartbroken to lose both you and your sister, but I will assure them the guilty parties have been brought to justice." He took a step into the room. "My poor brother was too trusting when he allowed his evil and powerful sister to live. I was able to crush her rebellion, but not before her assassins got to you. All of you. Such a well-coordinated strike, to attack the king and princes in the palace, just as the rest of you reached this island. I barely escaped with my own life." He shook his head. "And I pleaded with you all not to go, too."

"Assassins?" I broke into wild sobs as I leaped to my feet, gambling on my uncle's apparent lack of urgency.

He seemed to be reveling in speaking his mind after having to conceal his true feelings for so many years. I knew the sensation well enough to understand why he wasted so much time talking to his victims.

It helped that we were in a confined space, and William still held the Sword of Lanover. Attacking us would be a messy affair. If we wouldn't come out the front door on our own, I doubted my uncle intended to lead the charge himself. Which meant we had a few moments yet. I doubted he would consider any movement of mine to be a threat, so I scurried around the table and threw myself into my aunt's arms.

She staggered backward before regaining her balance and

patting me awkwardly on the back. Between the sobs I whispered in her ear. "Is there another way out of here?"

She stiffened, but only slightly before relaxing again. She turned her head, as if to comfort me further, and whispered, "Yes, around the corner, to the left of the fireplace. There's a back door."

"We'll have to make a run for it—there's no other way."

"No." Her arms tightened slightly around me. "You'll have to make a run for it. This is my chance for redemption."

Before I could argue, she snapped, "Celeste, stop your sniveling! It helps no one," and thrust me away from her. I staggered toward William, who caught me with his left arm, bracing me against him as he kept his sword arm steady.

Melisande stepped forward, pushing up her sleeves, her eyes locked on her brother. "You can't imagine I intend to simply give up on life without a fight, Horace. The real question is whether you are prepared to face me."

My uncle wavered, even falling back half a step. "You're bluffing."

I suspected he had been as unable to find information on Melisande as I had been. He didn't know what objects she might have been hoarding on this island all these years. What power she might still have.

I suspected now that his original plan had been to manipulate the situation to force William to use the sword against Melisande, before turning on us. If my mother hadn't told Celine and me the truth, we might all be dead by now.

While his eyes were glued on his sister, I stepped back, in the direction my aunt had indicated. I pulled at William, trying to draw him with me. He resisted. I tugged harder and then let go, taking another step back.

At the loss of contact, he finally broke his attention from the siblings and glanced my way. I widened my eyes, gesturing for him to follow me, and took another step back.

A spark flared in his eyes, and I hoped he had seen the door behind me and understood my intentions. When I took another step backward, he mirrored my movement, both of us keeping our bodies angled toward the front of the room in an attempt not to draw my uncle's attention.

"I've protected myself fairly effectively these last few years, have I not?" asked Melisande.

"So that hedge *was* you."

"My godmother seemed to think I might need the protection. Would you care to find out what else she thought I might need?"

Uncle Horace blanched and took a second half step backward. I could only hope Melisande was speaking the truth, and her godmother had left her with some magical aid. I didn't intend to stick around and find out, however.

My back hit the door, and I fumbled blindly for the latch. I caught at it and eased the door open as quietly as I could.

My aunt stepped forward threateningly. Not even by the flicker of an eyelid did she betray her knowledge of our actions. Apparently she trusted we were making our escape unnoticed. I appreciated her faith and her discipline. If we escaped this, it would only be due to her intervention.

I couldn't be sure that none of the guards had circled around to the back of the house, so I refrained from opening the door all the way. William took two more backward steps and caught up with me.

At the exact moment he reached me, Melisande screamed and launched herself at her brother, the two of them grappling in the doorway. I whipped around, not waiting to see the outcome of the conflict, and shoved the back door all the way open.

Two guards stood in the small cleared space at the back of the house, but they looked startled and distracted by the sudden commotion from inside the house. I could have taken them out, but I held myself back at the memory that I wasn't wearing a mask.

William stepped smoothly around them. "Go," he grunted, moving forward to engage them. I had enough faith in his abilities to take off toward the cover of the jungle.

At the last moment, however, I hesitated, and glanced over my shoulder to check on him. He was pulling his sword from the shoulder of the second guard, pushing the man to the ground. Looking up, he met my eyes, and something in his expression made me falter. A root caught my foot, and I tripped, sprawling into the beginning of the undergrowth.

William reached my side in several long strides. He leaned down and grasped my hand. For less than a second he paused, staring straight into my eyes with an emotion too intense for me to name. Then he yanked me to my feet, his gaze still fixed on my face.

"Aurora, RUN!"

He took off into the jungle, towing me behind him.

My body took over and propelled me forward without conscious thought, years of training kicking into motion. I threw off his hand, knowing we would run faster unconnected, but stayed as close beside him as I dared.

My mind was in free fall. Too shocked to comprehend our headlong flight. He had called me Aurora! Had it been a mistake? A slip of the tongue?

But no, the weight of his eyes from that single second seemed to burn me still. Something had changed inside Melisande's house. William had known what he was saying.

Loud yells, and the crash of bodies through the trees, announced that some, at least, of the guards pursued us.

A searing pain lanced through my left leg. I stumbled and then regained my stride, now a couple of steps behind William. The arrow had only nicked me, but the pain brought my full awareness back to our flight.

The impossible had happened—I had found someone who

truly knew me, the whole me—and now we were both going to die.

I threw my head back and screamed, the sound ripping through the jungle, laden with more anger than pain.

# CHAPTER 29

*I* refused to die. And I refused to let them kill William. I pushed my legs to move faster, despite the pain.

We ducked between trees, leaping over fallen logs and pushing through the ferns. I hoped desperately that neither of us landed on a snake. The sun had risen while we talked inside my aunt's home, so at least we had light enough to see our way.

Unfortunately, so did our pursuers.

"What in the kingdoms have they got chasing us? A dragon?"

I shook my head as I ran, but it certainly sounded as if one of the mythical fire beasts could be tearing up the forest behind us. Their archer had stopped firing, so I assumed they had lost sight of us and were following by sound.

I tried to examine our surroundings as I ran, looking for a place we could safely hide.

"We need to hide." Apparently William's mind was following the same track.

"Yes, but where?"

"We could climb a tree."

I grimaced. My leg was barely holding up for our frantic

flight. I wasn't sure if it would take my weight if I tried to climb on it. But I didn't see what choice we had.

"An arrow nicked my leg."

"What?" William faltered, so I gave him a shove, pushing him onward again.

"I'm all right. But I might need your help up the tree." Did the pursuit sound closer? We needed to hurry. "As soon as you see a good one, start climbing. I'll follow, but you might need to haul me up some of the way."

William glanced at me and nodded, before beginning to scan the trees. A few steps later, he veered to the left. I followed, listening intently for the crashing and the strange crackling that followed us.

Without slowing, he launched himself up a gnarled tree, grabbing a low branch and swinging himself higher. I followed, gripping the branch with both hands and attempting to use my momentum to run up the side of the tree. My left leg buckled, and I would have fallen if a strong arm hadn't gripped me.

With William's help I scrambled safely onto the branch. As soon as I had balanced myself, he swung up to the next branch, reaching down again to help me. We continued to move upward until the sound of the pursuit peaked.

William stopped, his back to the trunk, and pulled me against him. We both held our breaths, the discordant crashing of our hearts loud in our ears. The sound of our pursuers didn't falter. It surged ahead and gradually diminished.

The arm that gripped my waist relaxed slightly. I twisted and saw his lips open to speak. I smashed my hand over his mouth, and he raised both eyebrows at me. I shook my head.

The moment stretched out, our eyes locked, our bodies crushed together on the narrow branch, and his breath warm on my hand. Too many emotions surged through me, and I feared I would burst from the pressure. Something important prodded at my thoughts, but I couldn't wrest my mind away from William long enough to focus on it.

I felt his jaw move. Apparently he had decided he had humored me long enough. Before he actually spoke, however, a loud snap from below jerked both of our attention downward. Two guards walked slowly back in the direction of my aunt's house. They each carried long sticks and were beating the undergrowth around them.

"We're never going to find them this way," said one.

The other grunted.

"They could be anywhere by now," the first continued.

"The prince will have us comb the whole island if we have to, you know that. He can't let any of them get away. And none of us are getting those fat purses unless he gets his hands on the royal treasury. So keep your mind on the gold and stop complaining."

They moved further and further away, the first man continually glancing back over his shoulder. "I just think we should have stayed together. What if we actually find them? That prince still has that magic sword."

"Then we set up a racket and keep our distance. The dragon will get here quickly enough."

William and I exchanged a silent look of confusion. There was no way that had been an actual dragon behind us. Dragons were a bedtime story for children.

When the men dropped out of sight, William pulled his head away from my hand and lowered his lips to my ear. Despite the precariousness of our situation and the burning pain in my leg, the tingle of his breath against my skin sent a shiver through my body.

"We need to get out of here. Before you bleed to death. Do you see over there?" He pointed off to one side. "The ground rises slightly. I think I can see something. It might be a cave of some sort. If it is, we can lie low there for a while."

A cave sounded dangerous. We couldn't afford to get trapped

in a place with only one exit. But he was right about my leg. If I fainted, I could get us both killed. Reluctantly I nodded agreement.

William shifted his weight, half supporting me as I dropped down to the bough below us. Slowly, branch by branch, we descended to the ground. We moved much more slowly now, focusing on silence rather than speed.

It seemed to take an age to reach the place William had seen from the treetop. The uphill slope strained my leg, but I gritted my teeth and continued forward. We nearly missed the opening from ground level, hidden as it was behind several large bushes. A better hiding place than I had feared, then.

William helped me inside and swept the area outside the entrance with his eyes, looking for any signs we might have left of our presence. I pushed into the cave, looking for any unpleasant wildlife who might have made it their home. Nothing immediately greeted me, but the cave continued back a long way, gradually narrowing and disappearing into darkness. It looked like exactly the sort of place to house a colony of bats. I shivered.

Thankfully a couple of small openings in the rock let some extra daylight into the front section of the cave. I would just have to stay well away from the back.

Now that my body was still, the elusive thought from earlier took definition. I spun back around to the opening as William entered.

"I...I don't understand." My whole body trembled. "I gave myself away, but the curse hasn't punished me."

William ignored me, grabbing both my arms and wrenching me against him. His lips came down hard against mine, and the world spun away from me.

ire scorched through me. It lifted all my physical aches and pains, a sensation in direct opposition to the effects of the curse. I burned with energy and a new wholeness.

Only when every sense of time and place had fractured, did William break the kiss. His eyes locked on to mine. "I don't care what it takes. If that didn't break the curse, I won't rest until I find something that will."

"Actually, I think that did it." The feelings his kiss had ignited in me were the opposite of the curse in every way.

"Oh." For a moment he looked almost lost. Then a sly smile crept over his face. "Then I guess I don't have anything better to do than this."

Before I could grasp his meaning, he crushed his lips back down over mine. When my knees buckled, his arms tightened around me, taking my weight. I had spent so long trying to smother the fire he kindled inside me, that it swept through me now with a mighty roar, hungry to be free. I slid my hands around his neck and up into his hair, using my grip to tighten our kiss. Time slowed and then sped up.

Eventually, we had to come up for air. I regretfully put some distance between us. "As lovely as this is, we still have to get out of this jungle alive, remember."

He instantly sobered. Slipping out of his vest, he stripped off his shirt. I tried not to stare at his bare chest. I remembered when I had first seen it, in the practice hall of our faraway palace. How long ago that seemed.

He ripped the material into long strips and knelt. Wrapping the makeshift bandage around my dripping wound, he pulled it tight, murmuring an apology when I hissed at the pain. Once it was securely bandaged, he helped me to sit.

I closed my eyes and took deep breaths, willing myself not to pass out. Eventually the pain ebbed, and the dizziness faded. I opened my eyes to find William's blue ones staring at my face. I blushed.

He reached up to brush my cheek with gentle fingers. "Every moment you look more beautiful than the one before." He shook his head. "How is that possible?"

My blush deepened. Every fiber of my body seemed to quiver in response to his presence. I had found him hard to resist before —I knew I would have no hope now.

"You called me Aurora. How did you know? How long have you known?" My mind backtracked over all our recent interactions, stretching back to the capital. Had he known as we trekked through the jungle? When we talked on deck in the moonlight? In Largo?

"You confounded me from the beginning, Princess...Aurora..." He grinned ruefully. "See! I don't even know what to call you."

"I don't care what you call me," I said softly, and then wanted to roll my eyes at myself. I would have to be careful, or I would truly become the foolish court maiden I had mimicked for so long. Too many people already bent before William's natural charm; he needed someone who would stand up to him.

I swayed, exhausted from the blood loss. William scooted over to rest his back against the cave wall and then pulled me close, sitting me between his outstretched legs. He drew me back against him so that my head rested on his chest.

I sighed and closed my eyes as his hands settled loosely around my waist. We weren't safe yet, not really, but I felt more peaceful than I had in years.

"The beauty of the Lanoverian princesses is praised throughout the Four Kingdoms," said William. "Especially that of the Sleeping Princess. But, even so, I wasn't prepared for the effect of meeting you." He shifted slightly behind me. "I never thought mere beauty could impact me so greatly. I thought I had more substance than that. I always believed that when I fell in love it would be for kindness and intelligence and principles. A pretty face would simply be the dressing."

He cleared his throat. "But once I had seen you, you haunted me. I couldn't close my eyes without seeing your face. I tried to fight it, but whenever I was in your presence, it was like I couldn't see anyone else."

A small thrill ran through me, and he tightened his arms around me in response.

"I knew all about your curse from Rafe. I told myself that emptiness lurked beneath your beauty, though it was no fault of your own. But I couldn't quite believe it. Every now and then I caught a gleam in your eyes, or a seemingly innocent turn of phrase that intrigued me." He shook his head. "I told myself it was wishful thinking, that I was only seeing what I wanted to see. But even back then I thought the intensity of my attraction to you wasn't entirely natural. But still I couldn't stop the obsession. And then I met Aurora."

He dropped a light kiss on the top of my head, and I thought my heart would melt. Pain? What pain? I had entirely forgotten my wound, and the guards out searching for us.

"If I had thought myself conflicted before, it was nothing to how I felt after that. I told myself to be wary, not to trust you implicitly, but you were everything I thought I would never find. I had never felt a rush like when we fought together to free your agent—the fear when I saw you in danger, and the exhilaration when you held your own fighting beside me."

He stopped for a moment and swallowed. "I wanted to kill every one of them for daring to lift a finger against you, but at the same time I loved that you didn't need me to defend you. I told myself that my feelings for the princess were a shade compared to what I felt for Aurora. But my heart didn't believe me. I tried to avoid her…" He laughed softly. "…avoid *you* during the day, but I couldn't stay away. I berated myself every day for what I saw as my inconstancy, but somehow it didn't *feel* unfaithful to love you both. The best I could do was hold myself back from actually declaring my feelings to either of you."

His use of the word love made me shiver. The power of his kiss had already proclaimed the truth of his love, but I still exulted to hear it spoken. I had given up on love so long ago.

"I had never been able to shake the feeling that you, as Celeste, were an old friend. That I knew you, truly knew you. I realized that I saw you as two parts of a whole. Celeste was light-hearted and fun, but I couldn't truly love someone with so little substance. Aurora had all the intelligence, drive, and dedication I could hope for, but she never stopped to laugh. Together you were one whole, entirely perfect person. I told myself over and over again to stop such foolishness, but the seed had been planted.

"I didn't understand how it could be possible with the curse. And I didn't dare push Aurora for her true identity. I was too afraid of losing you altogether. I nearly went mad on board ship after we spoke to your uncle and you went into hiding. Not knowing what had happened to you, or if you were safe, was torture."

He paused for a moment, resting his chin on the top of my head.

"But I desperately wanted it to be true, and I wanted you to tell me the truth yourself." He paused. "I have a confession of my own to make. I saw you rescue your mother in the storm. But I didn't want to catch you out, I wanted you to trust me enough to tell me. So as soon as I saw you were safe, I ran. And then, when I saw you in Largo, I couldn't hold it in, I couldn't stop myself asking. Only, it sent you running, just as I had feared. And I started to doubt myself again. The storm had been intense, and the flashes of lightning so brief. Was I really sure what I had seen?"

I wanted to tell him how badly I had longed to tell him the truth. But I didn't want to interrupt his story.

"I told myself to stop believing in such ridiculous foolishness. When I talked to you that night as Celeste, I truly thought I was being driven out of my mind. My heart and my brain were completely at war with each other. One part of me was sure you were the same person, and the other part questioned everything.

"When you turned up at the hedge, my heart tried to claim it as a victory, but my head was firmly in control at that point. Our task was too dangerous, and I didn't want to see you hurt, as Celeste or Aurora."

"So what changed?" I tried to remember everything I had said or done in my aunt's house. What had given me away?

"When you conveniently 'tripped' next to the path, all my suspicions returned. I watched you carefully after that and, gradually, I felt more and more sure. But I couldn't say anything. Not with your aunt there. It wasn't my secret to tell.

"And then, when we escaped, any last doubt disappeared. You tugged at me, and I turned, frustrated, and saw the door behind you. And you gestured for me to follow you." He chuckled. "I had seen that steely look and that hand gesture several times before.

But never from Celeste. For some reason it was enough. I stopped worrying about the curse, and I just *knew*."

I snuggled back against him and smiled. "I've been thinking about that. How I gave myself away, and the curse didn't punish me. A long time ago, my godmother told me I had a lesson to learn. I think I might have learned it, just now, back in my aunt's cabin. I think the curse knew that all of its requirements had been met. That I was finally ready for true love, just as true love had found me. It seems to have understood that we weren't exactly free to kiss at that point and given us a free pass until we reached this cave."

"So a true love's kiss is all it took? Really?" William groaned. "I should have kissed you the day after I arrived. I've longed to do so often enough."

I giggled and paused at the sound. How strange to be free to mix my two personas, to snort or giggle as I saw fit. "I don't think it would have worked, then. It had to be true love—which meant you needed to love the whole me. You needed to know who you were kissing."

"I still don't understand how it worked. The curse I mean. And your being Aurora."

I drew a deep breath. "Get ready for a long story." And I told him everything. My searching before I turned sixteen, the deal I struck with the godmother, my efforts as Aurora. I even told him about my hatred and anger, about the truth I had learned from my mother, and the truth I had learned from my own heart.

He listened, and he held me, and he didn't judge. And I promised myself that if we got out of this alive, I would never stop loving this man.

When I had finished, silence settled between us. It couldn't last forever, though.

Reluctantly I pushed myself away from him, standing. "We've rested long enough. I've stopped bleeding, and the dizziness has passed. We need to find water. And we need to get back to the beach." Mention of the others twisted my stomach, my newfound peace disappearing. I had been trying so hard not to think of everyone we had left behind.

Even the thought of my aunt's fate brought a wave of fear. I couldn't ignore the sacrifice she had made for us.

While I was stuck in the cave, partially crippled and trapped, I had forced my mind to focus on William rather than my family. And it had been almost too easy. But the first heady joy had faded somewhat, and I could no longer ignore my suppressed fears.

William matched my change in mood. "I trust them—Marie and Rafe and Celine. The prince's guards won't find them as easy a target as they expect." He took my hand. "And the same with your father and brothers back at the palace. I fought your brothers in practice bouts; they're warriors. And you left them all a warning, remember."

The memory lifted my heart. I had given them an advantage my uncle didn't know about.

"You equipped them all," said William. "Now you need to focus on yourself. I'm not going to let you die just when I found out the truth." He pulled me in against his chest, seemingly unable to help himself. I let him hold me for a moment, drinking in some of his strength and certainty.

"You're right," I said at last, pushing back. "But my aunt is alone. She may already be dead even. But we have to find out. And try to rescue her if she's alive."

"Are you sure?" William looked into my eyes, and he didn't need to voice all the complicated questions and emotions behind the question.

I straightened. "She sacrificed herself so we could escape. You said it yourself—we have to trust the others. They're not helpless, but she might be."

"I love you, Princess." William used the hand he still held to tug me back toward him. "My Aurora." He dropped a soft kiss on my mouth. "Let's go get them."

## CHAPTER 31

We surveyed the jungle for some time before exiting the cave. The guards seemed to have moved on, presumably to search other parts of the island. Carefully we picked our way back in the direction of my aunt's clearing.

William kept shooting me concerned looks, but I ignored them. Now that we had staunched the blood loss, my leg would hold up for now. After his tenth look, I rolled my eyes. He replied with a small smile, before the expression dropped off his face.

"We..." He hesitated before trying again. "We might be too late to help your aunt. You said it yourself. But are you really prepared for it? Maybe we should head back to the beach, try to find the others. We could come back for her together."

I didn't break stride. "If we do that, it really might be too late for her. I'm hoping that he kept her alive because we escaped. He might be hoping to use her as a hostage or bargaining tool."

William sighed. "I feel like a fool for not seeing Prince Horace's true intentions."

I shook my head sharply. "No. You and Celine questioned the situation. You weren't sure about allying with him. I'm the one who let my hatred guide me. You bear none of the blame."

William took my hand and gave it a squeeze. "I still don't quite understand, though. Why did he wait all these years? He kept talking about a 'loose thread'..."

I had been thinking about that. "Horace is the youngest. Even if he killed both my parents, and all of us, he wouldn't be the next in line. Melisande would. Of course, the situation would be complicated given her banishment. But if there were doubts about the assassinations, she might have become a rallying point. The only way a Lanoverian princess can give up her right to the throne is by marrying into a foreign kingdom. Melisande's husband chose to renounce his Arcadian ties and join her in Lanover so, officially, she's still in the line of succession."

I rubbed my head which had started to ache, although a different sort of pain from the one the curse used to inflict. "At least that means Clarisse and Cordelia are safe. Uncle Horace will have no reason to go after them." The thought of my sisters made me glance surreptitiously at William. If we could just defeat my uncle, I would be joining Cordelia in Northhelm. I could start a new life away from the court who had known me under the curse. The possibility seemed too idyllic to consider while I trudged through the jungle with a bloodied leg and death hanging over my head.

"No wonder he was having his men keep a close eye on the situation with the hedge. He must have been trying to find a way to get to her for years. And then we all decided to sail over here. Imagine his delight when we not only took him exactly where he wanted to go but we went after the sword, too. His reluctance to give it to you must have been purely for show. You were the exact tool he needed." I paused. "I'm so sorry, Will..."

"Stop. No more apologies. You're too hard on yourself. You've carried a heavy burden for a long time, all alone. You might have made mistakes, but you've also done a lot of good. The kingdom needed Aurora, it seems. I'm just sorry you had to endure so much pain to create her."

I stilled, my attention caught by something to our right. "What's that?" I pointed toward it.

The small blackened section of jungle still smoked slightly, the acrid smell carrying on the breeze .

"Forest fire?" William's answer lacked conviction.

"It's a pretty small patch for a forest fire."

"Must have been that dragon, then." He chuckled, but it carried an edge of uncertainty.

I gripped his hand more tightly. "Let's keep moving."

As we moved closer to our goal, we passed several more patches of burned out jungle. I remembered the crackling sound that had pursued us through the trees. The guards couldn't have been lighting fires as they ran, it made no sense. And how come the entire jungle hadn't burned, if so?

We moved more slowly and cautiously the closer we got to the house. The tramp of feet and voices told us that some of the guard, at least, had remained there. For the last stretch we had to drop down and crawl along on our stomachs. Roots and rocks caught against my bandage, and I had to grit my teeth to remain silent.

A vantage point behind a large fern gave us a clear view into the clearing surrounding the house. A small knot of anxiety in my stomach loosened when I caught sight of a female figure lying on the ground, bound at the hands and feet. They wouldn't have bothered with that if she were dead.

She moved slightly, and the fern around us rustled at William's sudden jerk. I glared at him, but I had to admit I felt shaken myself. Her sleeve had completely disappeared, and a large fresh-looking burn covered her arm.

I squeezed my eyes shut and took several steadying breaths. If my uncle could do that to his own sister, what had he done to the rest of my family?

"You'll never find them, Horace." The hint of strain in her voice was the only indication of her pain.

"Of course I will. And when I do, I shall destroy you all."

A small knot of soldiers moved as my uncle spoke, giving us a clear view of him. He stood near the house, his hand resting, almost lovingly, on a large, black tube that leaned against it.

"What in the kingdoms is that?"

I didn't respond since I had no answer. I had never seen such a thing. It looked a bit like metal, but it absorbed the light instead of reflecting it. One end had been shaped to resemble the head of a dragon, and the words of the guards in the jungle came back to me.

Whatever it was, if my uncle felt so fondly toward it, it couldn't be good. Could it have anything to do with the burned patches and my aunt's injury? I surveyed the rest of the clearing. I counted ten guards, as well as my uncle. I was sure there had been more than ten chasing us. The rest must still be out combing the jungle.

One of the men present wore a bandage, and another lay prone against the house. Those must be the two William had fought when we made our escape. So, we really only faced nine, then. Still not great odds.

I carefully drew all of the knives except the one in my boot. I laid them out on the ground in front of me.

"What's the plan?" William produced a knife of his own which he placed beside the sword. "I don't like the odds for a frontal assault."

"No, definitely not." I looked back at the clearing again, assessing.

Two men seemed to be standing guard over my aunt, and one ministered to the injured man on the ground. The remaining six moved around the clearing at various tasks, singly or in pairs.

"We need to get behind the house, out of sight of the majority of them. Then we might have the chance to take them out slowly."

William ran his hand through his hair before nodding. He

knew we had no other choice. Retrieving our weapons, we crawled backward until we were far enough away to stand. Moving carefully, we circled the clearing before creeping close again, crouching this time, ready to leap to our feet.

My aunt and uncle, as well as the strange contraption, were hidden from view. None of the guards were in sight, either. But I once again laid out my weapons, content to wait.

A minute later, a lone guard came around the building, heading for the pool of water. I picked up one of my blades, testing the wind. Standing, I pulled back my arm and threw the knife. It left my hand before the guard had time to notice me.

It spun across the space between us, the hilt smashing against his temple. His head jerked back, and he fell to the ground, unconscious.

"Nice throw." William sounded impressed, and I hoped we lived long enough to have a true practice duel one day.

William crept into the clearing and slung the man over his shoulder, bringing him back among the trees. I removed his belt and used it to bind his hands. Ripping off several strips of his shirt, I managed to fashion a gag.

"One down, eight to go."

William looked back into the clearing. "I forgot your knife."

"Wait!" I reached for him, but he had already stepped back into view. Two guards rounded the corner of the building and froze in surprise at the sight of him. I grabbed another knife off the ground and threw it toward one of the men. It hit him, hard, and he went down.

William had at least had the foresight to carry the sword, and he ran toward the other man.

"Hey! They're here!" The guard barely had time to call the warning before William cut him down. He fell to the ground, moaning, but the damage had been done.

I rushed out to join William, my two remaining knives in my hands. I tried to remember if any of the guards had carried a bow. Hopefully the archers had all been sent out to track us down.

Three guards came around the side of the house at a run. William and I put our backs to the building and crouched. As they ran toward us, I threw another knife. These men were on the alert, however, and dodged the missile. I swapped my remaining blade to my right hand and reached into my left boot to draw my last one.

The three men closed on us, and I fought for my life, using every trick I knew to fend off their longer blades. William quickly dropped one of them, and the pressure eased somewhat. He had almost gained the upper hand on his remaining opponent, when the last three guards came into sight, my uncle trailing behind them.

Two of them carried the black tube on their shoulders, the head facing forward. Held that way, it looked a little like a cannon. A shiver rushed from my scalp to my toes.

The men fighting us fell back, clearing the way for their comrades. William and I held our position, our weapons gripped in our hands.

"Well, well, well. I knew keeping my sister alive would pay off." Uncle Horace waved the two guards carrying the tube toward us. "Destroy them."

The men angled the dragon's head in our direction, and a loud humming filled the clearing. A scream sounded from the other side of the house, sending another chill through me. "No! Celeste!" It sounded like my aunt's voice.

"Go!"

William and I dived in opposite directions, as a jet of flame erupted from the open mouth and blackened the stones where we had been standing.

## CHAPTER 32

*T*rolled and came upright, still with both knives in hand. One of the remaining men rushed me. I stayed low, swiping beneath his guard and then scuttling out of reach as he screamed and fell.

The humming sounded again behind me, and I spun in time to see the guards aim the dragon at William. An injured guard lay at the prince's feet, but he still battled with another and hadn't seen the danger.

I raced forward, aiming myself at the outstretched tube. I shifted my grip on my knife, raising it above my head and stabbing down at the contraption with all my force.

The knife bounced off, flying out of my stinging hand. I danced backward out of reach of the weapon and the guards.

"William!" I screamed his name as the rush of flame erupted from the spout again. His sword flashed out in one final, successful strike, before he dropped to the ground.

I had a better view of the weapon this time, and the flame that emerged burned with a terrifying purple and green tinge. The fire caught the edge of the fence around the garden, and the whole thing went up in flames.

For a second, I thought William had avoided the inferno, and then a small finger of fire leaped up from his left sleeve. He rolled over, crushing his left arm against the ground, but when he rolled back over, the flame remained. Leaping up, he threw himself into the water.

Horrified, I saw the bright flame shining from beneath the surface of the pool. I screamed, and then the flame disappeared from the dragon's mouth, the fence and William all at the same moment. An unnatural fire from an unnatural weapon.

William surged from the pool, a hole burned in one sleeve and an angry red patch beneath it. Our eyes met.

"Get him!" yelled my uncle.

Only the two guards holding the dragon remained. And it seemed the contraption needed a break between each attack. After a moment's hesitation, they lowered the heavy tube onto the ground. The time it took them to complete the maneuver gave William the chance to retrieve his sword and race toward them. They met in the middle in a loud clash of metal against metal. I lifted my arm, ready to throw my last knife and even the odds.

But I hesitated. The fight moved too quickly for me to be certain I wouldn't hit William. Before I could lower my arm again, the blade was ripped from my grasp.

I staggered, thrown off balance, and whirled to face my uncle. I expected to see the blade raised against me, but my uncle had tossed it into the jungle. Turning back to William, I saw that one of the guards lay unconscious at his feet.

A scuffling sound drew my attention back toward my uncle. He had lunged for the dragon, which was once again emitting a loud humming. He didn't bother trying to lift it from the ground, simply swinging it around to face me.

As the tongue of the flame emerged, rushing toward me, my eyes met William's. In the second before I was engulfed, time seemed to slow. Horror washed over his face, and he faltered.

The lone remaining guard raised his sword to strike at the undefended prince.

"Princess!" He screamed my name at the same moment I screamed his.

Our long ago fight in the gardeners' hut flashed before my eyes. But this time, only one of us had a weapon. William didn't hesitate, however, whipping back his arm and throwing the sword with all his strength across the space between us.

My knife had made no dent in the strange tube, but the Sword of Lanover cut through it as if it were made of air. The flame died just before it could lick the edges of my face.

I screamed and lashed out, striking my uncle where he knelt beside his broken weapon. He fell to the ground, and I raced toward William's attacker, roaring as I charged.

The guard, busy pulling his blade from William's chest, didn't even have time to turn. My fist caught him in the side of the head, and he dropped like a stone. I leaped over him and collapsed to my knees beside William.

"No, no, no, no, no, no, no, no, NO!" The tears poured down my cheeks, as I pressed my hands against the bleeding wound in his chest. He couldn't die. I wouldn't let him. Not after everything we had been through.

His eyes fluttered open and found my face.

"You fool," I wept. "Why didn't you defend yourself?"

He coughed, and a trickle of blood leaked out of his mouth. "I had to defend someone more important than me."

"No." I shook my head frantically while I tried to increase the pressure on his wound. "You are worth a hundred of me."

He reached up a shaking hand to cup my cheek. "Ah, but Princess, I thought I told you. You are my dawn." He smiled weakly. "True love's kiss, remember? There is no truer love than this."

His eyes fluttered shut, and his hand dropped, a sigh seeming to deflate his body. I pounded his chest and turned my face up to the sky as I screamed, "Godmother!"

I pressed my lips down hard against his.

Light encircled us. Bright, blinding light, sparking back and forth between us.

I fell back, blinking, dazed and confused. A familiar gray-haired figure stood beside me.

She surveyed the clearing, her interested gaze taking in the groaning figures scattered across the ground. Her wings twitched. "I see you've been busy."

"Godmother!" I gasped. "William!" I turned back to his body.

Brilliant blue eyes greeted me. "William!" I threw myself across his body and lay there, feeling the rise and fall of his chest, and gasping in my own great gulps of air. One of his hands stroked my hair.

Slowly I calmed and pushed myself back up. He propped himself up on his elbows and looked down at his chest. The slash in his vest remained, but the skin underneath looked whole and unbroken. Streaks of blood surrounded it and stained both of our clothing, but nothing new leaked out.

"I'm alive. That's a pleasant surprise." His eyes traveled from me to my godmother and his brows rose. "I suppose I have you to thank for that."

She chuckled. "I can see why you like this one, Celeste." She examined William. "I didn't do it on my own, though. The High King has rules about such things. But a final, ultimate sacrifice combined with a true love's kiss? The foundations of the kingdoms are built on power like that. You made it easy."

"Thank you," I said, helping William to his feet. "I can never thank you enough."

She looked me up and down. "Well. You're a sight to be sure. But somehow I find you more beautiful now than when we first met. Strange that." Her eyes twinkled. "I didn't give you an easy run of it all these years, so it's about time you get to enjoy some reward for all your labor."

A sudden thought shook me. "Uncle Horace!" I looked around, wondering if he had escaped in all the commotion.

He lay where I had left him, beside the two halves of his dragon. His eyes glared venom in our direction, but his hands and legs had been tied, and his mouth gagged. I looked around the clearing. Several of the guards had been similarly bound, although not gagged, and my aunt was busily engaged in trussing up another.

She looked in our direction. "I'm sorry it took me so long to work my way out of my bonds. I'm glad to see you're both all right. You had me worried for a moment." I tried to look her in the eyes, but my gaze kept getting stuck on her burned arm.

She glanced down at it. "Yes, I'm going to need some medical assistance."

"Let me take over with the guards." William tried to move toward her, but I clung to his clothing, holding him back. He threw me a quizzical look, and I reluctantly let go. I still couldn't quite believe he was alive. I wanted to count his breaths and feel his beautiful, living warmth beneath my fingers.

I turned back to continue the conversation with my godmother and blinked. She had disappeared. I bit my lip. I hadn't asked her about the rest of my family yet. But surely she wouldn't have talked so amiably with us if anything had happened to them?

Aunt Melisande approached me, and I told myself to focus on our immediate problems. "You need to get that arm into the water, Aunt. Right now."

She grimaced, and I pointed at the pool. She waded straight in, ducking her shoulders below the water and letting out a loud sigh. She closed her eyes and let herself float in the water.

William joined me, having tied up the last of the guards.

"Good thing your aunt had plenty of rope," he said. He

glanced toward the trees in the direction of the beach, and I knew his mind kept circling to the same thing mine did.

"I'm sure he had more guards with him," I said. "They must be searching the jungle for us, but some of them may have heard the commotion and be heading back this way."

His brow furrowed, and he scanned the trees closest to us. "What do you propose? If they come back in pairs, we could probably handle them. But if they come as a group...or start shooting from the trees..."

"We can't afford to wait anyway. I need to know that the others are unharmed."

"No arguments from me." I could tell from the set of his jaw that his thoughts were on his sister. "We can dispose of their weapons somewhere, though."

He moved among the bound men, gathering their weapons into his arms. He could barely carry them all, but he told me to stay with my aunt. He disappeared into the jungle and re-emerged some minutes later with empty arms and a satisfied expression.

"They won't be finding them in a hurry," he said, offering no further explanation. I didn't ask.

"Their comrades will probably release them before we can get back, but with only three of us, there's not much we can do to prevent that."

Aunt Melisande emerged from the pool and disappeared into her house. She emerged with a length of bandage which she attempted to wrap around her arm. After a moment William stepped up to assist her.

When he had finished, they both looked in my direction. My aunt stood in a puddle formed from the water that still streamed off her, but she didn't seem to notice her sopping state.

"We should go." She stopped, and her eyes darted between us. "That is..."

William looked at me, and I understood his silent message.

This was my decision, and he would support me either way. My body drooped with fatigue, my mind deadened by so many intense emotions in such a short amount of time. I couldn't rally the smallest spark of resentment toward her.

"You can come," I said. "We can't leave you here with mercenary guards still roaming the jungle. In my father's absence, my mother can rule on what to do with you now."

"Viktoria is here?" I couldn't read my aunt's expression.

I nodded and started toward the path back to the beach. I desperately hoped I was right, and we would find my mother whole and well, right where we had left her.

~

We moved much faster on our way back, despite our various injuries. William knew my identity now, and he knew I could keep pace. The daylight helped, too.

We stopped only once for a break. William plucked the brightest flower he could find and offered it to me, his eyes full of memory. I let him thread it into my hair, closing my eyes and enjoying the feel of his fingers among the strands. Neither of us offered an explanation to my aunt.

The closer we got to the hedge, the more jittery I became. No one said anything, but we all moved faster. When we finally broke out from under the trees, I couldn't help looking around nervously for bats. I could see none in the bright sunlight.

"My goodness." My aunt gazed at the wide tunnel William had carved through the hedge. "You don't do things by halves, do you?"

I didn't wait for either of them but ran toward the hedge. They both followed as I entered the arching leaves. The light shining through the tightly packed foliage created a green glow around us. A rustling, as if from a great wind, swept through the branches. I looked up to see the thorns and leaves writhing.

I put on an extra spurt of speed and emerged onto the beach. William followed close behind me, and my aunt behind him. As soon as she had stepped clear, a great creaking sounded, and the entire hedge buckled. The branches, leaves, and thorns collapsed to the ground and crumbled into dust.

# CHAPTER 33

We stared at the pile of dust in shock. That was more like what I had been expecting when William attacked the hedge with the sword.

My aunt stirred beside me, and a single tear slipped down her cheek. The godmothers had built the hedge for her protection. Apparently now that she had stepped out of its confines, its job was done. I didn't know if she felt exposed or relieved to be free.

A commotion from the other side of the rocks reached us. I stepped toward it, but William's hand grasped my arm, pulling me back. "We don't know what we're going to find. Best to approach with caution."

I didn't know what we would do if we were greeted by my uncle's mercenaries. I glanced behind us. The hedge was gone, but the protection of the jungle remained. We would run if we had to, despite the deep throbbing that had settled into my leg.

"Celeste! William! Oh, thank goodness!" My sister's welcome voice reached us the same moment she appeared, slipping and sliding across the rocks. She threw herself into my arms.

"We were so scared when we found you missing, Celeste! Where have you been?"

William raised one eyebrow at me, his expression judgmental, although I could see the laugh lurking in his eyes. "I thought Celine was the one who sent you along with me?"

I giggled and held up both hands, my relief energizing me more effectively than a long sleep. "There may have been one or two areas in which I was not entirely truthful with you. But, I blame the curse!"

"The curse?" Celine looked back and forth between us, her brow furrowed. "What is going on?" She stepped back to get a better look at me. "You look different, although I can't quite place it..." She wrinkled her nose. "And I don't mean all the blood, either. Please tell me none of it is yours."

"A little, possibly. But most of it is William's."

Her eyes flew to him, alarmed.

"Don't worry, I'm all right now."

When she didn't look quite convinced, he laughed. "You have a keen eye, Celine. But I'm surprised you don't recognize the difference in your sister. Don't you think she looks sort of...familiar?"

Celine rolled her eyes. "Of course she looks familiar, she's my sister."

I snorted, and her eyes flashed to me, startled.

"Yes," William said, the mischievous grin still tugging at his face. "On one level she is. But aren't you supposed to be good at seeing what no one else notices? Or is that Cordelia I'm thinking of?"

"Hey! I'm good at noticing things."

I kicked out at William with my bad leg and then winced. "Behave yourself. I want to hear what happened while we were gone." My eyes flashed briefly toward my aunt, reminding him we had an audience.

"You're injured, all of you. Come back to camp. I think the doctor has finally finished tending all of our own casualties, so we'll get you treated straight away."

I sobered instantly. "Casualties?"

"Don't worry," she said, gripping my arm to steady me across the rocks. "Injuries only. Uncle Horace took at least thirty of his guards with him, so the crew easily outnumbered those who remained." She squeezed my arm. "I'm sorry I didn't try to stop him, I didn't realize…"

"Don't be foolish, none of this was your fault. You followed the plan that I made, and you can't be blamed for that."

She almost tripped, and I had to steady her. "The plan that *you* made?" She looked back at William, visibly processing his earlier words. She gaped at me, her mouth hanging open. "Wait. You're—"

I cut her off with a shake of my head and another glance at my aunt.

"Bravo, Celine," said William behind us.

"Does that mean the curse is broken?" She whipped her head back and forth between the two of us. "You're really going to have to tell me everything."

"I will, I promise. But I need to know what happened to you first."

We stepped down off the rocks and could see the camp ahead of us. Several of the tents had collapsed, and bags and crates lay around haphazardly. Sailors moved slowly among the chaos, sorting and straightening. Others stood armed guard over a large group of men seated further down the beach.

"I waited for the hedge to collapse, or something equally visible, but nothing happened. Well, until just then, of course. It gave me such a shock, I can tell you." She let go of my arm now that we were back on the sand. "I didn't expect to see Uncle Horace until right before dawn, but he left quite a bit sooner than that. One of his men checked William's tent, and then they set off toward the hedge. I let them go, but the more I thought about it, the less I liked it."

She grimaced, and I once again assured her it wasn't her fault.

"I decided to wake up Tom. I'll admit I told him everything." She turned apologetic eyes on me, but I waved it away. I had left her with too great a burden to bear alone. I was glad she had reached out for help.

"As soon as he heard the whole story, he insisted on rousing the sailors. We did it as quietly as possible and managed to wake most of them before the remaining guards realized what was happening. They attacked anyway, but they didn't stand a chance and quickly surrendered. One of them has confessed since, and I think they only fought at all because they were scared Uncle would come back and find they hadn't even tried. We've been debating what to do now. Rafe is preparing a party to go after you."

I noticed another group of sailors milling to the side of the camp, many of them in the process of strapping on weapons. Rafe and Marie stood among them, looking grim. "William." I pointed to them.

"Celine, we need to send them, straight away. And any others who are willing to go. We disabled ten of them and left them tied up with your uncle, but the others were spread through the jungle. They may have already discovered and freed the ones we left behind."

"I can give them instructions on the fastest path to take," Aunt Melisande offered. "It will only take me a moment." She hurried off toward the group.

"Is that...?" Celine watched her go.

"Yes."

"You're really going to have to tell me your story."

"You finish yours first."

She shrugged. "There isn't much more to tell. The doctor has been busy patching up anyone who got injured in the fight. Mother's declaring calmly that she's sure you'll turn up any minute now. And Rafe's been prowling around barking at the sailors to hurry up, and alternating between glaring at the hedge as if he intended to tear the whole jungle down and trying to convince Marie to stay behind."

I snorted again. "How's that been going?"

She grinned. "Not very well."

"William!" Marie ran toward us and fell into her brother's arms.

Rafe, right behind her, swept me up into a hug. "Oh, thank goodness." He put me down. "That woman says she's…"

I nodded. "She is. But I'm not going to tell this story five times. Let's find Mother, and I'll tell you all at once. But you need to send the sailors out after the other guards first."

Rafe gave me an odd look before nodding. "They'll be glad to go. They've been itching for a fight with those guards since they first showed up on board." He grinned. "They weren't overly happy when the guards here surrendered so quickly. I have no doubt they'll have the rest of them rounded up in no time. I guess that's the thing with mercenaries—they aren't too keen to put their lives on the line once they realize which way the wind is blowing. I'll meet you all in Mother's tent in five minutes. Don't you dare start without me!"

In the end it took a lot longer before we could start our explanations since the doctor had to examine my leg first. My mother never took her eyes off me the whole time. When the doctor finally left, under instructions to find my aunt and keep her in the medical tent, she swept William up into a tight hug.

"I was hoping it would be you," she said.

"Thank you, Your Majesty." The panicked look he sent me over her shoulder made me giggle. "But what exactly were you hoping…?"

She let him go and mopped at her eyes. "That you'd be the one to give me my daughter back. I couldn't have asked for a more charming son-in-law." She rounded on me and enveloped me next, carefully avoiding my leg.

Rafe gave a choking cough, and Marie calmly patted him on

the back. "So you've finally gotten that sorted, have you? It's about time."

She didn't show any surprise, but she didn't look overly thrilled, either. I hoped she would warm to the news once she realized the curse had been broken.

"Enough is enough," said Celine, plonking herself down on a cushion. "I need the whole story—now."

It took a long time to get the tale straight. William and I were the only ones who knew everything, and the others all knew different parts. They kept stopping to exclaim and question, and in my mother's case cry.

"All those years!" She mopped at her eyes. "And you were trapped inside there!"

Between the true nature of the curse, my activities as Aurora, the truth about our aunt, and the betrayal of our uncle, everyone had exhausted their capacity for shock and amazement by the end.

But on one thing we were all agreed. As soon as the sailors returned with the remaining mercenaries, we were setting sail. I could see the concern for Frederic, Cassian, and our father lurking in everyone's eyes.

"You informed them, Lettie, that's the main thing," said Rafe as we exited the tent together. "They may not be as smart and strong as you, but they'll crush this so-called rebellion, don't worry."

He hurried off to tell the captain to ready the ship, and I forced my tired limbs toward the doctor's tent. Celine caught up with me, and we stuck our heads in together. The doctor shooed us back out and told us his patient was sleeping. "I had to sedate the princess to get her to rest at all, I won't have her disturbed."

"Oh, good." Celine tugged me toward the stream that now flowed freely down from the jungle. "In that case there's time for a bath. You look terrible, Lettie."

I arched an eyebrow at her, and she quirked a half-smile. "Well, comparatively to your normal self, anyway."

"Absolutely not." William blocked our path. "Those guards could still be roaming the jungle."

Celine rolled her eyes. "You can come along and protect us, then."

William glanced between us, a dull red creeping up his neck.

"Celine! He can't come with us to bathe!"

"Of course he can." She started dragging me again. "Look at him. He's nobility personified. He'll stand facing the other way the whole time, I'm sure." She looked him over. "Actually, it's a good idea. He can bathe after us."

I shrugged at William, and he reluctantly fell into step beside us. We didn't have to follow the stream far to find a small pool big enough for bathing. I gasped when the water hit my injured leg, but the prospect of being clean was far too enticing to stop.

When William took his turn, we diligently turned our own backs. Celine leaned in close to whisper in my ear.

"Should we peek?"

"Celine!"

She giggled. "Relax, Lettie, I was only joking."

I shook my head, but in reality a weight lifted off me. This rebellion might have forced Celine to grow up in some respects, but in others she remained her old self. The knowledge brought me comfort.

When we returned to the camp, we found half of it had already been packed away. The sailors moved quickly, apparently as anxious to be off the island as we were. William pulled me aside.

"Your mother needs to speak to Princess Melisande and make a decision about what happens to her now. We might not have much time later."

I nodded. When I checked back with the doctor, he exclaimed at the sight of my wet bandages and insisted I come in to have them redressed. William ducked out without my needing to ask and returned with my mother in tow.

My aunt had woken and sat on a small cot, watching us silently. My mother froze in the doorway of the tent, regarding her sister-in-law with wide eyes.

Melisande spoke first. "I'm so sorry, Viktoria. For everything. There is no excuse for me."

My mother shook her head, tears in her eyes. "And I am sorry, too, Mellie. It was so many years ago now, and we all made mistakes." She looked over at William and me. "And you have acted to rectify them now. Celeste told me what you did."

A sudden anger flashed in her eyes, and her entire body shook with strong emotion. "When I think of Horace…I could tear him apart with my bare hands."

I jerked, and the doctor, busy wrapping my leg, grumbled. I had never seen such a passionate response in my mother before.

Melisande sighed. "He never understood our kingdom. Father thought a tour of the other lands would help, but it only made things worse. King Josef would have swallowed the whole of the Four Kingdoms if his own family hadn't gotten to him first; it's no surprise he spread his infection to our brother."

My mother slowly returned to her normal state of calm. "Well, he shall have plenty of opportunity to reflect on his crimes. I don't care what Leonardo decreed all those years ago, you're coming back with us. Horace can remain here in your place."

No one questioned her pronouncement or our new passenger. And there was only the smallest of grumbles at the monkey she brought with her. We sailed out of the bay some hours later, our hold full of prisoners and a lone, angry figure on the beach.

We made straight for Largo, to deliver the mercenaries to the prison there. "There are too many of them for us," explained the captain. "The navy will send a couple of ships better equipped to transport them back to the capital."

When we sailed into Largo Bay, a shout went up from the harbor. By the time we had moored and disembarked, the governor of the city had arrived to greet us.

"Your Majesty! We were just preparing ships to set off after you."

My mother nodded. "You have word from Leonardo."

The man bobbed his head, wiping at his sweating brow. "It arrived mere hours ago, and we have all been scrambling since. With the greatest haste I assure you."

"The rebellion has been dismantled then?" I pushed forward.

He turned to look at me, and a slightly dazed expression took over his face. I waited impatiently for it to pass.

"Your…Your Highness." His expression told me he recognized who I was, and his stumbling words suggested he hadn't expected such a direct question from the Sleeping Princess. He looked at William, who hovered protectively at my shoulder, and his eyes widened.

How long would it take for word to spread throughout Lanover that the curse had been broken?

"Well?" I asked again.

"Yes, Your Highness. His Majesty uncovered the entire plot. His own quartermaster, too! Incredible! Ercole confessed to the whole thing, and the king sent his fastest messengers after you. We feared his warning had come too late!"

He didn't ask the questions I could see burning in his face, and I knew he would be left without answers. None of us wanted to stay for explanations. As soon as the prisoners had been unloaded, we would be off. My father could decide how much of the story he wished to share with his governors.

The *Viktoria* sailed from Largo with much more cheerful passengers than the ones who had arrived. A tangible weight had lifted from us all.

～

Two nights later I slipped out on deck and took a deep breath of the fresh, salty air. I leaned against the rail and gazed out at the moon. Everyone was still processing the many revelations, and I couldn't seem to escape their endless questions. They kept remembering this or that event that had occurred in the last three years and wanting to know what I had really been thinking.

Soft footsteps approached and strong arms slipped around my waist.

"Have I told you that you look enchanting in the moonlight? And that you'll make the most beautiful queen in the history of the kingdoms?"

I pretended to consider. "I remember beautiful and exquisite and *painful*, but I'm not sure I remember enchanting."

His body shook with his chuckle. "Allow me to rectify that." He spun me around to face him. "You look enchanting, Princess." He dropped a soft kiss on my mouth. "And I promise to tell you so every day for the rest of our lives." He chuckled again. "Even if you best me with those knives of yours next time we duel."

I smiled up at him. "Oh, especially then. I look particularly enchanting when I duel."

"Do you now?" His arms tightened around me. "I look forward to seeing it."

I opened my mouth to respond, but his lips closed over mine, and I forgot the words, along with any others.

Our ship raced through the waves, and my heart raced with it, swelling with happiness. I was free from the curse. And I had found someone who could love the inside of me as well as he loved the outside. How could I want for anything more? For the first time in my life, I felt truly content.

# EPILOGUE

rederic watched the ceremony from his place at the front of the room. Celeste looked stunning in her wedding gown, of course. Given her Christening gift, she quite possibly looked more beautiful than any bride had ever done before. The dress had certainly cost enough, despite being commissioned from some unknown seamstress in the city.

But beauty didn't move him. He had spent a lifetime with the foibles and wild emotions of his sisters, so he knew well enough that beauty meant little. His sister's intelligence and cunning meant more to him than her looks. And that was a problem that did concern him.

Now that the whole truth had been revealed about her curse and her activities for the last several years, he knew how much her loss meant to the kingdom. His father would have to find a replacement spymaster sooner rather than later.

Not that he could complain about his sister taking her place as the future queen of Northhelm. Her marriage provided an even more solid alliance than Rafe's had done.

He cast a regretful glance toward Prince Maximilian from Arcadia. He had hoped Celeste would succeed in winning the

Arcadian heir when she had visited the kingdom two years ago. That alliance would have been even more welcome, but the young prince had chosen a commoner in the end.

He examined Princess Alyssa, sitting beside Max. She was pretty enough, he supposed. The young woman leaned into her husband, her eyes misty at the romantic proceedings. Frederic noticed her hand had slipped down to cup her stomach protectively. Their own wedding had been almost exactly two years before, so he supposed that such a development was inevitable. Max's arm hugged his young wife to his side.

He had questioned the other prince's decision at the time, choosing a commoner over a princess and the alliance she would have offered. But Arcadia had prospered in the years since. His mother had been right. The High King and his godmothers still rewarded true love.

Frederic's eyes moved to King Hans and Queen Ava, sitting on the other side of the aisle to the Arcadian contingent. They both sat upright, but he noticed their hands were clasped, almost hidden by the folds of her gown. He caught Hans throwing her a quick glance, wonder and love in his eyes. That had been another marriage between a royal and a commoner. And another kingdom that had been turned completely around. Although almost anyone would have made a better monarch than Ava's now deceased father, King Josef. He had nearly managed to take all four kingdoms down with him, too.

He glanced at the eldest of his sisters, Clarisse. She stood at the front with the rest of their sisters, supporting Celeste as one of her attendants. He still felt guilty for not speaking against it when her marriage alliance with Prince Konrad of Rangmere had been arranged. The family had only found out years later, after she had been widowed, how badly Konrad had treated her. But Frederic had never liked the other prince on the few occasions they had met. He should never have stood by while his sister was sent off alone to Rangmere.

He had let his uncle influence him, and he regretted that doubly now. Uncle Horace's betrayal had cut deep, and he was determined to do whatever it took to right any wrongs his uncle had done to the kingdom.

Clarisse, at least, seemed much happier now, although she still looked sad watching her sister's radiant face as she spoke her vows. Or maybe that was just because of the contrast presented by Cordelia, standing next to her. The second youngest of his sisters looked almost as radiant as Celeste. He supposed she was remembering her own ceremony, only two weeks before. She certainly kept glancing at her new husband, standing across the platform next to William. Apparently he was the prince's oldest friend.

In fact, the ceremony seemed to be attended by a remarkable number of happy young couples. He was almost certain one of his sisters had told him that the two couples sitting behind Ava and Hans were merchant friends of the queen's who had married Rangmeran nobles. Although the couple on the end looked almost more like guards than nobles. He recognized it in their bearing and the clothes that looked like they wouldn't get in the way if the wedding turned into a brawl.

He couldn't see any sign of such a thing happening, though. In fact, he couldn't remember a time when all four kingdoms were so prosperous or so in harmony. He had always imagined that, as heir, he would marry to advance the welfare of his kingdom. And he had thought that meant a marriage of alliance.

But no marriageable princesses remained. The Arcadian twins were only thirteen, even younger than Celine. Although the three of them seemed to be getting along well. A little too well, if anyone asked him. They still had another week of the month-long festivities that had included both weddings and Midsummer Day. And he'd be astonished if they made it to the end without the three of them getting up to some sort of mischief. He barely saw his sister without seeing the three heads bent together, some sort of plotting underway.

No, the Arcadians weren't an option.

He looked around the huge hall again. Could he ask for any more compelling evidence? The welfare of his kingdom apparently demanded true love. It was a bit of a hazy requirement but, somehow, he couldn't bring himself to fault it.

His eyes caught on Celine, who had glanced in the twins' direction, and all thoughts of love were driven from his mind. As host to so many gathered royals, the responsibility fell to Lanover to ensure the smooth running of the event. Which meant, as heir, it fell to him to find out what sort of pandemonium his youngest sibling was planning. It was going to be a long week.

You can read about Frederic finding love in <u>The Princess Search: A Retelling of The Ugly Duckling</u>. Turn the page for a sneak peek!

Thank you for taking the time to read my book. If you enjoyed it, please spread the word! You could start by leaving a review on <u>Amazon</u> (or <u>Goodreads</u> or <u>Facebook</u> or any other social media site). Your review would be very much appreciated and would make a big difference!

To be kept informed of my new releases, and for free extra content, including an exclusive bonus chapter of my first novel The Princess Companion (Book One of The Four Kingdoms series), please sign up to my mailing list at www.melaniecellier.com. At my website, you'll also find an array of free extra content.

## THE PALACE OF LIGHT

"*T*he trouble in Lanover grows closer by the minute."

The gray-haired woman twitched her wings and frowned at her companion. "Yes, indeed, and what of it?"

The first godmother, her hair more white than silver, shifted uncomfortably. "Are you sure your goddaughter is up to the challenge?"

"She never had a Christening. Officially, she isn't my goddaughter."

The white-haired one rolled her eyes. "Don't quibble. You know she's still your goddaughter. Although I'm sure she thinks everyone has abandoned her."

The gray-haired godmother put her hands on her hips. "I may not have rescued her outright, but you know why. You know we've been weaving the threads into place for this moment for decades. Don't tell me you've gotten cold feet now!"

"Not cold feet, exactly." The first sighed. "It's just that my charges—all seven of them—have been through a lot lately, and I hate to leave them unaided at such a moment."

The second godmother frowned. "And my goddaughter has been through a lifetime of troubles. A lifetime she's about to be forced to revisit. Nothing about this is going to be easy for any of them. But they're not unaided because they have each other. Such challenges are not supposed to be easy. If they are to rule the kingdom someday, they must endure the difficulties before them and prove themselves worthy."

"Yes, you're right, of course." The white-haired one sighed again. "Only I do so enjoy helping to pave the way to true love."

The other shook her head. "If you find yourself so restless, why not pay a visit to Rangmere? I hear your widowed goddaughter there is on the painful path to love. And then you won't be tempted to interfere where you should not."

The first smiled. "Perhaps you are right. An excursion will be a great deal better than all this waiting."

The gray-haired woman twitched her wings again, observing the empty space where her companion had stood a moment before. Now that she was alone, her face lost some of its earlier assurance. "I do hope I haven't misplaced my confidence in the girl," she muttered to herself. "Or else a great many things will be lost that should not be, and it may take us generations to get things back on track."

*I* didn't need the tinkling of the bell above the door to tell me someone had entered my shop. For all she was only fifteen, Princess Celine knew how to make an entrance. I hurried to put down my work and greet her while my mind rushed to deal with the problem presented by her presence.

"Your Highness." I dipped into a curtsy, but the princess didn't seem to notice. She was examining a bolt of my newest acquisition—a deep midnight blue shot silk. It was certainly an impressive material, and a number of other seamstresses had already tried to prize its source from me.

Abruptly, Celine spun around. "I have a project for you. Your biggest yet." The excitement on her face made my heart sink even further.

Celine had surprising talent when it came to dress design. If she hadn't been royalty, I would have invited her to join me as a partner—her instinctive grasp of fashion would have made up for any lack of skill with a needle. As it was, her suggestions had sparked some of my most brilliant creations.

But I had received a visit the week before from no less a personage than Her Majesty Queen Viktoria herself. She had been flatteringly full of praises for my work, but I was fairly certain her commission for a ball gown had been intended to soften the blow of her true purpose. Because I had also been given extremely strict parameters to follow for any future designs made for the queen's youngest daughter. It was such a pity, the queen had said, that I kept creating such masterpieces that no one ever got to see.

I had winced at her words and rushed to assure her of my compliance. In fact, I agreed with her, even without the weight of a royal command. My excitement at our shared efforts had led me to create gowns for Celine that were—strictly speaking—too old for the young princess. One or two of them I had expected to create fashion trends and had been surprised not to receive a deluge of copycat orders. Now I knew why.

I had made a name and a living for myself through great effort and toil. I had dragged myself from the muck without assistance from those who might have been expected to help me, and I had no great inclination to take orders from anyone. But I would not disobey the queen. I needed to stay on the good side of the royal family—their patronage had established me here in the capital. And I wanted my best designs to go to someone who would be permitted to actually wear them. But that still left me with the problem of the youngest princess.

Celine spun around in a giddy circle, running her hand along several bolts of soft material. "I can't wait to tell you. You're going to be so excited. It's a challenge worthy of your skill."

I frowned. I hated to disappoint her because the young princess was one of the few people who had given me reason to be grateful. She was the one who had discovered my small, newly-established shop just over a year ago, and she had always treated me affectionately despite the difference in our ranks. Without her, I might still be struggling to gain noble clients. Without her, I would certainly never have received the commission for her older sister's bridal and attendant gowns the previous summer. And since Princess Celeste was every seam-stress's dream—a girl who would look stunning in absolutely anything—I had been flooded with orders ever since her wedding.

I considered my words carefully.

Before I could speak, however, the bell tinkled again, and a different kind of figure strode into my shop. Tall, broad-shoul-dered, and with a palpable air of authority, the young man was a far cry from my usual customer. I immediately sank into another, deeper curtsy to cover my confusion at his appearance.

I looked up again just in time to see Princess Celine roll her eyes. "What are you doing here, Frederic?" She put her hands on her hips and glared at her oldest brother. "I'm busy conducting business with Mistress Evangeline."

"Mistress Evangeline?" Although he said my name, Prince Frederic's eyes regarded his sister in surprise. "Since when are you so respectful? I'd expect to hear you calling her Evie or something."

I blinked at the sound of my nickname on his lips, my surprise overwhelming my amusement at the truth of his words. She did usually call me Evie.

Celine drew herself up to her full height and looked loftily at her brother. "I treat everyone with respect."

He chuckled darkly. "My dear Celine, you don't know the meaning of respect."

I dropped my head to hide a smile since I wasn't sure the prince had meant to be humorous.

He turned to me and gave an inclination of his head. "I apolo-gize for my younger sister, Mistress Evangeline."

Celine looked as if she were about to explode at this, but I quickly dipped into a shallow curtsy in response, hoping to head off any further conflict.

I tried to remind myself that an exalted position said nothing of the person within, and that my position in the capital was assured by my own skill, not by royal patronage—however much that patronage advantaged me. There was no reason for me to be intimidated by the crown prince. And yet intimidated I must be, since I could come up with no other reason for my heart to be beating a great deal faster than its normal rate.

The prince turned back to his sister. "You're supposed to be preparing for our departure."

"I am!" She narrowed her eyes and dramatically shook her head. "Which is the biggest of the Four Kingdoms, Frederic?"

He eyed her warily, sighing when she raised her eyebrows at him. "Lanover, of course."

"And which of the kingdoms is the most diverse?"

He sighed again. "Celine."

She put her hands back on her hips. "Well?"

"Lanover." He drew the word out slowly, clearly cautious of whatever trap his sister was trying to set for him with the obvious questions.

"Exactly!" She threw up her hands. "Unlike the other kingdoms, we have many different sub-cultures here. Tell me Frederic, what are the latest fashions worn on the islands?" She didn't wait for him to respond, and he showed no desire to do so. "What about in southern Largo? Or among the jungle dwellers? What about the nomadic desert traders?"

When he still said nothing, she gave a decisive nod. "Precisely!"

My eyes lingered on the prince's handsome face. He looked almost as confused as I felt. If the princess thought she had proved her point, she was sorely mistaken.

Celine turned to me. "Men."

I had to suppress another smile at her world-weary tone.

"I'm sure, if left to his own devices," she continued, "my brother would simply pull on the first clothing to come to hand each day. Hardly befitting the crown prince of the most fashionable kingdom in the land! Which is why it's such a good thing his sisters have always taken responsibility for his wardrobe. Only now that all the rest are married and gone, I'm the only one left. And the high and mighty Frederic doesn't like to admit that his baby sister knows more about some things than he does."

"Really, Celine. Please." Frederic cast an uncomfortable glance in my direction. I tried to maintain the blankest expression possible. Coming between squabbling siblings was always a bad idea, let alone when royalty were involved.

"Oh, don't mind Evie," said Celine. "She's my friend. And if you want this Royal Tour you've got planned to be a true success, then we need her. Because you're not going to remind all our different communities of the might and glory of the crown if we show up looking out of fashion and dowdy. And never mind impressing them enough to put an end to these rumors of a new rebellion."

"Celine!" Now Frederic sounded both shocked and angry.

His sister remained unaffected. "Oh, come on. You can't think I don't know the true purpose of this Tour. I'm not an idiot. And I already told you. We need her. And it's in our interest for her to understand how important this Tour and her role is. You put me in charge of the royal wardrobes for the Tour, and I'm here to beg her to close up shop for the season and come with us. Because we're going to need someone who can assess local fashions and ensure we're the most impressively dressed everywhere we go." She stared her brother down. "And that's no easy feat. Do you know any other seamstress up to the task?"

From the hopeless look on Prince Frederic's face, I doubted he could name any other seamstresses at all. He had probably only given Celine the role of wardrobe mistress to placate her, but despite her earlier accusations, he now looked ready to accede to her points. In fact, he looked quite struck by them.

"So, what do you say, Evie?" Celine turned to me eagerly. "Will you come with us? I know it's a lot to ask. We leave in only a week."

A week! I gulped. I had heard some talk in the capital about the crown prince's Royal Tour of the kingdom, but I hadn't realized Princess Celine was going too. And I hadn't expected it to affect me much, other than perhaps creating a quieter season given the absence of some of the royalty and nobility. It was a break I had welcomed after the hectic pace of the last year.

But now the princess was asking me to finish all my current commissions in the space of a single week so that I could then embark on an even bigger challenge. And she was asking me to leave the capital just when I had finally established myself here.

*But this could be your chance,* whispered an internal voice. *Your chance to prove your worth once and for all. If you succeed at this, no one could ever question if you deserve your place again.*

I bit my lip as I looked between the two royals. Celine was watching me with hope-filled eyes, Frederic with curiosity. Something about his expression roused a defiant determination in me. I could do this. I would do this.

"I am honored to serve the crown in any way I can."

The shadow of surprise in the prince's expression filled me with satisfaction. I would show him what I was capable of—him and everyone else.

"We are the ones who are honored, Mistress Evangeline." Something about the prince's grave voice inspired my imp of mischief. No wonder Celine couldn't resist teasing her oldest brother—his serious demeanor was almost irresistible.

"Oh, come, Your Highness," I said. "Surely you're not going to pretend familiarity with my designs. I suspect you didn't even know my name before your sister used it."

Frederic froze, and Celine giggled.

"Thank goodness you're coming, Evie," she said. "Frederic's picked all the oldest, most stodgy courtiers to accompany us. Every single one regards me with horrified judgment, I assure you."

"Celine," said Frederic stiffly. "You shouldn't speak of them that way. They are loyal supporters of the crown."

She sighed. "Of course they are. But they're also hideously boring." She shuddered comically, her eyes twinkling. "Which means I would have been entirely stuck with you and Cassian for the whole Tour."

Dawning horror spread across Frederic's face, and he gave me a half bow. "On behalf of myself and my brother, I must thank you again Mistress Evangeline. It seems we have many reasons to be grateful to you."

Celine winked at me behind his back, and I gave a small chuckle, looking up through my lashes at the tall prince. "Please, call me Evie, you might find it easier to remember."

He looked down at me, an arrested expression on his face. After a pause, he said, "Very well, Mistress Evie. Please report to the palace in six days' time. We appreciate your assistance."

He stepped back and grasped his sister's arm, attempting to drag her from my shop. She caught at the door frame and looked back at me. "I'll come past tomorrow to talk some more and arrange a time for you to inspect our current wardrobes."

I nodded, but the prince had tugged her away before I could actually speak.

I sank down into a convenient chair, my knees a little wobbly. Had I really just flirted with the crown prince?

*Well, why not?* asked that same inner voice. *He's a person, just like anyone else.* Only this time my internal dialogue sounded far too mischievous.

I had long ago decided that pain was best pushed from my mind—life was easier if viewed light-heartedly. But that didn't mean it was a good idea for me to offend the most powerful family in the kingdom.

But the thought of my past pushed a far more gripping concern to the front of my mind. I was about to have a great deal more to worry about than a prince who seemed as serious as he was hand-some. More important even than preserving my secret source of extraordinary fabric and ensuring no gown I created contained any poor stitching. Because I had just agreed to a full tour of Lanover.

Which meant the royal family—my most important clients—were about to find out exactly what had driven me to the capital the previous year. How long would it be before even Celine regretted befriending a commoner who she knew almost nothing about?

Read on in <u>The Princess Search: A Retelling of The Ugly Duckling</u>

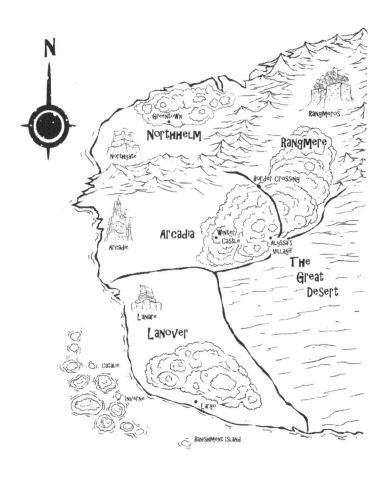

# Royal Family of Lanover

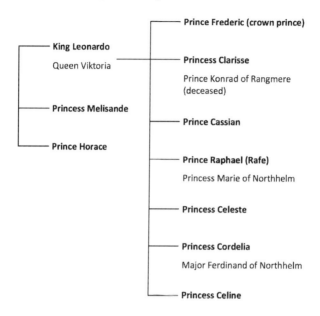

King Leonardo
Queen Viktoria

Princess Melisande

Prince Horace

Prince Frederic (crown prince)

Princess Clarisse
Prince Konrad of Rangmere
(deceased)

Prince Cassian

Prince Raphael (Rafe)
Princess Marie of Northhelm

Princess Celeste

Princess Cordelia
Major Ferdinand of Northhelm

Princess Celine

# ACKNOWLEDGMENTS

It has felt like a long—but fun—journey to reach book 4. The last of the princesses to be tested in The Princess Companion finally has her own story. Lanover has been a delightful kingdom to explore, with beautiful locations and a multitude of royals.

With the added complexity of the story, I have particularly relied on the excellent assistance of my team of beta readers and my awesome editors. Many thanks to my regular team: Katie, Rachel, Greg, Ber, Priya, and Debs. You guys never let me down.

Massive extra thanks also need to go to my new editor, Mary. Working with you has been a fantastic experience, and your insights have made this a much better book.

The perfect cover is thanks once again to Karri who has managed to bring all the characters from this series to life in such an amazing way.

Writing can be an overwhelming process physically and mentally—so a big thanks to Marc for keeping me (and our household) afloat while I dived into this book. And to the rest of my family for somehow remaining interested in the endless details of my writing and publishing journey. I couldn't possibly do this without my support network.

And, finally, thanks to God for somehow keeping me going and for allowing me a glimpse of the truest of loves.

# ABOUT THE AUTHOR

Melanie Cellier grew up on a staple diet of books, books, and more books. And although she got older, she never stopped loving children's and young adult novels. She always wanted to write one herself, but it took three careers and three different continents before she actually managed it.

She now feels incredibly fortunate to spend her time writing from her home in Adelaide, Australia where she keeps an eye out for koalas in the backyard. Her staple diet hasn't changed much, although she's added choc mint rooibos tea and Chicken Crimpies to the list.

Her young adult *Four Kingdoms* and *Beyond the Four Kingdoms* series are made up of linked stand-alone stories that retell classic fairy tales.

Printed in Great Britain
by Amazon